APPARATUS FROM ARUNA
Copyright © 2022 by T R Nickel

ISBN: 979-8-9864995-1-2

Cover Design by Lidia Puccetti

Edited and Formatted by Chelsea Lauren

Apparatus From Aruna

Book Two

The Legends of Limoria

Apparatus From Aruna

T R Nickel

XAVIER EFRAIM 2022

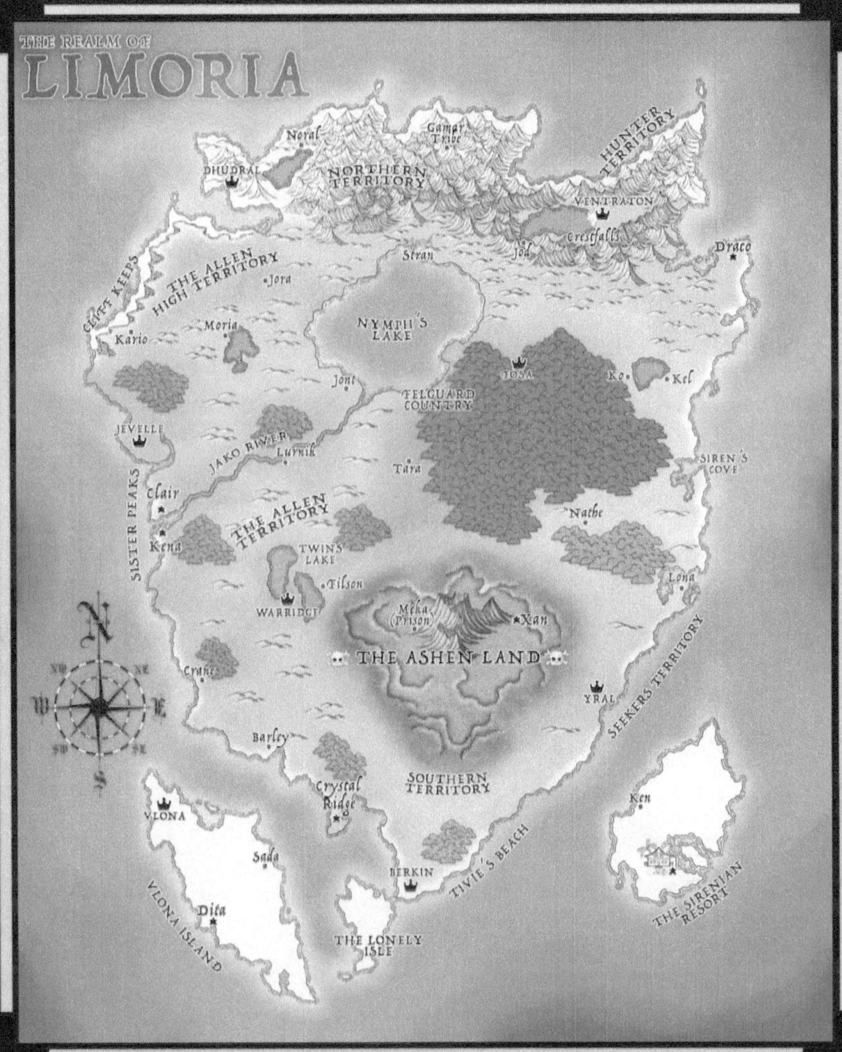

THE REALM OF LIMORIA
Noral
Gamar Tribe
HUNTER TERRITORY
DHUDRAL
NORTHERN TERRITORY
VENTRATON
Crestfalls
Jod
Draco
Stran
THE ALLEN HIGH TERRITORY
Jora
CRAFT KEEPS
Kario
Moria
NYMPH'S LAKE
TOSA
Ko
Kel
Jont
TELGUARD COUNTRY
JEVELLE
JAKO RIVER
Lurnik
Tara
SIREN'S COVE
Clair
THE ALLEN TERRITORY
Nathe
SISTER PEAKS
Kena
TWINS LAKE
Filson
Lona
WARRIDGE
Meka Prison
Xan
THE ASHEN LAND
N
NW
NE
W
E
Crane
SW
SE
S
YRAL
SEEKERS TERRITORY
Barley
SOUTHERN TERRITORY
Crystal Ridge
Ken
VLONA
Sada
BERKIN
ZIVIE'S BEACH
THE SIRENIAN RESORT
VLONA ISLAND
Dita
THE LONELY ISLE

AUTHOR'S NOTE

Wow, my second book. While I was writing it, I experienced a lot of doubt, worry, excitement, love and distaste for my own work. Even still, I think about ways I could improve or expand the world I am creating. I try to remind myself that this is a series, and the world is going to continue to expand and eventually all the rumblings inside my head will be out and onto paper in a format for people to read, enjoy, and be inspired by.... Well, that's my hope, anyway.

Xylia will always hold a special place in my heart as she was my first Dungeons and Dragons character and the reason the Legends of Limoria even exist, but Renatus is different. He is a true piece of me, created from the emotions and understanding of what it means to not have a voice, or at least be scared of using it. Afraid that whatever comes out would be the wrong thing, or stupid, or terrible. Writing became the way I could speak honestly and without judgment. It was a way for me to clearly string sentences together and know that they were not filtered because the only audience was me.

Many authors say that their second book in a series is their hardest, and I can see why. Renatus and the story told challenged me in many ways I was not expecting. One being that I realised I really have no control over my characters once I put them on paper. Sure, I created him and gave birth to the very story that was written, but it was a surreal feeling becoming Ren and expressing the emotions he needed to let out.

At the end of the book, you'll find an index that helps explain the unexplained and brings you closer to understanding the Legends of Limoria.

CHAPTER ONE

SHE IS CRYING AGAIN. Her face is blurry and no matter how hard I squint, I cannot see her any clearer. My heart hurts hearing her wail and having her bury her head into my chest. I want to hold her; I want to comfort her, but I can barely feel anything and the flames that are flickering around in my blurry vision feel cold. I open my mouth, but my words are silent. I feel a metallic liquid filling my mouth.

I must be dying.

As she sits up, a light erupts from her, blinding me completely until images of rolling hills, a small cabin somewhere far from others' gazes, youngins in the distance as she and I sit watching the sunset flash before my eyes. An urge comes over me to scream, cry and beg whatever goddess to let me live and stay with her. It doesn't feel right to leave her alone. I have to tell her. She needs to know that even if I am gone, I will not be far. She has to know.

I'm right here.

A hand smacks me across the face and I dart up, well-aware of my surroundings. The same dark broom closet I have grown so accustomed to waking in, at any hour the Master chooses to rouse me. The girl, the flames, the dream fades away as I stand from the cot I sleep on. Master is already far ahead, ascending the wooden spiral stairs. I look around and see the entry as it is, nothing torn, painting still hanging, carpet not disrupted from its resting place.

He's in a good mood.

I head to the large and sparkling clean room filled with the same pots and pans I find myself cleaning daily. I often wish I could stay here all day; it's quiet and easy to chop the day away. I take inventory for the morning, trying to think about what would best appetise the Master.

A knock at the kitchen's servant entrance rattles the door enough to make me jump. I glance out the window and see a familiar orange-hatted fellow walking away.

The fresh produce is delivered for the week.

I quickly scurry to grab the goods and bring them inside before any **cavrats** can get to them, again. I look over the contents of this week's selection.

Milk, meats, eggs, spinach, beets, potatoes, apples, and peaches.

While I prepare the Master's breakfast, I can hear his rushed footsteps above me.

Probably forgetting where he just set down his spectacles.

Despite being nearly a hundred sidereal years old, he sprints from one thing to the next. He has been slowing down though and has not been taking the herbs the healers brought him when I had to send for them in our last full mooncycle.

"Boy! I am withering away!" Master's words ring to my ears, even through the floorboards, and I place his food on a tray and rush up the spiral stairs, careful not to spill.

Walking into his somewhat tamed study, most of the papers are still all neatly filed away and only a few books are left stranded on the floor, in which the Master decided to leave them.

"Good. Set it there." The Master points to his cluttered

desk. Balancing the tray in one hand, I quickly clean the half-haphazardly written letters into a pile to the side so I can place the tray down. "Send those out while you are at it."

I nod and take the stack downstairs. Heading to the entrance, I glance at the names addressed on the letters and begin folding them neatly. I grab my cloak, slip off my sandals and lace up my worn green leathered boots. I rush out into the brisk autumn morning. A flock of birds jut out from the bushes by the front door as I close it. I can still see the delivery man making his way down the mountain as the vantage point from up here lets you see everything, even the ocean's horizon just over the mountain peaks. The city of Ventraton was built into the mountain and slowly has grown its way into the valley. The beautiful orange and yellow buildings give the naturally grey and black landscape brilliant colour. Even the castle that rests above the Crestfalls is visible.

I begin my long descent into the city, careful not to slip up on a step. I enjoy the stillness of the surrounding environment, much different from the dreams I see at night. They are as colourful as the world in front of me now, but nothing is truly familiar. There are moments where I think they could be memories, but that is probably the effect of having the dream so frequently. I shake my head, trying to rid my thoughts of her cries, and try focusing on the beauty around me.

There is nothing as beautiful as a quiet mountain.

Once my feet hit the city's pavement, I can hear it waking up. Boards being posted for the mornings market, youngins dragging their feet as they rub their half-awakened eyes and make their way to their studies, buckets being dumped from balconies.

Sir Daniel's was the nearest in the letter pile.

I rush down the main avenue before turning right and

climbing one of the large eastern stairs. A few youngins giggle as I jump around them while still avoiding their gaze.

Master will not be pleased if I take too long.

I take the eastern stairs to the top of the opulent sector and turn left. I slow my pace down as the Vets generally patrol this area more heavily. I get a few strange stares and lift up the parchment to signal my purpose. It has already been more than two sunshifts by the time I reach Sir's home. The entrance of the large estate is the only portion that is visible, the rest has been excavated into the mountain itself.

A Vet stops me as I approach it. "Hold it, son. What will be your business with this household?" the Vet demands, despite it sounding more like a question. I stand about the same height as him, but my eyes find the Ventraton symbol on his chest plate. A simple "V" surrounded by a stone circle.

I hold up the parchment, and he takes it from my hand.

"I will deliver this to the Master of this household." He unfolds it and makes a grunting noise. "Babylas," the Vet says to the other standing next to him.

I nod, confirming my master's name.

"Rich lunatic," the shorter and stouter Vet grumbles.

"Leave now; inform your master it has been delivered."

I nod once more, and begin the trek to Lady Courtney's house that resides just a little further down the road, and then to Sir Brandon, Lady Melinda, Sir Curtis and Sir Tyler's afterwards. Each house looking like the next and each Vet sounding the same as they say my master's name.

I would think they would sound more honoured since the Master founded this country and backed the monarchy that now rules it.

With the letters delivered, I head down the western stairs and make my way through the main avenue towards the tower. The city has come alive now that the sun is high.

"We ran out of baguettes over a shift ago."

"Watch your step!"

"Look at these pearls; they are so beautiful."

"Don't just be standing here, buy something or move on."

"Lovely weather we are having as of late."

"One drink now won't hurt anything."

I take in the people around me and listen as I walk down the road. I find it strange how so many lives can be lived in a place like this, yet not quite sharing and celebrating in each other's lives despite them living close to one another. It is as if proximity means nothing to relativity. The distance from one person to another does not correlate or demand a relationship.

I like to think that if I were to live close to so many people, I would begin to care for them as I care for the Master.

I finish my journey and hang my cloak back onto the hook it was hanging from earlier this morning. As I unlace my boots and slip back on my slippers, I can hear the Master throwing something upstairs. Before he can realise I am home, I make my way to the kitchen and slice up some of yesterday's bread and eat it ravenously.

I should have eaten this morning and not waited so long.

Once I feel as though I won't starve, I begin to prepare the Master's lunch.

THE LOUD AND rumbling sounds of the Master's snores keep the room from being silent as I quietly clean his study. Reorganising the torn-through books, realigning his quills, while cleaning the drips of ink left here and there, and piling his dirty dishes back onto the tray I brought them up on. I wipe my forehead, looking back at the work I've done, knowing full well I will be doing it all again tomorrow.

One might think that it's his making a mess that wears him out and not his age.

As I walk the dishes down the stairs, I see a small glass jar filled with ground herbs sitting on a shelf hiding behind a frame.

That wasn't there before.

Grabbing the jar and opening it, I can smell turmeric, digitalis lanata and lantana.

He really is going to get worse if he keeps refusing his medicine.

I shake my head and seal the jar up, placing it in my pocket. I will have to remember to give it to him once he wakes up.

After washing up the dishes and putting away the ingredients I needed for the Master's lunch, I head to my room and grab the broom resting against the wall inside it. My eyes fall onto my bed, which is nothing more than a cot resting on the floor.

I am grateful to him. He bought me when I was unwanted. I'm reminded of that often.

I leave the room and shut the door behind me. There is no point in wanting more than this. This is my life, and I am wanted nowhere by no one, other than here by my master's side.

Sweeping around the house, I notice some of the paint on the walls by the skirting is peeling.

I'll need to go get the spare paint from the shed. Though, I am sure the Master could care less.

I clear some of the spiderwebs that are beginning to form in the entry hall and dust the multitude of paintings on the first floor. The Master only allows me to clean the first two floors of the tower. He has mentioned that any higher could very well get me killed. He has yet to divulge what exactly would be murdering me.

Though I imagine the dust and mess left in his wake would actually be the reason.

Noises from up above shake me from my thoughts.

The Master is up.

I check the dial in the yard and see that it's about time to get supper started. I place the broom back into my room, throw the gathered dust out onto the step and make my way into the kitchen. Lighting the stove, I fry up some of the meat we received today, along with some green beans I collected yesterday from the garden. Thumps and bangs rattle the ceiling above me as I finish plating his meal.

I'll check in with him before I serve his meal. I should have asked if he was hungry.

I climb the stairs, hearing his mumblings as I get closer to the second floor where his study resides. The door is left open, expecting my entry. I walk into the dimly lit chamber. Tables and desks are overrun with parchment, bottled liquids and jarred animal parts.

I just cleaned this room, yet it never seems to be when I step back inside. Must be cursed.

I stand still in the entrance, waiting for his instruction, watching as the long grey-haired elder scurries from one messy pile to the next. He pulls parchment after parchment, bringing them all curiously close to his face to read his own mad scribbles until he finds the one he was apparently searching for.

"Yes! Yes, this is it, the one. I need this one. This is the one that will work," Master exclaims excitedly. "Boy! Come here."

I widen my eyes, not sure where this tangent will lead now that I am involved. I hurry to his side, trying not to be obvious as I peer over his shoulder at whatever is making him so happy.

Master shoves the parchment to my chest.

He rarely allows me to be a part of whatever thing he is thinking about.

He nods excitedly as I observe the parchment, wriggling his fingers towards it. A beautiful chalice is drawn on it, along with scribbles of words in a language I do not understand.

"This is the key. This is the start of everything I have been working towards. The Chalice of Broken Wills, or originally known as the **Contritos Spirit**, created by Aruna and her sister Ayla. Many don't know it by its true name, or the sisters themselves, but it is the last piece I had been missing." Master tugs the parchment away from me and puts it close to his face once again.

I have never seen a chalice quite like it. It's beautifully ornate.

Master begins to cough, a splash of red colouring in the rough sketch. I rush towards him, holding his now crumpling form. His shoulders are thin; I feel as though I could break him if I just applied enough pressure.

He shouldn't be worrying about some chalice when his health has been declining like it has been.

Master gasps for air, trying to cling on for dear life. I take the paper from his hands and set it on the table, leading him towards the large chair sitting next to his desk hidden under a mountain of research. He grunts, sighs and settles in.

I rush away towards the kitchen, skipping a few steps as I head down. I grab a glass and use the indoor well to fill it with water.

I carefully make my way back up the stairs with the cup filled to the brim. I pull the medicine out of my pocket and finish my careful jog to his side. Master holds his hand out expectantly, but groans when he sees the jar in my hands. I stir a bit of the mix into his water using a leftover spoon on his desk. Handing over the glass, his scrawny fingers touch mine and they are cold. I glance around and see the throw I normally cover him with is laying on the ground.

I know my life ends when his does. No one will want me or take me in. My own parents didn't want me. All the nobles that I have met through the Master are scared of me because of my silence. Master likes it though; he taught me that it is best to listen, and I am very good at that.

"Boy," Master calls as I grab the throw from the floor.

I gingerly walk towards him, his eyes focusing on something far from this room.

"There are few I trust to have good morals, boy. I'd say you are part of that few." He coughs again, and I furrow my brows. "Speaking is easy when you have nothing to say; that is why I raised you to be the way you are. Someone who, when they speak, will have something to say. They will listen to your thought-out words." Master takes a deep yet shaky breath. His eyes focus on mine. My knees hit the wooden floor as I feel the weight of his very present gaze.

"I was dying long before anyone caught on, before I bought you. I knew a time would come where I would acquire the knowledge, but would likely not be able to utilise it. That is the purpose for you." My eyes break away as the words leave his mouth.

A purpose? My family did not want me. I was sold and shipped away. I do not have a purpose. He may propose, even offer one, but it is not mine. No purpose belongs to me. I am going to die the moment he does. There is no need for a purpose, anyhow.

"You are mindful, careful, thoughtful. I know you are already aware of what is going to happen to you."

He speaks to me, but his words feel like they mean nothing. Though, I have never heard him speak the way he is speaking now. His normal odd ramblings often fill every inch of this tower, but these words are quiet and are barely leaving his lips.

"Renatus," I shudder, hearing him say the name he once gifted me, "you will live and leave this place. Before I take my last breath, you will take what is needed and follow the map I provide. We won't have much time, but there are things I must teach you, skills you need to master." I can feel his hand grip and pull my hair. Forcing my head upwards. "Look at me."

I do not understand. What does he think I am capable of? I have nothing, am nothing, that is why I do not speak. I do not believe I have anything to say, to offer.

"Go find the **apparatus from Aruna** and bring them back to me." He reaches towards his desk, dropping me and grabbing a large scroll resting on the desk in front of him. "Cure death, save your master, save yourself."

I take the scroll from him, slowly rolling it out. A map of the Realm of Limoria. There are X's labelled on the map near Kena, Xan, Berkin and Yral.

"Mark an 'X' on Fosa, boy." Master coughs. "It is where you will find the Chalice of Broken Wills."

I stand and lay the map onto the desk, grabbing the ink quill and lightly putting an "X" near the capital of the Felguard Country.

Does he truly believe I will be able to travel such distances? The furthest I travelled was from Draco to Ventraton after the Master bought me, and even then I was unconscious for the majority of the trip. I cannot do this.

"Boy!" I hadn't realised he was calling me until he grabbed my wrist with the shaking quill in my hand.

Or perhaps it is my hand that is shaking the quill.

"Fetch the books sitting on that chair over there." I set the quill down and do as I am instructed. At the far end of this room, I see a chair with a stack of books taller than I. I glance back and see him staring off. Grabbing an arm full, I race back to the desk, knowing I'll have to go back and grab the rest. Once all the books reside by his side, he waves his hand downward, beckoning me to kneel. "Read these books. I want every moment spent on this until they are done."

I open my mouth to protest, but close it just as quickly.

Never speak.

"I taught you to read for this purpose. Now read."

I nod.

Now I understand why he would go through the effort and cost of educating me the way he had. I overheard many conversations from tutors that would mention the waste of teaching a servant. Especially one that chooses to be mute. I thought the same as them, and still do. The Master is not a kind man; I should have figured my lessons were out of purpose.

Grabbing the first book I see, I look at the spine; it reads ***Understanding the Four Elements and Precious Materials***.

Is he planning on teaching me Forged Magicae?

"Now you understand what must be done." He leans to his side, his face inching closer to mine. "I chose you because I saw what was inside, boy. This practice is your purpose. You will understand as you develop why immortality is a gift, and why I must have it."

I nod slowly.

What is inside me?

My hands won't stop trembling under the weight of everything unfolding in front of me.

"We do not have much time," he mutters into a cough. "Begin."

Chapter Two

The reading is intensive. Long drawn on sentences speaking about Fire, Water, Earth and Air, and the magicae that naturally flows through each of them. How to harness it, how to manipulate it, the necessary tools and ingredients needed to do any of it. There are mathematical equations and picturesque diagrams. Formulas of different manipulated ingredients to create different spells and tonics. Preaches going on about one's mind, soul and body. The tutors the Master had brought on to teach me back when I was a youngin were fast-paced and inpatient. They often scolded me for just putting the quill down to stretch my fingers or rub my eyes when I had been reading for too long. They taught me a lot, and by the end, I had exceeded the pace they had originally set. Though what the Master is asking of me now... well, this is something different altogether.

We have spent the last week from the beginning of the sunshift to the end of the moonshift reading, reciting and writing down the formulas I was able to memorise, while he would drill the ones I did not.

Every once in a while, I swear I see the Master smile.

Surprisingly, I have enjoyed the bulk of it. It's exciting to hear some of the Master's old stories he rambles on about when telling how he came across certain materials that helped him increase the effectiveness of certain spells. I've only known him as an old man, but I suppose he was once young and adventurous.

It's nice not always being alone, and I hadn't realised how much I had missed learning. I don't deserve the attention or resources the Master is giving me, but he says it's for a task I must complete to save his life. To save my life. As quick as I am catching on, I still do not see how I will accomplish his ask. I do not see how I will be able to fulfil this purpose he claims is mine.

Today is the first day of real practice. Trying to actually bring one of these spells to life. I doubt I'll be able to do it, but the Master is adamant about me getting it. We have been practising this same growth spell for a little over a sunshift.

"No. Again." The Master smacks my head with his cane he has needed to start walking around with. "You used too much salt in that vial, and your sigils were not proportioned."

Everything has to be so precise.

I grab some mud from the pile I dug up and flatten it across the stone in front of me, covering up my last attempt underneath it. I take a deep breath and shake my head. I stretch out my fingers before reaching for an empty vial. I put some of the rosemary seeds my master gave me and put them inside. I sprinkle a pinch of salt, exactly nineteen grains.

"Now only three drops, boy," the Master whispers, peering closely over my shoulder.

I grab the wet rag sitting in a bowl beside me and hold it loosely as I drip three drops of water into the vial and sigh with relief when the third drop goes in, with no others following suit. I cork the vial and set it down in my lap, straining my tired eyes as I focus back onto the mud in front of me. Wiping the sweat from my forehead, I draw the main circle in which I am casting my growth spell. I take my finger and draw a straight line from one side of the circle to the other.

"Now you got it. Carefully pour out the materials into the centre of it," Master says, slapping my shoulder.

I widen my eyes, realising how close my finger was to ruining the sigil once more. I shake it off and grab the vial from my lap, uncorking it and spilling its contents in the dead centre of my circle. Setting the vial down, I grab another handful of mud and place it on top of the materials.

"**Incrementum**," I mutter just under my breath.

My hand, still placed firmly on the mud pile, begins to heat up as a green light illuminates it. I remove my hand quickly when the heat intensifies and suddenly multiple shrubs of rosemary begin to pop out of the ground. Some of the shrubs are pushing through and cracking the stone path I am sitting on. I stand and look down a few metres where the shrubs finally stop.

"Hmph, finally. Faster than most could have learned it, but too slow for the schedule we need to keep," the Master says, standing from the chair he was sitting on. "Lets have you make up some lunch."

I look back at the shrubs and then to my hand.

I did that? No. The Master must have helped in some way. Right?

I close my hand into a fist and look out ahead and see the whole city of Ventraton far out in front of me. A city I've never thought of as home, but always as beautiful and curious. I know their thoughts on my master and of this tower.

Deranged, terrifying, foolish, rich.

I've only ever seen an old man obsessed with scribblings, but now I am slowly beginning to understand those scribblings. Languages that looked like a cluster of dots are now becoming letters. Simple items like herbs, lead, dirt, all now have a powerful purpose. I admit that when I started learning it, none of it made sense. It wasn't until my master showed me the growth spell a few days ago that I realised that Magicae is real. Though, it's still hard to believe the Master when he says he believes I am to succeed him. That I'd be able to create things out of a couple of materials and the Natural Magicae residing in the elements.

I know where I belong, and it's not out there. It's here in this tower.

"Boy!" the Master shouts, a loud cough following suit.

I drop my hand and make my way inside the front door, closing it behind me. My heart drops seeing the Master inside the kitchen rummaging around. I rush into the room and catch the bread that is falling from one of the cupboards.

"Hurry up now," he mutters and makes his way up the stairs.

I'll be done by the time he gets to the second floor. With every new day, he is growing weaker.

I quickly cut up the bread and take out the roasted lamb I prepared this morning. I slice a few pieces against the grain and make the Master a sandwich, eating the rest of the lamb as I load it onto a tray.

Once I am upstairs, he will make me do something else, so now is the only time I'll be able to eat.

I pass my room, which makes my eyelids feel heavy. I cannot remember the last time I slept a full night, but I shake my head and continue upstairs.

The Master is flipping through a red-dyed journal as I set the tray down on his desk in front of him.

"Here, read through this. It talks about the foundations of combatary Forged Magicae." The Master extends the journal out to me.

Combat?

My lip trembles and eyes widen, realising the extent I may have to go to in order for me to obtain the apparatus.

"I thought I had taught you to be smart." He sighs. "Through all this talk of immortality, I figured you would understand that you will most likely not be the only one looking for these items." I take the journal from him and turn it around in my hands.

Not only am I already unworthy of this purpose, but now I must compete with others to obtain the apparatus.

He grabs the sandwich I prepared. "Wipe that worried look off your face. As long as you keep quiet, no one should bother you." He takes a bite of the sandwich. "Sit, read. When you are done, we will go out and practise what you learned."

What if they find out, though? Does he expect me to fight?

"I said sit," the Master commands.

Looking around, the chairs are piled with dirty plates and the floor is covered with read-through books and reports. I scoot a book to the side with my foot and sit on the ground, leaning against his desk. With my studying and practising, it has not left me with much time to clean and organise.

Opening to the first page, I can tell that this is the Master's handwriting. It's messy and strangely worded, just like all of his reports and notes seem to be.

After
~~Had~~ a little bit of experimenting with the heat
spell I realised I could combine it with the
movement spell.

With precise direction, it could cause a
ball of fire that would then become a
projectile.

Required Materials:
- Ash
- Powder
- Ground Eucalyptus

3 Directions:
Combine all ~~the~~ materials into casters hand.
Focus Energy on paper with the Sigil Drawn on it
Paper should burn.
Once paper catches fire, blow materials out of hand and
the fire should expand.
Be purposful with direction for accurate aim.

1098/3/15

To burn someone to death. That's what this is for, right?

Just the thought makes me think I can smell the scent of burning flesh. A shiver runs through my body. My body recoils into itself, my knees now pressed against my chest. I try to calm myself down by flipping the page, looking at the next spell. Though the next one talks about electrocution, and harnessing the power of the sky to strike down multiple enemies at a time. The next page speaks about weaponizing an enemy's fear, making them visualise it inside their own mind, essentially blinding them for a mere moment.

A moment to kill them.

I swallow hard, my breathing uneven and barely reaching my lungs. The lamb in my stomach feels like it's about to come back up.

The thought of hurting someone has never crossed my mind.

I've read about violence in the textbooks my tutors once had me read through, but even then it was almost talked about as an afterthought.

But these spells are meant to be violent.

I turn to the next page and see a spell where it shows me how to disrupt the ground beneath me, shifting and shaping it to my will. The intent is to trap enemies under the earth or even crush them.

Has the Master taken someone's life before?

From the way these pages look, they seem to have seen more of this world than I have. Precautionary no longer feels like the truth of the matter.

I'm scared. I'm a servant. I have to do as I'm told. I'm not worthy of this purpose. I shouldn't have one. He intends for me to kill anyone who becomes an obstacle. I cannot do this. I will fail because I don't think I can take someone's life.

"I'm all finished boy." The Master grunts. I hear his chair squeak from his shifting weight. "You're still reading? What's the matter with you? Should be finished by now." The cane smacks my head, and I bend forward away from him.

This is beyond my capabilities. I cannot hurt someone for these things.

I turn to slightly meet his gaze, a tear falling from mine. The Master grunts and suddenly his elderly fingers are gripping the journal, pulling it towards him.

"So fragile," the Master mumbles. He flips through the pages. The sigh that follows relaxes his shoulders, and he slumps back into his chair.

"I want you to answer this question for me," the Master says, ending in a cough. He grabs the napkin that he used during lunch to wipe some of the blood from his chin. "Why are you afraid?"

Because I am not meant for this.

"Don't just stare off in space. Answer me."

"I am afraid that I am incapable of completing the task. That I am not worthy of a purpose. That I'll have to..."

"Wrong," the Master cuts me off. "You are afraid because you have been spoiled with contentment. Wasting what has been in front of you this entire time. Renatus. You naïve boy. Life is about the circumstances of birth and what one chooses to do about it. Worthy has little to do with anything. You don't live in a fairytale. Plenty of those without a single heroic bone in their body achieve greatness. Look at me. I know you do not see me as a good man, and I am not one."

Even if we take worth out of the picture.

He throws the journal onto the desk and looks down to meet my gaze as I peer up just over the desk's edge.

Is there really a choice here?

"My circumstance of birth was that I was born with intelligence, ambition and more money than some countries had access to. I could have chosen to have lived life as my mother did. Surrounded by the simple things, books, her children and a husband who adored her. Or I could have chosen to have lived as my father had. Someone who paid no mind to the money he spent hosting guests and buying every luxury that crossed his path." The Master rubs his eyes and looks back to me with his eyes lulled and tired. "Instead, I chose to be neither. I chose to use my intelligence to study forgotten texts, used the wealth that was left to me to found a country where I could make Forged Magicae a legal practice and my ambition to make it all happen and teach others my learnings."

I rest my head against the edge of the desk, taking in his words.

I am none of those things. Not ambitious, not rich; I hardly have intelligence. Why does he think I can do this? I've never done anything outside of what I was told to do, and finding these items leaves too much open for me to decide. If the time comes, how am I supposed to decide if someone lives or dies?

I bite my lip, gripping the desk tightly.

"Stop that pouting! You have your own set of circumstances you were gifted with. You were born with perspective, naturally gifted at anything you handle and sold to someone who is giving you the tools to be something." He slams his hand on the desk, bringing my eyes up to meet his once more. I've never heard the Master yell like this. His eyes are wide and hands are shaking. "Now you have a choice. Consider your circumstance, consider the options laid out and those unspoken. Decide for yourself how you will accomplish the task your Master has given you." The Master grabs the journal once more and throws it at my head. It bounces off and lands on the floor. My eyes fall to stare at it.

"Lastly, I'm sure the thought of killing someone doesn't please you, but one day, it might be necessary. You will know when that time comes and kill." He stands with a few grunts and slowly makes his way out of the room and up to a higher chamber where his bedroom resides.

Perspective, naturally gifted, in the hands of someone powerful. Is that really what he thinks?

I take the red-dyed journal in both hands.

Decide how I want to do this?

My life has been living by his commands. The most I've decided is what to cook, or what order in which I accomplish the chores around the tower.

How am I supposed to choose what is the best course of action regarding this?

I stand from my kneeled position and quietly walk down the spiral stairs. The Master's words were said harshly, but were meant to be kind and encouraging. He seems to truly believe in my ability to accomplish this, but how do I decide? What don't I want?

I don't want to hurt anyone. I don't want my master to die. I don't want to leave the tower. I don't want things to change.

What are things I can decide on?

Whether or not I hurt someone. Whether or not the Master dies forever.

How do I bring back the apparatus?

I'll ask first and take it if I have to. Run and flee instead of staying and fighting.

I open the door to my room, leaving it slightly ajar to let the flickering firelight in. Sitting on the cot, I cross my legs and stare down at the journal now resting in my lap. I open it back up.

I'll learn what spells can help me the way I want to do this.

I wonder if the Master meant what he said.

Though maybe that is just the means to obtain his selfish goal.

CHAPTER THREE

THE WOODEN CEILING above me is the same one I have stared up at since I was brought here. Duller in colour and stained from a leak we experienced one winter, but still the same. I turn to the side, my back stiff from laying in the same position for too long.

I've changed too.

Grown taller, stronger and smarter since my master bought me. My eyes rest on the journal laying next to me, and I put my hand on top of it. I didn't realise how much I've changed until the Master tasked me with assembling immortality. I've been tested in my ability to retain information, have pushed myself beyond my normal duties, studied a skill set that almost seems unattainable and had to make an actual choice. Even if that choice was just a small one in the large scheme of the Master's plans, it's still my own.

What else can I make mine?

I turn back to face the ceiling once more. It's changed even though it did nothing but exist in this world. I wonder if by just existing, the world outside this tower will change me even more. Come back duller in colour and with a stain from bad weather. Another choice I cannot make, but something that will happen, regardless. I close my eyes, images of the last week appearing behind my closed lids and the Master's words ringing in my ears.

Wasting what has been in front of you this entire time.

He meant the knowledge that resides inside this tower. Master has boasted about how expansive and rare his collection of knowledge is. He, himself, is a great resource as well, being one of the first mass producers of the Forged Magicae education and the leading advocate to make it a legal practice all throughout Limoria.

Like last night, I could choose what I learn. Grasping the knowledge on subjects that I want to learn. What do I want to learn?

My eyes dart open as I hear the Master's footsteps hit the stairs. I rise from my cot, grabbing the red journal as I do, and open the door. It's not until I am standing that I realise how tired I am. Sleep did not come to me last night.

I stand at the foot of the stairs, waiting for the Master to appear. As his head finally comes around the bend, his eyes greet mine. He pauses for a moment, eyes drifting to the journal in my hand. A smile creeps across his face and nods. A shiver runs down my spine seeing that smile.

I wonder what thought ran through his mind.

"Bring me my breakfast in my bed." I try not to look completely shocked, hearing him say this. I have never once travelled above the second floor, though, oftentimes, my mind wonders how dusty, dirty and detestable the higher floors must be.

The Master turns, breaking for a second to adjust himself and climbs back up the stairs without need of confirmation from me.

His condition is getting worse.

I rush to the kitchen, set the journal down on the counter, and begin to prepare some eggs and slices of ham. I fill up a cup of milk and prepare some tea with the herbs the healers said he needed to take.

I put the journal and his breakfast on the same wooden tray I use with every meal and make my way to the stairs. My feet drag with every step up towards the third floor. The Master values his privacy over all things, even his reputation. He once told me that secrets are one's most valuable asset, and that is why he keeps all of them close to his chest. Won't even allow his servant to clean his chambers.

What secrets will I uncover? What mess lies just beyond the bend?

The last steps creak as I find myself at the third floor platform. A single door curved at the top and a golden handle with the Master's initials, BA.

Babylas Amara.

When he first brought me to the tower, he made sure I knew my new name. Renatus Amara. He quickly added that he wouldn't be addressing me formally, but that I needed to know it. When he does call me by my name, it's always unsettling. Like a curse just escaped his lips and something terrible was going to follow.

I'm not sure why it feels that way.

The stairs continue further upwards after this platform. I peer over the corner slightly, knowing full well I won't be able to see anything anyway, but getting a peek at the third floor makes me curious about the one after.

What lies beyond the spiral? Is that something I want to learn?

I shake my head and knock on the Master's door lightly, hearing some disgruntled noises come from inside as I open it.

There is hardly anything in the room.

There's a large red wooden canopy bed sitting in the centre, a matching wardrobe to the right of it, and an ornate rug that is nearly large enough to fit the floor of the room perfectly.

No dust, no mess, just this.

I was expecting books littered among a dozen or so wardrobes filled with clothes never worn or worn through. Mountains of dust and unidentifiable things covering the floor like the rug that is actually there.

"Stop gawking and deliver me my breakfast." The Master grunts, readjusting to be in a more upright position.

Walking over, I notice a small portrait sitting to the right of him in bed.

Don't stare. He's probably only having me here because he is getting weaker.

I place the tray in his lap and step back a few inches. He nods at the food before turning his gaze towards me.

"Did you finish reading?" the Master asks, tucking a part of the napkin cloth into his nightshirt.

I nod my head.

"You decided to go the escapist route? Your demeanour last night spoke louder than any word you could have muttered."

I simply nod again at his words.

I don't want to hurt anyone. The Master gave me a choice, and that's what I want to choose.

"Regardless, you need to learn those spells and prepare yourself for a fight." He doesn't look towards me this time for a confirmation. This is something he is requesting of me.

"We will get to that a bit later. While I eat—" He takes a bite. Master chews for a moment before continuing. "Take my keys and go look up on the floor just above this one. I want you to really look, not organise or clean, but look for something that draws you into it." He reaches over to where the portrait is, and I can hear the muted sound of metal clanging. Master pulls the keys from under the covers and tosses them over to me. "I mean it. Do not clean," he says through another bite. "In fact, don't touch anything at all."

So up there is where the mess is hiding.

I nod, somewhat understanding his request. I take my leave and close the Master's door behind me, looking now upward towards another floor that was once off limits.

I guess I do not need to choose this time. I will be learning what's just ahead, per the Master's request.

Beginning my ascent, the noise the stairs normally make is not continued on this next flight of them. It's quiet, only my unsteady breaths are audible. Rounding the curve of the stairs, I see another top round door at the summit of the stairs, but this one is not off to the side like the Master's. Without the keys, there would be no way to continue upwards. The door matches the Master's, but the doorknob is different. There is not one at all, just a keyhole in the shape of a square. I look at the keys he handed me and there are only four with a similar block shape, though each has a shape protruding off of it. An S, N, E, and W.

A lock only works with one particular shape of key, right?

Deciding on the S-shaped key to try first, I slowly insert it – a bright blue light shines through the door instantly. I look away to shield my eyes; turning back, I see multiple towers of items in front of me. They stretch upwards and outwards, taller and thicker than I am. I turn around and the stairs are gone; a similar shaped door is in front of me instead. The key hole is the same squared shape, but an engraved "N" is residing just above it. Slowly turning back around, the room expands, the floor barely visible with the number of objects in this room. There are cases lining all four walls, corner to corner.

There are corners?

I shake my head, trying to ignore that fact for a moment and focus on the sheer amount of things. Pile after pile of strange-looking items, display racks randomly placed throughout the room, mounted creature heads on the walls.

I do not think I am in the same tower as I just was.

As my eyes do another scan of my surroundings, I notice now the amount of natural light coming in and illuminating the space around me. Leaning to the side, I can see a window on the other side of the room. I begin walking towards it, and notice two more windows on either side of me.

The Master's tower does not have this many windows.

Finishing my tentative stride to the nearest window, being careful not to step on any cloaks, stray darts, daggers or swords. A sigh of relief comes over me as I pry the somewhat sticky window open; the need to obtain a grasp on my surroundings nearly causes me a moment of panic. Looking out to the left, the right and straight down, the only thing viable is water.

Nothing but water.

The sound of crashing waves hitting the ground and stone walls beneath me makes me wonder if the Master is that powerful. If he could move the oceans as easily as he just moved me with the turn of a key. I let the cool sea breeze wash away the sickness of nervousness coming on from staring at the height in which I am at. A screeching noise drives away the little calm I am soaking in, and I whip around and see a flying creature coming straight towards me.

I'm going to die!

Ducking out of the way, the floor catches me with a loud thud and the creature flies past me and out the window. I scramble to my feet and look to see it flying straight up, the sun illuminating the mesmerising green and blue feathers that run the length of its slender, near malnourished body. I can now see its pearl white horns and its four raven black talons. It flies up so high it disappears from my sight. I finally exhale the breath caught inside of me from when I saw it coming towards me.

Now the Master said not to touch anything, and I am hoping that letting this thing out does not count as touching.

Pushing the thought of something mauling me to the side, hoping nothing will, Master instructed me to look and find something that draws me in.

Whatever that means.

Walking around the room, it's almost impossible to even see anything, really. There are dozens of bows, probably a hundred swords amongst everything, some horns, helmets, gloves that have somehow stayed with their match, but they are all resting on top of each other. I understand why the Master said not to touch; pulling anything out to look would cause all of it to come crashing down.

I'd probably be impaled by an unsheathed blade.

I wander around the different piles for a while, nothing that I would classify as drawing me in. Though I have never had much interest in material things, nothing has ever been mine. I sit down on the ground and lean back, looking upward. There are tropical flowers painted all across the ceiling. Each one looks slightly different from the last.

Maybe that creature was it, and I just let it go.

I lay down as my stomach begins to ache. My mind was so distracted this morning and then too eager to see what was here that I forgot to eat anything. Though this was definitely the mess I had imagined his room to be. It is a room filled with weapons, apparatus, clothing and items that the Master must have collected over his nearly hundred years of life.

Nothing looks all that special. Nothing glowing or brilliantly shiny, and no blades bursting with fire.

A laugh slips my lips for a moment as the story my mother used to tell me as a youngin comes to memory. A heroic knight with a sword that burned like fire and a suit of armour that shined like the sun. He saved any and all who found themselves to be in trouble.

Master's red journal also comes to mind. That heroic knight killed the villains in the story so he could save innocent lives, save kingdoms.

Would I be able to kill someone if it meant losing the apparatus that the Master is looking for? Is it a good enough reason?

I turn my head and see the end of a green handle sticking out from underneath the pile of items. I roll over onto my stomach and reach for it. The leather on the handle is soft and fits my hand pretty well. I pull it towards me; it somehow comes loose from the weight that should have been pinning it down.

A whip?

Though it's unlike any I've ever seen. The butt end is silver, its handle green with brown and green leather woven together and a thin silver band wrapping around in a spiral. The thong of the whip is what is truly strange. It looks like it's made out of deep green wood. My hand grazes the thong, the texture definitely that of wood, but it bends and twists like a normal whip would. The end is dipped in silver and it appears extremely sharp.

My curiosity is not that hungry to find out just how sharp.

A green flash illuminates the room as my eyes lock onto a strange marking carved into its handle. I stand up and walk to a different window than the last one I was at, and open it. The view of the sea is still there. I take a few steps back from the now opened window and fix my grip on the handle.

I lift my hand up with the whip, bending at the elbow and

bring my hand back down. The whip comes to life, shooting out the window, extending further than what the original length of the thong was. It sounds like wood cracking. I pull the whip back and the whip listens to me, coming back in with accuracy and retracting back into its original size. I look down at my hand and the whip.

What did I just do?

I drop the whip and step away. My eyes focus on my trembling hand. I have never used something like that. Sure, I've seen a whip and read about the anatomy of a whip, but it didn't explain how to use it.

Why did I even grab it?

It was underneath a pile of the Master's things and it just pulled out as if nothing was on it at all. I've never read about things like this.

Is that normal?

I close my open palm into a fist and try to swallow down the large lump that found its way into my throat. Glancing back at the whip, I move towards it once more. I carefully inspect it before grabbing it by the butt. Maybe the Master would know what had just happened.

This must be the draw Master was talking about. I can still feel it, but much less now than when I first saw it.

I let out a sigh as I look around the room; the door is hiding to the side of one of the mounds. I start making my way over to it, though the sound of a bird's wings flapping wins over my attention. The blue and green feathered creature, with pearls for eyes, looks right at me.

So it just wanted some fresh air.

I walk over to it, timidly extending my hand towards its head. It quickly flies past me, my breath catching as it does, and dives into one of the larger piles. I rub my eyes, not sure if I saw that right.

Not a single item moved. Just like when I pulled out the whip.

I shake my head, knowing I'll need to ask the Master about that one, and continue my way back to the Ventraton tower. I use the key and I come face to face with the magicae door once again.

CHAPTER FOUR

I walk down the stairs, where I can hear soft snores echoing from inside his chambers. Sneaking past the doorway, I head straight for his study, knowing the Master must have a book regarding the apparatus sigils and enchantments. I place the whip on the Master's desk and begin looking through the dozens of bookshelves that are overflowing with texts.

There are at least twenty books in the first two cases on sigils.

I take a random guess and pull the book titled **Cognisance of Sigils**. I flip through the first few pages and realise that it's breaking down the language of a sigil and how, over time, they have become more complex due to the loss of ties to the places beyond the doorways. It's interesting that even Forged Magicae has been somewhat affected by the depletion of Natural Magicae, but it makes sense because Forged Magicae was created by harnessing the Natural Magicae that used to run rampant simply by manipulating through it using sigils, enchanted apparatus and spells.

Placing the book back where I had taken it from, I pull the next one off. **Symbols and Sigils**. Flipping through this one, it shows where sigils originate and talks about the mothers of Forged Magicae, Aruna and Ayla. I sit for a moment as I read a few passages talking about the twin sisters from Caelum that gave birth to the new age of magicae. Not much is known about them, but it's believed that most of the apparatus created were forged by them. They had very few mentees and helped establish some major military forces as well as governments, including some involvement in the old world's capital.

It's almost unbelievable there are folk that are that powerful. Makes even what the Master has accomplished seem like only a fraction as impressive.

From what the Master told me, Aruna was the creator of the apparatus that, when used together, can cure death.

Does that mean Aruna and Ayla are still alive? Did they use it themselves?

I shake my head. The whole vitaterrium would know they were still alive if they had.

What will happen when folk find out the Master is immortal?

Creaking wood pulls me away from the text, and I see the Master leaning against the curved door frame. "What are you," he coughs for a moment, "getting into?" His eyes squint, like he is trying to recognise the book I have by shape and colour alone. I hold it up, making the cover visible to him. "Hm. Did you do as asked?"

I nod and point to the desk.

I am really hoping he forgot about the whole don't touch rule.

Master walks over and sees the whip laying there coiled. He looks at it carefully, eyes wide and nose pointed upwards, before picking it up. "**The Kindled Whip**."

I stand and place the book I have back where it belongs, rushing over to the Master after I do. Looking at it again reminds me of the feeling when I first saw it, but it's only a remembrance and not the feeling itself.

It was like I was, possessed? No, like I was determined to use it. I've never been so confident about anything before.

Master turns the whip over so both of us can see the sigil resting on the handle. "The magicae that is bonded to this whip by the sigil is old." He clears his throat before continuing. "Look at how spaced the design is. Thick, deep-rooted lines mean the more magicae it intended to store and absorb. You have been practising complex, tight designed and more nature-based Forged Magicae that now requires a dependence on the life force of all living things." He hands me the whip and takes a seat at his desk, sighing heavily as he does.

I look at the old man in front of me, his already thin frame looking thinner, weaker and tired.

How much time does he have left? How much time do I have left to learn?

"I used it," I whisper, glueing my eyes to the floor.

"That is because of the magicae that resides over that room. Enter it again at another time in your life and something else may draw you in instead." I look up and see that weird look on his face again.

He's smiling at me.

Whatever that magicae is, it drew me to the thing I needed or maybe even wanted at the moment of me entering it.

He knew I would touch something.

"When I inserted the key," I start to explain, and the Master nods.

"You were taken from this tower and transported to the other one." He states like it's an obvious fact. "It resides in the Seeker's Territory, far off the coast."

My jaw opens slightly, hearing the distance I travelled in that brief second.

How did I get there, though?

The Master laughs and then coughs. "You need to work on

not giving your thoughts away by the looks you wear. If you want to know more about it, go look for the answers." Master gestures to all the books riddled on the shelves and throughout the messy room.

I nod.

Just like I did before.

The Master tries to stand but is visibly tired. I rush to his side and assist him, walking up the stairs and laying him in his bed. I walk downstairs and grab him a glass of water.

This mess is quite bothersome.

The kitchen is messy. Dishes in the sink, crumbs and food sitting on the counters.

The Master probably hasn't eaten enough today.

With a heavy sigh, I pull more mess out of the cabinets and make the Master some soup. I swallow the contents of my own bowl quickly, burning my tongue, before taking the Master's bowl to him. As I go to enter the Master's room, I see him holding the frame that was resting next to him earlier.

"Are you waiting for me, my dear Leana?" His voice is a whisper. "We will see each other soon; Aruna's apparatus will be ours." He chuckles to himself.

Ours?

I knock on the door, and the Master puts the frame next to him. "In, boy." His tone is back to its normal stern one.

I bring the Master a glass of water and a bowl of tomato soup. He gives me a list of titles he wants me to read, along with my independent study into the magicae that transported me across the realm.

I leave the room, closing the door behind me. Making my way back down the stairs to the study, I find the titles the Master had instructed me to read. Making sure to also keep an eye out for something regarding teleportation or movement magicae. Unfortunately, I don't see anything amongst the shelves. I walk over to the Master's desk and set the large pile of books on the ground next to it. I glance over some of the titles that the Master had always insisted should stay on his desk and would never let me put away. I see one that reads ***Teleporta-tion, Movement and Evaporation Magicae***.

This must be the book the Master wanted me to find.

I turn to the first page and notice my master's name printed as one of the writers of this book, along a Leana Varis.

That was the name the Master muttered earlier. He seemed to talk to the memory of her sweetly, and the words he used made it seem like she was no longer amongst the living.

I shake my head to rid myself of the thoughts for the time being.

Reading through the first couple of pages, I understand now just how complex this type of magicae really is. So far, I've noticed a pattern that most of the more complex spells are generally built on top of a simpler one. This book explains it outright. The basics is movement, which can increase and decrease a user's or target's speed. The step above that is tele-portation, which depending where you are, what is used and when it is cast can determine the distance, how you travel and the number of people transported. Teleportation is a skill that is nearly impossible without an enchanted item, sigil or script. It reads that the item method is when an item is crafted from the Natural Magicae users' magicae itself, though that method has long died out. The sigil method allows a Natural Magicae user to attach their magicae to an object, creating an apparatus. Then the script method is when a Forged Magicae user spends a period of time solely concentrating their energy, mind and soul into channelling the vitaterrium's life force as well as their own into a script in which they recite to teleport. The text says that script method is one of the most advanced techniques of magicae control and that very few have been able to accomplish a successful script.

I wonder what method the Master used. The sigil seems to be the easiest, but you need to find someone who has the capabilities of teleportation. If I could find someone like this, or learn how to do it myself, it would make finding the apparatus a lot easier. I wouldn't have to fight anyone as well.

I keep reading on, now invested in understanding the step above teleportation; evaporation. The book warns me that evaporation magicae is deadly and hard to control. Something that only well-trained and expert Forged Magicae users can even muster. My heart sinks, seeing that it is intended to evaporate an enemy or monster instantly.

Why would someone need to go to this extreme of a measure?

I swallow hard and close the book, my curiosity over fed. I close my eyes, leaning my head back. Not just today, but the last week has been unlike the rest of my life. I have read things I can hardly believe, created things I didn't think possible, done things I had never done before.

I feel like I want more, but it is also terrifying. Terrifying not just because of what I've learned, but because I actually want something.

Putting the book to the side, I look at the pile of books I need to read.

THE MASTER's thunderous snores pull me from the text talking about the different herbs and where to find them. As interesting as the world of herbology is, the Master's whispers and the name "Leana" keep rattling in my mind. I sneak away from the desk, being mindful of where the floorboards normally creak. Climbing back up the stairs, I feel my heart racing.

I really shouldn't be doing this, but this is something I am choosing to learn. So the Master cannot be mad, right?

I open the door and see the sleeping form of my master. I stand there for a moment watching him, making sure he hadn't woken up to my presence. Slowly, I make my way to the right side of the large canopy bed. The painting is still where I saw it before. I pick it up and look closely at the beautiful red-haired woman smiling back at me. Her hair falls to her waist, her eyes a striking golden colour, her lips and cheeks perfectly rosy.

She looks young in this painting, maybe in her twentieth sidereal year or perhaps her thirtieth?

I memorise her soft features.

She is very important to the Master, that much is clear.

I set the painting back where I had taken it from.

"Getting comfortable, are we?" the Master grunts. I jump from the side of the bed and immediately fall to my knees, bowing my head towards him. "It's easy to get swept up in the curiosity of things. I don't seem as crazy now, do I?" His laugh ends with a soft cough. I raise my head and see him smiling at me again.

No, not so crazy.

"I am glad you still have the mind of an innocent boy. The potential power you could have is not intoxicating you like it has me." I look back to the ground as I listen. "As you collect the apparatus, the power you wield may become tempting, so keep in mind the morality you have decided on for yourself."

Not to hurt others, to complete the task, to save the Master and continue living on like I always have.

"If that's the morality you still want, that is."

My eyes widen hearing the Master's words. I stand and look at him now.

Maybe not like I always have.

There's that smile again.

CHAPTER FIVE

THE MASTER's cough has worsened in this last week, and even the small amount of training we have done today seems to have worn him out. As we barely climb to the second floor landing, the Master's knees buckle underneath him.

"My chair," the Master mumbles weakly under his breath.

I do as I am told, and with what strength I do have, carry him over to his seat in the study. I take the red journal I had been using to practise earlier out of the back of my belt and place it on the desk. Rushing down to the moulding kitchen, I grab a glass of water for the Master and rush back up.

How much longer do I have with the Master?

I hand him the glass and he takes a few sips before clearing his throat. "You've changed. Forged Magicae has opened something within you, as I knew it would. Despite your timidness, you've grown curious, and I—" a rough cough interrupts him. He takes another sip of the water. "I know it means that you are ready. Curiosity is another shade of courage; it'll push you forward even when you are scared."

No, I'm not ready! There are so many questions I don't have answers to. Problems, if they were to arise, I would not have solutions for. A lack of confidence that is needed to travel all across

Limoria and do whatever it takes to obtain the apparatus. I'm scared.

The Master reaches down towards the red journal, knocking some of the papers on his desk to the ground, and hands it to me once again. "Fear is what keeps power in balance. Be afraid, but remain curious." He pats my face a little too hard and leans back in his chair. "Now go fetch some more of that medicine the healers forced on me. It seems to be the only thing keeping me out of that bed and talking. You may be ready, but we might as well use the time we have left."

This medicine is giving us borrowed time, and I am thankful for every second.

I nod and head down the stairs towards the entryway. Setting the journal onto the entry table, I grab my cloak, pat the already attached Kindled Whip on my belt, throw my satchel over my shoulder and tie up my leather boots. I head out the door but look back at the journal sitting there.

I'll probably have to wait for the medicine. I can continue studying through it then.

I grab the journal and put it into my satchel. I close the door behind me and begin my trek down the path towards the city.

The healers building is in the centre of Ventraton; it'll take me a few sunshifts to get there and back.

I don't normally travel out this late in the day, but I am just glad the Master has actually been taking his medicine.

The sun sets just beyond the castle, the orange sky blending with the orange-dyed stone the city is made out of. The grey natural stone that surrounds Ventraton, and that the castle rests on, glimmers at this time of day. It all looks so warm, unlike the cool wind that nips at my ears and nose.

Walking down the somewhat overgrown path, I recognise most of the flora from that herbology book the Master wanted me to read. I bend down and pick up some mint and sage, placing my findings in my satchel.

As boring as some of that reading is, it all has its purpose.

I pick up the pace a bit and start jogging towards the city, being mindful of the uneven road. As I reach the city's pavement, a few Vets look in my direction. I avoid their eyes and just keep moving in the direction I need to go. The city is busier than I am used to. Most of the produce and merchant stores are closed, and they are all coming out to enjoy their evenings. I pass by the Tipsy Port Tavern; the door is wide open, letting the cold in to cool the loud laughing crowd inside. The smell of cooked meat and alcohol fills the air.

That seems more like a nightmare than a good time. So loud you wouldn't be able to think, and so crowded you wouldn't have space to breathe.

I move through the thickening crowds of people walking up and down the main road as I get closer to the centre of the city. My shoulder hits against something and I look over at a woman dressed nicely, but has a face filled with disgust. A hand appears to the side of me and grabs the collar of my cloak.

"Watch it!" A man that must be accompanying the woman shouts as he pushes me backwards, and my back hits something that topples to the ground behind me, making me almost fall on top of whatever it is. "Look, there he goes again, running into people."

"No manners," the woman chips in with a scoff.

I turn and see a brunette girl sitting on the ground. Her golden paled over eyes narrow, not at me but the man who pushed me. I offer my hand to assist her up, but she slaps it away and stands on her own. She walks up to the man and punches him in the face.

"Next time, watch where you shove somebody." Despite her heavy breaths and angry expression, her voice sounds even and nonchalant. A shiver runs through my body as she glances towards me for a moment, smiling a half hearted grin before focusing back onto the nicely dressed woman who shrieks seeing the same thing I am.

I should get out of here before the Vets come.

I turn and begin walking again towards my destination, but I look back and see the man slowly standing with the help of the lady he is accompanying. The girl is gone, though.

Guess she had the same thought I did.

"You are tall, but when you hunch like that, it makes you look weak," the golden-eyed girl says from next to me. "You should also meet people's gazes." I freeze, and she chuckles with a monotone laugh, stopping with me.

Why is she talking to me? I hunch so people don't pay attention.

This is probably her way of trying to give me some advice to not wind up in a similar situation. I nod and start walking again, looking off in another direction, hoping she will get the hint that I am not wanting to continue the conversation.

"Alright, well, see you around," she says from slightly behind me.

Don't look. Don't look.

I lower my chin, looking slightly off to the left to glance over my shoulder at her walking just a few metres behind me. Her focus is on a street vendor selling an assortment of ornate things. I glance her over, her simple clothes, hair pulled back tightly with not a single strand loose, and her golden eyes are as dead as a corpse. I focus on the pavement, glimpsing up at the traffic I'm fighting through occasionally.

What if she is following me?

Shaking my head, I try to push past the notion that I am any more noticeable. I turn my head upwards towards the night sky. The bright lights shining from the thousands of lanterns here in the city nearly outshine the stars themselves.

"Oh, wow!" a woman standing next to me says. I look over, with just my eyes, and see her staring right at me. "You look so handsome!" she says, giggling, her hand coming up to cover her smile slightly.

I widen my eyes and put my head back down, picking up the pace and weaving in and out of the crowd to get away from her.

Handsome? What is that even supposed to mean for someone like me? She just wasn't looking close enough to see that I am nothing, a nobody.

"Can't take a compliment, huh?" The mysterious girl's voice rings out from just behind me. I jump a metre ahead of where I was and turn around to face her. She is smiling, her lips obey, but her eyes do not. She steps closer. "Did I spook you? I thought you knew I was right behind you."

Yes, but not that close.

"I told you that if you stopped hunching, you wouldn't look so weak. You got a girl's attention just by looking up." I look over, hearing her comment, and my mouth runs dry as I watch her eyes take in every inch of me.

She sighs and continues walking alongside me the rest of the way to the healers building. A large building that is circled by pavement, six different roads leading to this one spot.

Please turn down another road.

"Are you sick or something? You should have said something if you are. Should have probably said 'thank you' too after I helped you out back there." Her voice is still in the even pitch.

I glance up for a moment with my brow furrowed and eyes shifting from hers to the door. I give her a simple wave before turning away from her and walking inside. The smell of boiling herbs and ointments hits my nose almost instantly. I wiggle my nose a bit, trying to adjust to the intensity of the smell.

A younger looking male with curly long hair greets me with a smile. "Welcome, you two. How can the healers help you today?"

Two?

I freeze and glance back over my shoulder once more to see the girl standing right behind me.

What is happening? Why is she following me?

She notices me looking and gives me a tight smile again before gesturing for me to step forward towards the man. I turn back and walk up to the desk.

"I am here to pick some medicine up for my master." The words come out soft, making the man lean forward to hear.

"Ah, I remember you! The quiet demeanour and those eyes. They just pop out against your skin; I'm sure you attract plenty of attention with that combination." He smiles brightly at me. His words sounding far too friendly. Though I recognise him too. He came to the Master's house with the healers last time. He was studying to be a healer at that point.

He probably still is.

"I can get working on that for you. There is a seating area just through the curtain over there." He points in the direction of an orange curtain that stands out amongst the white ones that are strung up everywhere else.

I nod my head and walk through the curtain. I hear it shift again, as I am sure the girl from before just followed me through it. There are five benches in this cube of sheets. There are already four people in here, so I take the last empty bench near the back corner.

"Well, now I know you have the ability to talk." She sighs, sitting on the bench. She scoots close to me, and I turn my head. As our eyes meet, I can feel something sharp press up against my neck. "I think it's so funny how small Vitaterrium really is. I was on my way to see you and Babylas, then like out of some miracle, you were right there in front of me." She smiles, not like the tight one she's flashed at me before, but one so big her eyes are wide.

My whole body is shaking.

Why is she doing this? What does she want? What is she planning on doing?

She laughs and puts the knife she is holding in her hands down. "Just kidding." Her eyes shift forward, and so I follow her gaze and notice one of the other visitors looking at us.

She wasn't kidding; she just didn't want to get caught.

"I was hoping we could talk. If you help me out, I can help take care of you once your master dies. I just need you to know how serious I am and what I am willing to do to succeed in getting what I want." The sound of each "I" comes out harsh and demanding, but every other word was still in that even tone. "Though now that I've actually met you, I think we could be a lot more than just two people put together due to circumstance."

What does that mean? And if she is looking for information and help, I doubt threatening someone is really the best way to get it.

My heart is beating so fast I'm afraid she might hear it.

I need to do something.

"What's your name?" My voice is just as shaky as my body. I avoid her eyes and look ahead at one of the orange hanging sheet dividers.

"Seodi. I already know yours. I had a few questions for your master, but it's well known how secretive he can be. Do you think you could answer my questions?" Seodi leans closer, setting her head on my shoulder and wrapping her arm around mine.

In the corner of my eye, I see the visitor who is watching us turn away.

I'd be uncomfortable staring, too.

"You are very warm. Are you feeling alright?" Seodi hums close to my ear.

No, not really. I'm sweating and shaking. I want to go back to the tower, alone.

"We can make this quick if you want. Just answer my questions. Where are Aruna's apparatus? He's been looking for them since he started his Forged Magicae career, and someone was kind enough to let my little group know that he's close to start his hunt for them."

I try not to, but I stiffen, hearing her ask about the items the Master is charging me with finding.

He was right.

People are after them, just as he is. She's already threatened me with a knife, and doesn't seem scared to hurt people like I am.

That's a problem.

I can feel her grip on me tighten. "You are a handsome guy, even if you are just a servant. I'd hate to see anything happen to that face of yours." She giggles, her lips grazing my cheek and her free hand resting high up on my thigh.

There is a lump rising in my throat; my legs bounce up and down.

Can anyone else hear all of this? Someone, just look, listen, help me!

Her hand begins to wander up the inseam of trousers. "You look so... nervous."

My lip begins to tremble, and I close my eyes tightly.

Stop, please.

The curtain opens, my eyes opening to see, and the man from the front desk steps through. "Renatus?" He scans the room until his eyes land on Seodi and me. He diverts his eyes quickly.

I stand, hoping to pull myself away from her grasp, but she stands in sync with me. We walk over to the man together; him holding out the jar of herbs.

"I was right! Even with that shy personality, those looks of your shine through. Congrat—" his speech slows as our eyes lock "—ulations." He looks over to her and knits his brows.

"Funny! I was just telling him how handsome I thought he was," she says, removing one of her hands from my arm to brush some of my hair back away from my sweaty brow. "I try not to be so affectionate when we are out, but I can't help myself." Seodi laughs and smiles at the guy.

"I bet." He laughs, it comes out a little forced. "Oh! I almost forgot. I promised Master Babylas I'd get him something the last time I saw you. Just stay here, and I'll quickly grab it."

"Okay," I spit out, noticing Seodi about to say something.

If I can tell there is concern on his end, I'm sure she's noticed, too.

"Hm, I think we should get going instead, Renatus." The hand Seodi still has on my arm starts tightening, almost too much.

"I'll answer your questions after." I turn to her and whisper. Her eyes are half-lidded, but look up into mine.

A sigh leaves her mouth, and she drops my arm and goes to sit back down. I follow tentatively behind her.

I'm just hoping that it really is a concern that man was feeling.

I ball my hands into fists, trying to stop my body from shaking so much.

Seodi pats the spot on the bench next to her, inviting me to sit closely. I stop walking for a moment, and her eyes harden. I take the seat and stare forwards once more.

"I'm not a very patient gal, Renatus. Please keep that in mind." She admits, no, more-so warning me. She rests her head back on my shoulder and yawns.

It's like she knows what makes me uncomfortable. She wants me on edge. I need to try to show her I'm not afraid, even if I really am.

"What does your group do?" I tentatively ask, turning my head to her. She leans her head back, our faces only a few inches apart. She smiles at me, her eyes gleaming up at mine.

"You don't need to worry about that part yet. I'll tell you things as I see the need to." I can feel her warm breath.

I should be ready to defend myself by now, the Master said so himself. Why am I so terrified?

I lean a bit closer, swallowing hard as my forehead rests against hers. My breath is uneven, but I need to show her I am not scared of what she is doing, even if I really am.

Be brave, brave, brave.

"Oh?" she says with a bit of surprise in her tone. "Maybe you are not as timid as I thought."

I grab her arm, my hand wrapping around her smaller frame, and squeeze tightly. She laughs and brings up one of her hands so her fingers intertwine with my hair, pulling it slightly.

"I could kill you right now if I wanted to. It would be messy and cause a scene, but I'd do it if I needed to. Or even wanted to. I'm a trained killer, and you are just a servant boy. I like this side of you, but do not test me." Her lips graze mine; she's still wearing a smile. "Now I am being a good girl and sitting patiently, per your request. Don't push me." Her lips press against mine; I try to pull away, but the hand that was playing with my hair is now holding my face firmly in place.

Let go of me!

"This is a place for healing, kids." The same visitor who

was watching us earlier says just loud enough to draw our attention.

Seodi tugs my hair once more, pulling my face away from hers before dropping her hand and putting it onto my thigh once more. My whole body is trembling.

"You are right. We apologise," Seodi says with an overjoyed look on her face.

The visitor gives us a brief smile before turning away from us again.

"Some people just don't know how to mind their own business," Seodi whispers, staring daggers into the back of the woman's head as she massages my thigh.

The curtain opens and my heart lightens seeing two armed men stepping in. The front desk worker right behind them points towards us.

Seodi stands, pulling out her knife and walking up to the woman who has been eyeing us, yanking her head back and pressing it against her throat.

"Careful boys, this may be a place for healing, but I wonder how well they could heal her with her throat cut."

No, no, no, no.

Before I even can process what I am doing, I am on my feet, grabbing the whip strapped to my side. It unfurls itself and wraps around Seodi's wrist, yanking her back to me. She screams out in pain as blood rushes down her arm. Once she is in my grasp, I hold on to her as tightly as I can, hoping it will be enough to keep her from moving.

"So the puppy can nip." She cackles.

Seodi throws her head back, hitting me in the face. I recoil back; my vision goes blurry for a second. I delayed her just enough, though. The Vets moved as I did. She is being pinned down, her hands pressed against her back. She wrestles with them a bit, but she turns her head towards me.

She's smiling.

I take a few steps back; the bench hits my legs and I buckle into the seat.

"I'll see you around, Renatus," she yells as they pick her up and start dragging her out of the curtained off area. Her eyes don't leave mine until the curtain falls, cutting us off from each other.

I let out a loud breath and relax onto the bench I am sitting on. My body is shaking to the point where I don't think I can move. My vision blurring from the threatening tears. I look down at the now recoiled whip.

I just did that.

I look back up and see the front clerk checking in with the other visitors, everyone visibly unsettled by what just transpired, but no one is hurt. He walks over to me and gently puts his hand on my shoulder, and I flinch away from it.

Please, no more touching.

He holds up his hands so I can see them. "Did she hurt you at all?"

I shake my head and focus on trying to even out my breath.

He gives me a tight smile and kneels down in front of me, waiting for me to calm down. "You acted just in time. That lady over there might have died if it weren't for you." He glances over his shoulder at something. "The Vets are going to ask you some questions, is that alright?" the man asks, as if I actually have a choice. They just saw me attack someone who was attacking another person after they were caught harassing me.

The Vet that has both questioned and accompanied me back to the tower gives me a wave before heading back down the path. My head is pounding, my limbs feel limp and the last thing I want to do is talk to the Master. Though I know I will have to. I unlock the entry door and make my way inside. The interior is dark.

I forgot to light the candles.

I walk in and rummage around for the matches that should be in the kitchen. They are normally in the cupboard with the extra candles, but I cannot find them.

Maybe the Master has them.

I carefully make my way up the dark staircase, stumbling on a few of the steps, and feel relief as I see a faint flicker of light coming from the Master's study. I turn into the room and the Master is lost in the book he is holding in his hand. The floorboards creak as I approach him and pull him from his trance.

Please, just let me go to bed.

"About time! I had to light the candles myself. Took me ages to find where you hid this stuff." He slams the book onto the table and looks towards me, expecting some sort of answer. Though his eyes travel up and down my body and then back to my eyes. I shift uncomfortably under his stare, and not for the normal reason.

I feel bare.

I set the medicine down on his desk, resting my body against it.

"You have dried blood on your neck," the Master states calmly.

I immediately begin wiping both sides of my neck frantically with my shirt, my skin beginning to feel raw.

Get it off, get it off, get it off!

"Speak, Renatus." Hearing my name just reminds me of the way she would say it.

Sharp and short, each consonant sounded like an attack.

I begin to tremble once more, tears sliding down my cheeks.

There was so much happening, I don't even feel like I've really processed it yet.

"Speak."

I take a shaky breath. "A girl about my age named Seodi followed me to the healers building, said that her and her group heard about Aruna's apparatus and that they wanted answers from both of us as to where to find them." I glance at my sleeves; the right one now has a crimson stain. "T-then, then she was t-touching—"

A growl-like sound escapes the Master's lips, halting me from explaining the next part. He tries to stand, but falls back into his chair. I assist him up and he pushes me slightly, probably out of frustration.

"Damn them! I figured they would know, but this is just. Too soon! You have to leave now, boy," Master shouts and mumbles at the same time as he makes his way to a locked cupboard.

He pulls out a small set of keys, different from the ones he shared with me last week. I peer around him and the only thing inside is a large travel bag with a bedroll tied on top. The Master pulls it out and throws it at me. I catch it, but my eyes are still focussed on the Master.

Leave now? After what just happened?

"Master." He ignores me and is grabbing a few journals and map scrolls. "Master, please!" My voice reaches every inch of the room this time. He turns to me with wide eyes, anger raging through them.

Master rushes to me, dropping the things in his hands, and grabs a fistful of my hair, pulling my head back roughly. A part of me wants to slap him away, not wanting to be touched, but I can't bring myself to do it.

"I said, now!" The "now" being the loudest word, sends chills down my spine. "They will kill you if you do not leave this tower. You will leave, you will retrieve, you will do whatever is necessary and kill anyone who gets in your way. Do you understand?" My face feels wet and my heart is throbbing. "Do you understand?" The Master pulls my face back in; his words so sharp, spit follows them out of his mouth.

I nod, a sob escaping my lips. Tonight was almost like a test, and I failed.

I'm not ready to go.

The Master is rough as he throws things in my direction, but as he does, I put the items in the bag. Pouches filled with spell components, journals, books, maps, dried rations, clothes and a pair of boots that are of a much higher quality than the ones I currently wear.

"That should hold him over for the first long trek."

The Master mumbles to himself as he makes his way around the room. For his current condition, it's pretty quick, but in reality, this goes on for at least a moonshift. Many coughs and moments of rest in between each item selected and thrown my direction. He takes out the small set of keys again, but this one is for a large chest he likes to hide under a few blankets and pillows. He throws the blankets to the side; the pillows following suit. The Master opens it, pulls out a large sack and walks it over to me. I can hear the clinking of coins as he places it on the floor next to me.

"Do not be stupid with this. Use it as only necessary." His words are a bit softer than the rest have been. He sighs and leans against the desk. "I'm sorry you were cornered, Renatus, and I know the comfort of something safe and familiar is what you were hoping to come to. This tower is neither of those things for you now. It will become an empty shell that might once have been something extraordinary." The Master rubs his face, his eyes locking onto something resting on his desk.

He wouldn't.

"By the time you recover all of the apparatus, I will probably be dead. Regardless, our plan will stay the same. I will tear down as much of this tower as I can. Keep those keys I gave you, though; I will make sure to not damage the door."

"No!" I cry out. "This is everything I know. Where will we go when I bring you back?"

The Master smiles at my broken voice. "We will rebuild. For now, this is what will protect you," he states, standing back up with some difficulty. "We need to go. I doubt I'll be able to make the trek on foot, but we will try."

I let myself crumple onto the floor, tears soaking the exterior leather that the pack is made out of.

This is it, and I'm not ready. I thought I would have more time to learn, more time to understand. I just got used to the taste of curiosity; the fear will overwhelm the taste.

"It's moments like this one that you need to remember to trust your body to move, even when your mind doesn't want to." I lift my head, hearing his words. "Trust that it'll keep moving, even if you are too afraid to."

I nod and stand up, steadying myself.

My stomach is turning and my head is spinning, but the Master is always right with these kinds of things.

I take a step towards the Master.

My body can still move.

CHAPTER SIX

THE DEAFENING SOUND of stone shattering and windows breaking echoes through the cool autumn night. The Master casts a complex spell I have not seen, almost like a mixture of a few I know, in order to create this destructive spell that is carefully destroying the only place I truly know.

The ceiling. It's not just stained and dull, but completely dismantled. Unrecognisable.

The tower that once stood tall and overlooking Ventraton, is now nothing more than a pile of rubble. Everyone who once looked at it with disgust of the wealth and the neuroticism the Master stood for will no longer have to be hindered by its shadow cast from the rising sun.

Will they notice how bright the sun shines in the morning or will it take them time to see there is nothing in the beaming light's way?

I look amongst the demolition and see the door the Master gave me the directional keys for. The entire frame is still intact. Left for me, in case there is a need for something inside it. A part of me wants to hide in there. Ignore the responsibility and purpose the Master has given me.

I still don't think I am deserving, still doubtful I will have what it takes. The only thing pushing me forwards are the

Master's words. Despite him knowing every flaw, he still believes I am the one capable of doing this.

"Boy." The Master coughs, kneeling on the dirt path. "Carry me to the castle." I widen my eyes, looking over my shoulder to where the Crestfalls are normally visible during the day. A few lights can be seen from this distance, but it looks like they are just stars because of how far away they are.

Moving the pack from my back to my chest, I walk up to the Master and squat down so he can climb onto my back. His arms wrap around my neck, so I grab hold of his shaking legs and hoist him up higher on my back so I can stand. He's not all that heavy, but I am also not all that strong. It might take us a while to reach the castle, but I think I can manage.

"I doubt that girl you spoke of is travelling alone, so be mindful of your surroundings," the Master mumbles into my ear.

I start to sweat, not sure if that is from carrying the Master or hearing his words. My stomach becomes uneasy and everything in me is just telling me to run.

Seodi was unlike anyone I've ever met. The look in her eyes and, despite the intense situation, her calm voice. Violence was something she was born into; I could tell that much.

I nod, understanding him though, and swallow the lump in my throat.

She did say she was with a group.

I stumble a bit on the uneven path I am walking down. The Master grunts at the sharp movement I had to make to ensure we both didn't fall.

"I said be mindful, boy," he coughs out.

I want to mumble an apology, but there's no point since I feel like it will happen again. It's hard to focus on the dirt since it's so dark, and the moon is hardly visible as we are midway through the mooncycle.

This will be the last time I will make this descent for some time.

Normally, I admire the view, taking in the beautiful colours that the mountains and Ventraton produce. The wind is starting to pick up, and it smells like metal, dirt and a hint of the wild mint that grows like weeds here.

I'll miss this familiarity. Miss the contentment I felt being the Master's servant.

I can feel the near mooncycle of late nights and early mornings catching up with me.

How am I supposed to sleep knowing people are coming after me?

I make one step at a time, pushing myself to keep moving forwards. Seodi knew what I looked like, knew my name. She had to have been watching the tower, or someone would have had to paint a pretty good picture in her mind for her to recognise me on the street like that.

Stop thinking about her.

The fresh memory of her touch, lips and breath makes my legs feel like they can barely support just me, let alone the Master riding on my back.

It was like she knew exactly how to make me feel weak, knew what would make me falter.

I tried to push back, which surprised both of us in that moment. Then having used the whip on her like that was nearly mind shattering. It was that same pull I had felt when I saw it for the first time. The need to use it with no hesitation.

I just wanted to save the woman. Right?

My steps falter for a moment, and I trip over the beginning of the cobblestone path. The stone is cold and dry. The Master cries out in pain briefly as he hits the stone next to me. I drag myself towards him, ignoring the discomfort my face is feeling, and begin assisting the Master, but the sound of metal jostling makes me turn my gaze towards it. A Vet begins running to us, my guess from hearing the Master's cry. Something warm drips onto my mouth. I bring up my hand to touch it.

Something is coming out of my nose.

Pulling my hand back, I see crimson glistening in the soft lantern light.

I'm bleeding.

My mind spins for a moment, seeing the blood.

I made her bleed when I used the whip. I hurt her.

"Hey, what's going on here?" the man wearing the Vet uniform asks, looking down at me and the Master.

"I am Babylas Amara," the Master grunts out. "I am having my servant carry me to the castle. It's an emergency." Hearing the Master's words, the Vet's eyes widen under his helmet.

"Oh, uh," he stutters as he looks at the Master. "I can carry you the rest of the way, sir." His tone is as uneven as the path I just stumbled down.

I move out of the way so he can help the Master, putting the pack back onto my back. I pull my handkerchief out of my pocket and hold it to my nose as I stand. The Vet quickly lifts the Master onto his back, and we start walking again.

This seriously hurts.

I pinch the bridge of my nose to try and help stop the bleeding.

I wonder if her wrist hurts. Would they have bandaged her wounds? What if she gets sick because her wound gets infected?

"Is Ventraton under attack, Sir Amara? What's this emergency?" the Vet asks, the same unevenness in his voice.

"You are asking questions above your station," the Master spits out.

The Vets body completely tenses. "Right. I apologise, sir."

It's so different seeing the Master actually interact with other people. The normal disdain they openly show towards my master is now replaced with something else. Fear?

The Master's demeanour has completely changed, along with his normally grumbled tone. Where I am normally avoidant and scared, and what I thought he might be from his lack of human interaction, he is confident and certain of his station.

The streets of Ventraton are far quieter than before. Only a few people left who are too deep into their cups to notice us making our way through the city. A few other Vets notice us, though, and generally stand on guard until the Vet who is carrying the Master waves them off.

I pull my handkerchief back; my nose has stopped its bleeding. I hesitate before putting the bloodied cloth back in my pocket.

Orangish hues in the sky begin to reveal themselves as we are now reaching the grand stairway. This will lead us up to the top of the Crestfalls, where the castle was built. I've used these stairs a handful of times before, but it's the first time I've ever climbed them with the Master. Looking up, I see the tips of the sharp points on the squared towers of the castle. As we get closer, the white and orange dyed bricks become clearer in their distinction, the multi-levelled structure resting on top of a mountain-esque bridge that arches over the small lake the Crestfalls form from.

I remember the Master telling me that there are rare materials that are charged with magicae that act as a watermill and recycle the Crestfalls water back into the lake from underground.

As we climb the final step, the Vet looks out of breath; his brow full of sweat and mouth wide open to allow as much air in as possible. I look back at the monumental entryway. Large bright orange doors that stand far taller than me and wide enough to fit two carriages through at the same time. The lanterns, hanging from their decorative iron mounts, flicker in a strange and almost unnatural way. Ornate flowers and mint leaves, crafted from what appears to be silver, are decorating the doors; ten or so armed guards standing in front of them. A few of the castle guards notice our approach, one of them stepping forward.

"What business do you have with the crown?" A woman guard shouts out the question. She holds up a hand, signalling for us to stop.

"I am Babylas Amara. I seek immediate counsel with the royal family," Master speaks clearly, though a cough he is trying to hold in peeks through.

The guard lowers her hand, turns and runs back towards the entrance. A few of the guards look at her and she appears to be telling them something. Two of them open one of the doors, they both enter.

"Will it be just you, Sir Amara?" The guard turns back to us.

"My servant will join us," Master states to the guard. "You can put me down now," he mutters, talking to the Vet.

The Vet nods and slowly sets him onto his own two feet. I walk up closely behind them and wait for the Vet to step away before I take the Master's arm and place it over my shoulder. The Master and I walk together through the strangely lit entryway.

The ceiling, walls and floors are all white. Not a single speck of dirt, stain or smudge on any of the surfaces. Opaque glass orbs light the interior with that same unnatural flickering as the lanterns outside. In the centre of the room, is an orange rug with a yellow detailing of the Ventraton symbol. It runs the length of the room and stops in front of a set of smaller doors just ahead of us. On either side are paintings of the beginning of Ventraton. One of the pictures shows a small group of people wandering into an open mint-filled valley. The next painting has a few wooden cabins built, and a larger group of people gathered around a slightly older gentleman standing on a platform. The one next to that is of miners digging into the mountain's side.

I'm guessing that's where the opulent sector is now.

The painting after that is of the castle being built. They are all beautifully done and give me a glimpse of what Ventraton really looked like all those years ago. The last painting that rests above the two doors ahead of us is that of the royal family. A man and a woman, both with brown hair and bright green eyes. The woman is sitting in an ornate chair while the man has one hand on the edge of the chair and his other hand resting on her shoulder. There is a youngin standing on either side of them. A boy with the same brown hair and green eyes, and a girl with a lighter shade of brown and blue eyes.

They all look so beautiful.

I open the doors and reveal a short staircase just behind them. I look to the Master, whose focus is forward. Walking up the steps, I can tell it is taking a lot out of the Master, but he is pushing through it. Grunts and coughs escape his lips as we reach the top. The room expands forwards, a large foyer looking area. There are cushioned chairs surrounding small wooden tables and a fireplace on both sides of the room.

Everything in here looks expensive.

There are three sets of doors; none of which are open or show signs someone has walked through them. I wander over to one of the chairs, not sure of where to go from here, and set the Master down on one of them.

"They will come," the Master whispers, not sure if it was to me or to himself.

I stand there looking around the room once more; large landscapes are painted on the ceiling high above us. A view of mountains, flowers and an ocean just behind it all. One of the doors open, and a tired-looking man walks through with the two guards who were sent to notify the royal family. The brown hair and green-eyed man approaches us with his brow knit and eyes narrowed on the Master.

This is the King.

I kneel down immediately and glue my eyes to the floor.

"Beaumont," the Master says; his way of greeting the King.

"Babylas, what is this? It is hardly the beginning of the sunshift and you rouse the castle awake." His voice is deep and calm, a slight roughness to it.

Perhaps from him just waking up.

"You know I wouldn't if I didn't think it dire," the Master grunts. I glimpse up slightly at him and see a stern look across his face. "Where is Reine?" the Master asks while he gestures for the King to sit in the chair across from his.

A sigh escapes the King's lips before I hear the muted sound of clothes against the chair's fabric. "Babylas, in her condition—" the King halts his sentence by clearing his throat. "State your purpose."

"I was attacked. My tower was destroyed. I'm sure with the new day's light, it will be visible." The Master lies, though the King wouldn't know that.

I shift my eyes slightly, looking to the King where I see his green ones wide and mouth slightly open.

"Who would attack you?" the King asks, his voice much quieter than before. He looks over his shoulder at the guards who have kept their distance. He waves them away and they nod, exiting the room through the entry doors.

"The Domi Nostrae; the group I warned you both would come for me one day. I am not the young Forged Magicae Master I once was," the Master coughs, "but I was able to fend them off. It was clear they were after something other than just my head."

I look to the Master, who is now looking at me. I widen my eyes.

Is he saying that something is me?

I look at the King, who has his attention on me. My hands feel instantly sweaty as I swallow hard under the pressure of his gaze.

"What would they want with a simple servant?" the King asks, peering at me as if trying to find something.

I probably have dried blood all over my face, which probably helps the Master's story.

"He is not just a servant, but my apprentice. I've told very few of him, but word must have got out somewhere. Perhaps one of my letters was stolen," the Master explains. "He is in the possession of knowledge that is immensely powerful. I have tasked him with gathering the key materials for this knowledge to become tangible."

"What is this knowledge?" the King asks.

"Nothing I can share with you. Telling you may only threaten your family's safety. We must get him out of Ventraton. I have close connections with the King of the Felguard Country. Would you be willing to spare a carriage and guard to escort him there?"

"And give that knowledge to another kingdom?" the King scoffs in disbelief. "And what is to be done with you? If this group is as tactful as you say, then your presence is a threat all on its own."

"Beaumont. I founded the Hunter's Territory; my loyalty will always lie here. Getting him away from the assailants is my main concern. The Domi Nostrae are bold, but they wouldn't openly attack Ventraton."

I wouldn't think the Master is talking to a king with the tone in which he just spoke.

So demanding and harsh.

The King growls. I glance up once again and see a scowl on the King's face as he glares at the Master. "Fine, Babylas. Though I do hope you can be a little more revealing of information, since I assume you will be staying with us until the repairs of your tower are complete."

I look to the Master, who nods.

"I will tell the guards to prepare something right away." The King glances back at me. "Seems you had enough time to pack a bag."

"Something I had prepared for this very scenario," the Master quickly explains. "As I said, we knew this attack was coming."

Is the Master still lying?

He said he had mentioned it to the King before, that this group would be hunting him down.

Maybe he is lying by saying it was the Domi Nostrae when it was someone else all together.

I look at the ground. My reflection in the marbled tiles is blurry and incoherent.

Lying to a king. Will the Master expect me to do the same?

I shudder.

The Master's words ring in my head, "Do whatever is necessary."

CHAPTER SEVEN

THE MOUNTAINS HAVE BEEN EASIER to travel than I had expected. There has only really been one road we have needed to follow. It is heavily guarded and having a carriage makes it easy to sleep as we travel. The cushioned seats are more comfortable than the cot I used to sleep on in the tower. Though without the Master or practising Forged Magicae, I am really only left with my thoughts. I try to read through the books the Master gave me to take, but my last moments with the Master make it hard to focus.

This is all really happening.

I'm leaving the Master's. I'll be travelling the realm, and I will need to do what is necessary in order to collect Aruna's apparatus.

"Guards!" the King shouts, his voice echoing through the foyer. Multiple guards from the other two doors in the room quickly enter the foyer; some even have their weapons drawn. My muscles tense seeing the intensity of power this man holds with a simple word called out.

Does he realise the Master lied? Will he want us thrown in prison?

"Take our guests to one of the suites. I also need a

carriage and a few guards prepared for travel to Fosa." The King stands, commanding the people to move and do his bidding; and they do. One of the guards rushes to our sides, all of the weapons now seethed.

I guess being tasked with protecting such an important family comes with its own kind of stress. The King calling out of nowhere in the middle of the night must have put them all on edge.

"This way, please," the guard says as they begin to guide us through the large set of doors the King had entered from. The halls past here are far less decorated than the first one we entered through, but all still that perfect white with details of silver and orange. There are plants and vines that decorate in between doors and stairways.

"This door here," the guard says, stopping our walking abruptly. "I am sure one of us will come to fetch you when the carriage is ready."

The Master nods and opens the door. The interior is dark, but the Master clicks something to the right of the entrance, and the whole room lights up with that same strange unnatural flickering.

Why are the flames doing that and how was it lit so fast?

The Master steps into the room, allowing me to look around at how the room was lit up automatically. My widened eyes take in the glass orb that appears to have a flickering lightning bolt captured inside of it. A metal pole connected to it leads into the ground.

Is the whole castle lit up by this lighting?

I look at the Master, who is grumbling to himself as he glances out the window.

He must have drawn back the curtain.

A part of me was hoping he would just go into an explanation of how this light works. Taking a gaze around though, the room is about the same size as the Master's old room was. It has a large bed pushed against the wall. There is a fireplace on the opposite side of the room, a painting of the castle hanging above it.

The Master should be comfortable in this room.

Walking up behind the Master, I can see the sunrise more clearly now that we are slightly elevated than we were at the castle entrance.

It's beautiful.

The soft orange and pinks bounce off the ocean just beyond the mountains, colouring their tips and leaving their grey bases.

"Use your words wisely, Renatus. Truths, lies, secrets are all made up of the same words, just used in different contexts. Remember which is what."

I nod, glancing at the Master, hearing his words, before turning back to the view in front of us.

The carriage stops, and I am pulled from my trance. I draw the orange curtain to see what caused our abrupt stop and see a few of the guards huddled together, talking. I drop the curtain and lean back in my seat.

Maybe they need a break.

A knock at the carriage door makes me jump, but I quickly open it. One of the guards is standing there with a furrowed brow.

"Sorry to disturb you, but there seems to have been a mudslide. It'll take us quite a bit of time to clear it," the guard admits, their voice firm in tone.

They have all been more than respectable, despite knowing I am just a servant. I can tell the longer we travel, though, the more tired they grow of keeping appearances up.

I move from my seat, surprising the guard, and they take a

few steps back, allowing me to exit the carriage. The handful of guards the King sent with me all look towards me as I step out. Avoiding their eyes, I glance around the carriage and at the large mound of mud stuck in our path. With mountains on either side of us, there isn't really an option to go around.

There is a spell I could use, though.

I step back into the carriage and rummage through the pack that Master gifted me, looking for one of the prepared spells he packed.

*The **terramotus** spell will work.*

I find the small vial with the prepared spell components already mixed, awaiting the sigil and activation to bring it to life. The terramotus spell will allow me to manipulate the ground to my will.

I step back out of the carriage and start walking to the mound of compact dirt. The sigil is still fresh in my mind from rereading the journal a dozen times already on our trek to Fosa.

The guard, who is still standing near the carriage, follows closely behind me. "We can handle the removal," they state simply.

I look back over my shoulder and give them a small smile before turning back to the mound. I reach down and grab a handful of the dirt, smoothing it out in the palm of my hand. I draw the sigil for the spell, uncork the bottle with my teeth and pour the contents right on top of it.

Closing my eyes, I focus on the shape I want the earth to move, and as the picture solidifies in my mind, I slam my hand onto the ground. My hand feels like it's burning for a moment as a flash of green light appears. Suddenly, the earth rumbles, the mound of dirt shifting from my intent.

"Another mudslide!" the guard shouts, throwing themselves over my back. They tuck my head in close to my chest with their firm hand trying to protect me.

"It's alright," I mutter, pulling my head out of their grasp.

The mound begins to clear out and lay tightly compacted against the sides of the mountain, leaving a smaller but clear path for us to travel through.

The guard lifts themselves off of my back, and I stand, admiring the success of my spell. I glance down at my muddied hands before closing them into fists.

This was one the Master and I practised quite a bit, and it seems to have paid off.

"Was that Forged Magicae?" the guard asks as they step up from behind me. Their greyish eyes are wide. They take off their helmet, their amber hair tumbling out and falling to their shoulders. "Incredible." That last word fell out into a whisper.

That look in their eyes. Something changed from before.

"Em! What just happened?" Another guard runs up from the group that was staying back.

The amber-haired guard turns around and smiles brightly at the one approaching. "Our path was just cleared, Al." A higher pitched, almost excited sounding laugh escapes Em's lips as they turn towards me.

I give another small smile and begin walking back towards the carriage.

I'm glad I was able to help them in some way.

My eyes find the ground again, trying to avoid the pressure of everyone staring at me.

"Wait. Your hands," Em says, grabbing my wrist. I feel something soft push against my dirty palm and I glance at my hand.

They are cleaning the mud off.

I pull away from them and take out the handkerchief I have in my own pocket, dried blood staining it from the last time I used it. I begin wiping my own palms as I turn back and climb into the carriage.

Closing the door behind me, I sigh in relief.

I could feel everyone's eyes on me. Is this the reaction that is to be expected when I showcase what I've learned?

I help the Master into bed, pulling the sheets back so he can climb in. As he swings his legs in, I pull the sheets over him.

"There is a strength in depending on actions to speak for you, Renatus, but actions won't always be enough. Some need reassurance. Simple replies that let them know it's alright." The Master coughs and grunts as he shifts. I try to help make him more comfortable by grabbing the other pillow and placing it under his head. "Show them what you can do so they see the gap in power. Use what I have taught you and make your own path to Aruna's apparatus."

There is a knock on the door, causing both of us to jump. It opens slightly, and a guard with grey eyes peeks into the room.

"The carriage is ready."

"Go, boy. Fulfil your purpose," the Master says, placing his hand on my wet cheek.

I'm crying?

"Remember everything I've taught you. You are ready."

There are still so many questions I want to ask. Despite disagreeing with the Master's words, I nod, believing that the Master must be right.

What would the Master say about the spell? Was it done right? Could I have had a wider influence?

I OPEN MY EYES; the carriage rocking back and forth as we progress on our journey to the Felguard Country. From what the Master told me, the Felguard Country is a powerful

Limoria leader. They have the largest Natural Magicae army in the world.

I think the Master referred to them as the Magicae's Guided Assembly.

A room full of powerful beings that can just will magicae to their fingertips. A shiver runs down my back, thinking of being in that room.

What if the King knows I'm lying about what I plan to use the chalice for? What if I can't even speak? What if he takes one look at me and decides I'm not worth his time?

I swallow hard and wipe the sweat from my forehead.

The Master said I could do this.

Practising what I want to say could probably help.

What would a king want to hear when you are asking for an item with magicae coursing through it?

I grab my master's journal. The loose papers of Aruna's apparatus are laying neatly inside along with the map of where they all should be. Fosa is in possession of the chalice. The Master mentioned once before about the apparatus having multiple purposes, but it was bringing them together that would create the cure of death.

A life that would never end.

The Master has so much knowledge and power to share with the world. If someone could live forever, it should be him.

"It's just down this way." The guard guiding me to the carriage mutters as we approach a side entrance to the castle's stables.

We push through the doors, and I stumble for a moment, seeing a familiar brown-haired man standing by the carriage. His eyes lock with mine, and I instantly bow towards him.

"Please, stand straight and join me in the carriage for a moment," the King says.

I stand, but my gaze focusses on where I need to go instead. I enter the carriage; it shifts from my weight but settles as I take my seat. I feel it shift again as the King comes into view, taking his seat and closing the door behind him.

"Now, Renatus. I am quite familiar with you. Where you are from, the names of your parents and where you were born." My eyes glance towards his, hearing him say all of that clearly with little interest.

I haven't heard my parents' names since I left.

"I say this because I want you to know that I've been keeping tabs on Babylas, and in extension, you. That little commotion you had last night in the healers ward was the start of this attack, correct?"

I need to lie to a king.

I nod.

"I was told you were a quiet one." He hums under his breath. "Can I really trust your master's words when he says his loyalties lie with Ventraton?" I meet the King's eyes.

If I had to take away one thing from the ten sidereal years I've spent with the Master, it is that he loves this country. He spent most of his life cultivating it. I can understand the basis of concern and fear since the Master has always been off in terms of his obsession, but I can not and will not understand the distaste the city of Ventraton has for him.

"This country means everything to him." The words being as true as I know them to be.

The King nods and reaches into his pocket. "You'll need this letter of integrity in order to enter the high society district and get to the castle."

I take the letter from his hand and look it over. It simply states what it is, my name and has the King's signature at the bottom.

"You are being endorsed by the Hunter's Territory and

Ventraton's Crown; behave like it." He opens the door to the *carriage and leaves, slamming the door shut.*

"We're gonna rest here for the night!" I hear Em shout from outside in front of the carriage. A knock sounds from the roof above me, signalling for me that it's alright to come out.

Since I cleared our path, the guards have changed their tune. I'm no longer a servant living well above his means, but someone who does what it takes to keep moving forward. They all formally introduced themselves as well, though it's taken me a while to memorise their names just by going off their voices since the majority of their features are covered by their helmets.

Of course, the Master was right. My actions and gifted power speak louder than I ever could.

I climb out of the carriage and start helping them make camp for the night. Finding what dry brush I can to start a fire with.

"Don't you have a fancy spell to just light fires?" Ni asks in a joking tone.

"Oh! Even better, if you had a spell that made a buffet in an instant," Al adds in.

I smile at them and bring back the brush. We light a fire and place canned meats in the embers for it to cook. The group of guards chat about some of the things they saw during the day. A pack of **lureas** running around the sides of one of the mountains, some strange-looking bird creatures flying around the mountain-based trees and a funny-looking mushroom.

Maybe I should peek out the window more often.

"The Felguard Country is just a day away. We will stop in Jod before making our way to Fosa," Em informs us.

"An actual bed." Ni sighs, a far off look in his eyes.

"I could care less about a bed; I'm excited for the drinks,"

Al says, shoving Ni a bit. "This stale stuff is killing my tastebuds."

The group chatters for a bit as we eat our food, and when the fire dies down, some of the guards wander off to sleep while others start their watch.

"Renatus," I jump, hearing my name. Em laughs and stands, offering their hand to help me stand as well. "What do you do all day while you are cooped up in there?" Em asks, turning their face towards me as we make our way to the carriage.

I open the door and reach in, pulling out one of the books resting on the seat, and hand it to them.

"**Storing A Spell**. Is this really what entertains you?" they ask, laughing a bit.

Entertainment? It's valuable information and something that will help me with the purpose the Master gave me.

I shrug my shoulders and take the book from them, placing it back onto the seat.

"Maybe you should sit out with us tomorrow," they suggest, patting my shoulder. "Get some sleep, though. We won't arrive to Jod until late into the moonshifts."

I wave goodnight and enter the carriage, Em closing the door behind me.

Sit out there with them?

Laying down where I am normally seated, my eyes begin to feel weighted.

She is crying again.

CHAPTER EIGHT

HER FACE IS BLURRY, and no matter how hard I squint, I cannot see her any clearer. My heart hurts hearing her wail and having her bury her head in my chest. I want to hold her; I want to comfort her, but I can barely feel anything, and the flames that are flickering around in my blurry vision feel cold.

I open my mouth, and where I normally cannot speak, my words are clear, "Who are you?" My words echo as the flames disappear and I am now standing in front of her blurred form, some place where there is nothing but light. The vision of her begins to come into view. Her blonde hair, the few scars riddling her otherwise perfect skin, the golden gleam of her eyes.

"Renatus, we need to get going!" Em shouts as they open the door.

I jump up, smacking my head on the roof of the carriage, and look at them with wide eyes. Em bursts out laughing and closes the door. I sigh loudly and rub my head; it stings from the abrupt bump.

I finally saw her, even if it was just a glimpse.

Climbing out of the carriage, I see the rest of the guards are on top of their mounts, and Al and Em sitting at the reins of the carriage's horses. Em is still snickering, and Al stares at me curiously.

"What, did they find you naked or something?" Al asks with a furrowed brow. I shake my head and watch his tense shoulders suddenly relax.

He seems upset about the thought of that.

"No, he was sleeping like a youngin. Startled him so much he smacked his head," Em says again, laughing just as loud as last time.

Al shakes his head with a scoff. "Not that funny."

"You didn't see his face! I've never seen him so expressive." Em sticks out their hand towards me, offering to help me up to sit by them. I take their hand and I am hoisted up onto the seat.

Al glances my way, and I give him the small smile I have been providing them all throughout our journey.

I hope this is enough reassurance for him.

He gives me the same smile back before whipping the reins, causing the cart to jerk forward.

Looking around as the horses pull us along the path, it's upsetting that I wasn't out here this entire time. Everything is so bright and beautiful. The mountains are far less dense and there are more valleys and breaks between them. Though ahead, I can see a large range of mountains that look like it is going to cut us off from our destination.

"Look at that," Em says, pointing forward towards a small opening in the mountains.

I squint my eyes, trying to focus on whatever they are seeing. There is a large twisted tree sitting a little further back in the clearing. Its bark is deep green and leaves black.

"I've never seen a tree like that before," Al mutters under his breath.

Neither have I. Not that I've travelled much, but I haven't read about a tree that looks like that either.

"We should take a look." The words come out soft, but Em seems to have heard me.

"Hold up!" they shout.

"Come on, Em; we are almost there," Al whines, but slows the carriage down nonetheless.

I hop off the still somewhat moving ride and start walking over to the tree. The colours of the tree become more complex as it is a metre away from me. The black leaves now have strands of purple that travel down into its stem. The deep green bark looks to have dark brown spots hidden by the rough texture of the tree. I feel at my side the Kindled Whip strapped to my belt. This looks like that same kind of wood.

"Interesting," Em says, reaching out and touching the bark with their fingertips. "Ough!" They quickly shout, inhaling sharply as they pull their hand back to them. Al is right there beside us and grabs their hand from them, bringing it close to his face.

"Idiot," he mumbles, a soft agitation in his voice. "We don't even know what this thing is, and you went and touched it."

"I wasn't expecting it to be sharp," Em says, the sting lingering in their voice.

There is a chance it could be poisonous.

Inspecting the area where Em was running their fingers, I can see the faint shine of a sap-like liquid on the sharp points of the tree's bark.

We should be safe rather than sorry.

I take Em's finger out of Al's hands and put it in my mouth, sucking out the potential poison. Al stops me, shoving me back by my shoulders. I spit Em's blood out to the side and look back at him. We are about the same height but he is far bigger than me, so I take an additional step back, seeing his face turn red and his teeth bared at me.

Em quickly stands between us and looks to Al. "What the infernum was that?" Their voice is stern and short.

"What?!" Al shouts down at them. "You are upset with me? He just stuck your finger in his mouth!"

"Poison," I mutter, gaining both of their attention. Al's expression changes from enraged to confused. "I was getting the poison out."

Al looks down at Em, who has their eyes still trained on me. I look away from both of them and back to the tree we came over to inspect.

I don't really know if it was poison, but that's too much to say. I think this got the point across.

"Thank you, Renatus," Em whispers. I can hear footsteps leading away from me, but when I turn, Em is still standing there, and Al is the one who has left us on our own.

I nod and give them a smile and begin walking back behind Al.

As I take a few steps away, something grabs my wrist. I look over my shoulder and see Em with a strange look across their face. Nose scrunched, eyes narrowed, mouth pinched closed. I turn to face them completely.

"I'm sorry about Al. He can be a little, well, overprotective. I'm sure you've figured it out by now, but please don't say anything to the rest of the guards. They would separate us if they knew."

What?

I nod, not really understanding what Em is talking about. It's clear that Al cares about Em, but I don't see why that would be a bad thing.

Maybe that Al would prioritise Em over his duty?

We walk back to the carriage, Al not glancing our way as we return.

I think I should ride in the carriage the rest of the way.

I walk past the front reins and open the door to the interior of my ride.

It's been a few moonshifts since the last update Em gave me on our nearing destination. Jod should be less than a moonshift away at this point.

Technically, I've ridden through Jod before, but I do not remember much of my journey to Ventraton.

Pulling back the curtain, the mountain I had seen is now right there, and we are still heading towards it. I open the door and lean out slightly to see an archway carved through the stone. There are woodpillers on either side that go from the top of the archway to the ground.

Just through it, stone buildings are all lit up and there is a faint sound of music playing, though the guards are all hollering in excitement as we pass through, so I cannot hear what song is being played.

I close the door as I duck back inside.

People will be staring at me if I'm hanging half in, half out like that.

The carriage rocks back and forth, stopping a few times before starting up again as we make our way through what I assume is traffic.

I'd open the curtain, but someone might try to look inside.

I quickly begin packing the books and papers I have lying around the other seat, the mess reminding me of the Master's study. The more I have taken to learning and understanding Forged Magicae, the more I come to understand why the Master was prone to leaving things left where he finished with them. Knowledge has become a desire, not just a need, to complete the task. Learning what I want is a choice the Master said I can make. How I obtain the apparatus is the other one. Regardless of my choices, the outcome is what must remain the same. Bringing the Master back.

The carriage stops, and within a few moments, a knock sounds at the door. I open it and see Em smiling at me. "Al went into the Regnant Night. It's a higher up place but still has a tavern at the ground level. They should have enough rooms for the lot of us. I'm sure some of us will be sharing, but that's fine." Em stands there but turns their head towards something else.

Peeking past them, I see oil lamps lighting the streets and people dressed in puffy-sleeved blouses with motifs carefully sewn in with beautiful colours of thread. Some of wheat, roosters, crosses, an eye, stars, circles, all woven together to make an ornate pattern. I look up from one of the women's blouses and meet her eyes. Her face is red with eyes wide.

I was staring at her...

She quickly walks away, her arms crossing over her chest.

Well, that's not good.

I turn my gaze back into the interior of the carriage, making a mental note to apologise if I ever run into her.

"We are all set," Al says, breaking my concentration. I look over to him as he finishes his walk over to Em and myself.

Well, probably just to Em, who happens to be standing next to the carriage door.

Al hands them a set of keys. "Thank you. Renatus, we will head in. Al, please move the carriage around to wherever the proprietor said we could park it."

Al and I both nod before Al heads towards the front of the carriage. Stepping out onto the cobbled streets, I get a few glances. The King's carriage is definitely extravagant, and I'm sure they are more interested in the wealth it proposes, and not the servant boy exiting it.

"Here is your key," Em mutters, handing me a small key hanging from a chain with a wooden piece connected to it. A number five carved into it.

While I try to avoid eye contact with anyone on the streets, I tighten my grip on my pack and watch Em's feet for reference as where next to step. I hear a soft chime as Em must have opened the entrance to the Regnant Night. The bustle of noise outside seems quiet compared to the condensed noise of the excitement that is coming from the main floor of this establishment.

"The boys will have a good night." Em laughs.

I take a peek and see multiple groups of people laughing, spilling drinks, dancing and hanging over each other. The smell of alcohol is strong and makes my nose scrunch up.

I'd rather not be down here.

Looking around the bustling room, I see an opening in the back. My feet begin to carry me in that direction, hoping it is where the rooms are, but my path is stopped by a tall, burly man. He has reddish brown hair and a beard to match.

He holds up a mug and smiles at me. "Hey kid! Why in such a rush?" He offers me the cup in hand, but I simply glance at it before returning to his gaze. "What? Did a feserpentline catch your tongue?"

I shake my head, not sure what that even means.

He shoves my arm a bit and laughs. "You really should learn how to lighten up! I'm just having some fun."

"Renatus," Em says from behind me. "You know him?"

I shake my head.

"No, we just happened to bump into one another. Though I think he looks a little worrisome to be in such a joyful place!" the man explains through a hearty laugh while taking a drink of the same mug he offered me. He lets out a satisfied sigh and looks to Em. "Make sure to get him a drink. Might lighten his spirits."

"Alright then," Em says.

The man gives me a wink before turning and heading towards the bar.

Ni puts his arm around my shoulders. I try to pull away, but he keeps his arm firm. "We are gonna get you talking tonight, bud! Just need a few drinks in ya."

I give him a widened stare.

This is terrifying.

"Remember, we are back on the road tomorrow morning!" Em shouts over their shoulder as they walk past us and towards the bar.

A gentleman with long curly hair and large tusks peeking out from his bottom lip walks up to Em from behind the bar and leans in to hear what they are saying. Ni pulls me away and towards a table with the other guards, minus Al.

I just want to go to my room.

"Renatus, you can drink, right?" Se asks with a furrowed brow. His normally metal-covered head is now showing his muddy brown hair. A few pieces are longer than others, resting just above his honeydew-coloured eyes.

I nod, answering his questions before taking a seat on the bench next to him.

"I'll go get the drinks," Le mumbles under her breath and steps away. Her hair is a deep burgundy colour. It's kept quite short though, only the top portion of her hair keeping its length and resting just below her ear.

My gaze follows her to the bar, seeing Em and Al now standing next to each other. Al is leaning in close, like he is whispering something in their ear. Al's hair is buzzed, but the hair that is left is black.

"You are always looking around." Ni laughs, pulling me back to the table I am sitting at.

I shrug my shoulders at him and smile.

"What's caught your eye this time?"

"I'm sure you've figured it out by now, but please don't say anything to the rest of the guards." Those were Em's words.

"Why do all of your names only have two letters?" I ask, hoping that my speaking and asking a question will deflect from where I was actually looking.

"He spoke!" Se's excitement causes a few of the other patrons to look towards us; I'm sure expecting to see some sort of animal talking and not just a boy.

"Oh, that? Ventraton's Guard Commander started it a few years ago. We just abbreviate all our names to the first two letters. She said it was to keep our privacy and keep things less personal. It's why we hide our hair in our helmets too." Ni smiles at me with his cheery-sounding voice in response.

"Though out here, we are free! No more having to have that stupid metal digging in while we sleep," Se adds, clenching his fists and raising them both in the air.

"Calm yourself," Le mumbles as she sets the drinks in front of us. She takes her seat next to Ni.

I take the mug in hand as all of them begin emptying the contents of theirs.

It's like they are dying from thirst.

I look at the dark and foamy liquid inside before I take a sip. The bitter taste bites my tongue and the heat from the alcohol burns my throat a bit as I swallow it.

I see why they drink it fast. You probably don't taste it as much.

Following suit, I tilt the mug back, drinking the contents of my own drink as fast as I can. As the last bit slides down, I put my mug back on the table and cover my mouth with my hand. My eyes squint shut as I wait for the bitterness to subside.

Ni, Se and Le are all chuckling, and I open one of my eyes to see the laughter pointed at me.

"Not your kinda drink?" Ni takes a break from laughing to ask.

I shake my head.

"I'll get you something sweeter, but it costs more," Le mumbles as she gets up from the table and back to get another round.

"I'll give you props for finishing, though!" Se says, shoving my shoulder.

My stomach churns, feeling the weight of the drink just sitting there. I shake my head again, not liking this environment nor the attention they are putting on me.

I just want to escape from them.

"I sure hope you aren't making our ward do anything he isn't up for," Em says.

I look up and see Em and Al standing at the edge of our table, glancing at all of us. Both their cheeks are a bit red, and they both are carrying similar mugs to the ones Le just took with her to get more drinks.

"Of course not! He is drinking as much as he wants to tonight!" Se shouts.

Way too much enthusiasm.

I hiccup and feel my cheeks beginning to warm.

Great.

"Out of the way, Captain," Le mumbles, wedging herself through Al and Em to set the drinks down.

"Sorry, sorry," Em says, spilling some of their drink.

"We should probably get to bed," Al says, a smirk tugging at his lips. Em smiles up at him and then goes back to the group.

"You all should follow suit after a few more drinks. Early morning!" Em says in a peppy tone.

The guards at the table all groan and nod. Em and Al wander off to the opening in the back of the establishment I saw earlier.

Definitely where the rooms are.

"How much you wanna bet they are gonna be up later than any of us?" Se chuckles, an eyebrow raised.

"That's too obvious to be a bet," Ni sneers, chuckling slightly afterwards.

"You all shut your mouth," Le growls, her face scrunched up as she glares at Se.

"Oh, you are just jealous the Captain doesn't give you the same kind of attention." At Se's retort, Le stands, downing her drink, slamming the mug down and storming off.

"Now you did it." Ni lets out an exasperated sigh.

"It's the truth." Se pouts, sticking out his bottom lip, looking over to where Le just stormed off.

It seems they all know about their closeness.

"Is Le jealous that Al gets to talk to the Captain more?" The words slip out of my mouth and I look to Ni, who is just as surprised I asked the question.

"Ugh," Ni mumbles, rubbing the back of his neck. "It's more that she's jealous that Em and Al do a lot more than just talking. Though, it's forbidden for us to have relationships like that with each other. They have been on and off since we were youngins, so we all just keep quiet about it."

"You should too," Se says, patting my shoulder.

Nodding my head, I take the fresh mug in my hand and take a sip of a much sweeter liquid. The burn is just as intense, but it has more of a fruity flavour to it.

Why did I even ask?

I imagine Seodi's lips pressed against my cheek, and I shudder.

I'm sure it would be different with someone you trust. Someone who isn't threatening you at the same time and only doing it to intimidate you.

MY HEAD IS POUNDING. I lean against the stone exterior wall of the Regnant Night. The sun is just cresting, a greenish hue colouring the sky. Em said they were going to get the carriage and bring it around while we all settle ourselves for the next portion of our journey. Al mentioned there are a few villages we would pass, but we will be pushing through as much as we can for this next leg of the journey.

"This night shift stuff is going to suck," Ni groans, leaning on top of Se, who is sitting on his pack. "Sleeping on top of a horse does not seem like fun."

"You aren't sleeping on top of a horse." Le butts into the conversation. Pushing Ni off of Se from a slight shove to his shoulder. "Renatus said he will share the carriage with us when we need it."

There is plenty of room for two of us to fit in comfortably. I can ride a horse or at the reins if needed. I don't think it is fair for me to always have the good seat.

"That's because he is a saint," Ni whimpers from the ground.

The carriage pulls up; Al is slightly behind it with the reins of the other horses. Ni and Se hop into the carriage, ready to sleep some more, knowing they will cover the majority of the night shift. I climb up onto one of the horses, as do Al and Le, while Em stays at the reins for the carriage.

"Sorry about yesterday." Al rides up next to me, his helmet still off so I can see his grim expression.

I nod, accepting his apology.

I can't blame him for not understanding my intentions. We hardly know each other, and I didn't really explain myself.

"I'm not sure how you do it, but you managed to get the whole team to like you. Without saying a thing," Al tells me, his gaze looking forwards now. "Even I have some respect for you. I didn't know it at the time, but you were trying to save Em."

Do they all like me? Respect me? I thought they just stopped hating me.

CHAPTER NINE

My stomach turns, my hands clutching the edge of the seat, seeing the shadow from the walls begin to cover the ground outside of the carriage. From afar, they didn't seem so terrifying. They remind me almost of mountains, strong, sturdy and unmovable. Maybe they were at some point in history, carved away to create the secure gates I approach now.

Little they did, though, to help the late King Torrin. Being torn down from the inside out is how his reign ended.

As we have approached Fosa, memories of stories shared about this kingdom by the Master are coming back to me. Master said that the new king, King Felguard, withheld the information of how the coup d'état occurred, simply stating that King Torrin's life was taken by Lady Xylia. She liberated her country, and he took the crown.

I wonder if she wanted it, or if she simply thought herself unqualified. Just like I do with this purpose the Master gave me.

Master said that if she had taken the crown, the demise of Stran would have never happened. Saying a woman thinks with her head, where a man thinks with his lust.

Master sure does.

I wonder what the kingdom would look like if she were still around. Master said he met her once before her death, at the

89

coronation of King Felguard. He only spoke highly of her beauty and the strength she exuded. Whereas the King was charismatic and poised. Master teased and said their roles were reversed, that the king should be the intimidating one, and the queen, the socially graced.

Though she never was the queen, the Master referred to her as one.

I hear a few knocks sound from the top of the carriage, meaning we are almost to the gate. I reach into my satchel and pull the letter the King of Ventraton wrote me to bypass the gates.

The carriage slows to a halt. I look out of the window and see a sentry approaching the carriage.

I'm really hoping this letter works.

Opening the carriage door, the sentry bows his head towards me.

That feels weird. To be the one bowed too versus the one doing the bowing.

"Sir, your guards say that you are here to seek counsel with the King?"

I stiffen; a lump in my throat begins to form as the sentry's full attention is on me. I nod my head, and the guard extends his hand towards me, expecting the papers I realise I have now crumpled in my sweaty hands. I swallow the lump and hand him the papers.

The sentry takes them, his brow furrowing as he reads it carefully. "Ventraton, huh?" The guard turns from me, facing the tower slightly to our left. "Geraad! This sir needs an escort to the castle. The Fel Watch will need to take it from there." The sentry hands my papers back to me before reaching into his satchel and handing me a blue slip.

I exit the carriage, Em just right of the door.

"Sir Renatus, we will be taking respite here in the capital

before heading back to Ventraton. We will have the Fel Watch notify you when we secure lodging," they say with a smile and a slight bow.

I really don't like that. This carriage draws way too much attention.

"It is quite a hike to the castle," the sentry says to Em. "Are you sure he would not prefer to ride there?"

"He likes his walks," Al says from the reins of the carriage. He gives me a smile before looking down at Em, who is looking up at him.

"Well, alright then," the sentry says with a nod towards another sentry that is walking up to us. This sentry is slightly wider than the other, though they come to about the same height. "Geraad, please take Sir Renatus to the castle."

"Follow me, sir." Geraad doesn't hesitate and turns around, walking through the gate's door and onto the cobbled stone streets.

I jump and quickly follow suit, glancing and waving goodbye to Em, Al, Ni, Se and Le, who are all waving back at me.

I'm glad I got to meet them. Maybe when I am done with King Felguard, I can stop by and see them one last time.

Walking through the merchant district, the streets are packed. So many people are shouting about deals and trades they have. I keep my head down, a tight grip on my pack, and remain close behind Geraad, who is keeping a brisk pace.

Fosa is much more lively than Ventraton is. Almost twice as much.

It takes a lot to not be swept up by the crowds. Luckily, Fosa is also much larger than Ventraton. As we pass through another gate, Geraad just waving to one of the guards stationed at it, we start our walk through the residential district. Kids' laughter resonates throughout the streets as others enjoy a stroll down the less crowded cobblestone roads. All the houses are pretty uniformed; the only difference is the colour of roofs. Some have plain colours of red, blue, green, but others have a mixture of colours creating zig-zagged patterns.

It takes us over a sunshift to arrive at the castle's gate. It is more decorative than the others we walked through; golden cherubs holding flowers and pitchers. As decadent as it is, though, the castle most definitely draws my gaze towards it. Its circular spires and golden bars around the top pose just as intimidating as the walls surrounding Fosa.

That same lump returns.

I am supposed to just waltz in there and ask the King for a favour? I am going to get my head chopped off.

"Sir, your papers." The guard extends his hand in my direction.

I blink a few times before rushing to his side. I hand the papers to the Fel Watch towering over the both of us. He takes them with a short smile and analyses them. He nods and hands them back.

"Renatus?" the guard asks hesitantly, his left brow arched slightly. I nod my head, letting him know he pronounced my name correctly. "Alright, you can come with me. I'll walk you to the next set of Fel Watch." Geraad bids his adieu as I follow the Fel Watch through the gate.

My heart is in my throat! How am I supposed to do this?

I struggle to keep up with the fast pace the Fel Watch is walking as his leisurely stride is a near jog for me. As we approach the castle, more and more Fel Watch appear into eyesight. I quickly count twenty or so just here in the front garden.

I can't imagine how many must be roaming inside.

A few other Fel Watch are bunched together, all laughing over something. There are five men all about the same height, towering over me and the short-haired brunette standing next to them with her arms crossed. Our eyes meet, her eyes furrow slightly.

Why are all the Fel Watch so giant?

"Hey Madi, this kid has papers to meet with the King. You mind taking him in?"

The woman turns and gives the Fel Watch standing next to me a once over. "General to you." Despite her shorter appearance, her presence is strong. She glances over to me once more. "This kid?"

"Come on, Madi, you should know not to judge a person by their size!" The group of men laugh at the nearest Fel Watch's comment. She throws her elbow into his side, making him whimper and fall to one knee. "Good... shot."

Madi rolls her eyes and beckons me to follow her. I rush to her side as we make our way to the castle's entrance.

She may be shorter than me, but she is terrifying.

"What business do you have with the King? I can tell from your clothes that you aren't from around here." I look down at her and offer her the same papers I offered all the other guards. She raises her hand, dismissing them. "I can't walk and read at the same time."

Right.

"You being shy or something?" Madi doesn't glance up or even slow her pace, but I know she is expecting an answer.

"I, well, need something." The words feel harsh coming out, like I choked on them.

"Don't we all," Madi chuckles a bit, shaking her head. "Though, not many get to ask the King of Felguard for something they need." Her eyes flicker towards me for a second, and I swallow hard.

She's right. I shouldn't say that I need something from him, but simply to talk.

We reach the grand entrance, ten guards lined up in front of the entry. They all nod towards Madi as she raises her hand to them. The two guards directly in front of our path stand to the side, and Madi walks past them, ahead of me, and opens the doors.

This is it.

My heart begins to pound as my foot steps over the threshold.

There is really no going back now. I must do anything it takes to obtain Aruna's chalice.

Madi puts her hand on my shoulder, stopping me from taking another step.

Am I sweating so much that she can see my nervousness?

She moves away to approach another Fel Watch. They chat for a moment, just out of earshot. Madi nods at something the other Fel Watch says, and she looks towards me, beckoning me once more.

Are they going to arrest me?

I swallow hard and try to keep my hands from shaking as she leads me down a series of hallways, all looking quite similar; the only difference being the paintings hanging on the walls and the vases holding different flowers that seem to be from other regions of the realm. We reach a larger set of doors with vine engravings on them.

"I am going to check with the King before taking you in."

I nod, taking a step back, and she walks through the door.

Would she be saying something bad about me? Like how I look like a servant boy but have papers to see a king?

I can hear muffled talking on the other side. I bite on my lip to stop it from trembling. I try to focus on a painting that's just down the hall. I can't make out much detail, but I can tell it's some landscape that looks dry and abandoned. I start to tap my foot, and before long, my entire body seems to be moving.

I am about to meet another king. Though this time I cannot just hide behind my master. My entire journey could come to a halt if he doesn't like me or something I say. What if he hates the Master like all the folk back home do? What if I lie and he knows it?

"Well, don't you look nervous!" I jump and look onwards where the words originated from.

A boy about my age is leaning his side against the hall's wall with a bright smile. Slicked back blonde hair frames his face. He pushes himself off the wall, his dangling earring on his right side sways as he does. He approaches me with his arms crossed and head cocked to the side. "I would guess you are waiting for a life's sentence the way you are jittering out of your skin."

My mouth falls open, not sure how to respond.

Should I say something? Who is this guy? Does the King have heirs?

"I'm Zain. I thought I would come talk you off whatever ledge you seem to be standing on in your mind," he says, tilting his head to the other side, opening his arms up towards me. I shut my mouth and look back at the door. "Ouch, and here I am, trying to be friendly." Without moving my head, I glance to the side, seeing him begin to move even closer. "Come on, at least tell me your name!"

I reach into my satchel, pull out the papers once more, and offer them to him. He laughs and takes them.

"Renatus, huh? Well, I'll call you Ren." He grabs my wrist and puts the papers back into my hand.

Ren? The majority of my life I've been referred to as "boy" and very rarely "Renatus". Not that he knows that, but why not just call me by the name that's written?

"My parents are a pretty big deal around here. So if the King gives you a hard time, I would be your best bet," Zain says, pointing both his thumbs to his chest. "Having a good friend like me could come in handy."

He's a little overwhelming. Though he said he knows the King well enough to talk about him so casually. Maybe I should ask him about the King. What if he could help me? Or worse, what if he hinders me?

I look to the ground, intertwining my fingers together.

This is not helping matters. I'm only getting more nervous.

"Come on, Uncle Kage is not that scary of a guy. Just don't talk about Stran or Aunt Xylia, and you'll be fine." Zain slaps my back, his way of encouraging me. I think.

Uncle Kage and Aunt Xylia? Who is he? Did the First Prince Torrin have a son before he passed? The Master didn't mention anything about that if he did.

The door opens and Madi comes out, looking from Zain to me and me to Zain.

"Leave this poor boy alone, Zain."

"What! He happens to be a newfound friend, Mother. You always assume I am up to no good."

Madi arches her brow and chuckles before grabbing the boy's collar and pulling him away from me.

So he's the son of the General? Maybe the King and her are close? Though how does he know Lady Xylia?

"That's because you are always up to no good. You have the same look in your eyes your father does when he's doing something he shouldn't be." He laughs with a guilty smile. Madi shakes her head before looking back at me. "He is ready for you. Head on in." She points with her nose and turns her attention back to Zain.

Her parenting style is... aggressive.

I put my head down and count my steps as I push the door open and sneak between the smallest crack I can manage to make it through.

The room is massive, and every inch covered in books. Makes the Master's study look like a single shelf compared to this. Though the sight of knowledge simply displayed in this room makes me tempted to start reading the bindings. My eyes dart to the single figure standing in the centre behind a large red desk. His long raven-coloured hair meets his shoulders, where a navy jacket proudly displays the Fosa's crest. His golden trousers stand out against the darker tones his top half wears. His eyes are a deep green, a scar resting just below his left one, and they both look tired. Though they widen when they meet mine. He stands there for a moment, watching me.

Is there something on my face? I should have washed up before presenting myself in front of royalty! I must look like a homely servant more than I normally do.

My thoughts are cut off short when he clears his throat. "General Madi explained to me that you were needing something? She's not one for elaborating, so I am hoping you will." He smiles and gestures to two large chairs sitting in a nook off to the right of the room.

Master was right. Intimidating is not the word I would use to describe King Felguard, but he is most definitely still a king.

I bow towards him and follow his lead to the chairs. As we sit, setting my pack onto the ground, he smiles again; his full attention is on me. I can feel that lump rising again.

Don't mess this up, Renatus. The Master said you could do this.

I reach in the pack, not breaking his gaze, and pull out the red journal that belongs to my master. King Felguard looks down towards it, his brow now furrowed.

Just get it out

"I belong to Master Babylas Amara. He sent me to request a favour from you, Your Majesty." The words come out fast, the journal shaking in my hands.

Breathe, Ren, breathe!

"Hm, and what is the name of the boy who belongs to Sir Amara?" King Felguard asks, his tone deeper than before.

"R, Re, Renatus."

Saying my name should not have been that hard.

He smiles again and shakes his head, looking just past me, tempting me to turn my head and see what he is looking at.

"You travelled all this way to ask for something? Seems like a letter could have sufficed." His eyes draw back to mine. "Though perhaps that means what he is asking for is much more than what he should be."

Sweat begins to drip down the side of my brow.

That doesn't sound great.

The King chuckles and pats my shoulder, a confused look on his face. "Words seem to fail you, my youngin." He stands and walks over to the desk. His back to me. "Speaking to a king can be... daunting, but keep in mind that I am still just a man. Say what you came to so I can assist where I can, for Sir Amara's sake."

I'm wasting his time; the Master's time.

"The Master is looking into certain items embedded with magicae." My voice is quiet. Quiet enough that I am worried the King might not even hear me.

Nothing to be nervous about. I'm not lying. Speak clearly.

"He came across one that was last known to be in your family's possession." The words come out loud to me, but a normal pitch and volume of anyone who speaks.

"My old family had collected a hoard of items that are now in Felguard's possession." King Felguard turns around and leans against the desk, so he is now facing me. "Could you be more specific in both describing the item as well as his intent of asking about it?"

I nod and begin flipping through the pages of the

Master's journal until I land on the one with the image of the chalice. I turn the journal around and show the King. His stale smile fades to a frown, his eyes taking in the image. He closes his eyes, bringing his hand to pinch the bridge of his nose.

Does this item mean something to him?

"The intent?" The King walks over to the windows in the back of the room. He leans on his arms that are pushing against the pane as he stares out of the glass.

I should probably just remain sitting.

"He's sick," I mumble. "He said it would help him."

"I am familiar with that item." King Felguard looks back to me and sighs. "Could you explain how exactly it would help him? As far as I understand, the ability of the chalice is that it can restrain the abilities of Natural Magicae users."

No, I can't really explain it. Maybe I should have gone a different route? What am I supposed to say from here? I am aware of what Aruna's chalice is capable of on its own, as the Master told me, but I should have guessed so does its owner.

"Did he even share that information with you?" the King asks, staring at me with a raised brow; his arms now crossed in front of him.

I'm going to have to lie and pray he doesn't notice.

"He said that with an item like the chalice, you could manipulate the Natural Magicae that has been restrained inside of it."

The King's eyes widen at my response. He glances back at the journal in my hands before meeting my eyes once more.

"Is that so..." his words fall into a whisper.

I swallow hard and slowly nod.

I lied.

My heart feels like it is going to beat straight out of my chest, or worse, come up out of my throat. My stomach is in knots and I can't even meet his gaze now; my eyes fixed on the marble flooring.

He walks briskly towards the door and opens it. "Madi, take him to one of our guest rooms." The King faces me. "I apologise, Renatus. There is a pressing matter I must see to. Go with the General for now."

The King gestures for me to exit the room. Madi is leaning up against the hall's wall and looks into the room at both of us with her eyebrows raised.

Did I say something wrong? Maybe he didn't hear me.

"We will meet at dinner when I am available."

I open my mouth again, but he's already turned his back on me, walking over to the large desk once more. I stand, grabbing my pack and rush out of the room, nearly running right into General Madi as I didn't notice she had stepped towards me.

"Come on, kid." Madi ruffles my hair with her hand roughly, making me bend my head down to her.

I've already failed. The King knows I lied or perhaps doesn't care about the Master's circumstance. I should have done better.

Putting one foot in front of the other, Madi leads us down several hallways. Zain peeks his head around every corner we turn. Eventually, I see him standing in front of a solid oak door.

"That didn't take very long. What did you need to talk to him about, anyways?" The kid laughs.

It doesn't matter.

"Zain, knock it off." General Madi smacks Zain's head and pushes him to the side. "Head on in. If you feel like exploring, I suggest not going with my son. He will get you into trouble." Madi smiles and grabs Zain by the collar again, dragging him away alongside her. "Make yourself comfortable!"

She is different from other mothers I have met.

My mother was always somewhat distant, but remained

present. Never affectionate like that, but was with me almost every shift of the day.

The door opens with a light creak, bringing me back to this current moment in time. Walking into the room, it's dark. The curtains are not drawn, but the light from the hall gives me a good enough idea of what is what. There is a round table near the far right corner with two chairs on either side. A fireplace with a large decorative painting of a forest hanging above the mantel. The enormous bed, with at least ten decorative pillows resting on its head, makes my eyes droop.

Not even the Master's bed compares to the one in this room. There is no way they are expecting me to stay here. This is just a place to keep me for now.

I set my pack and Master's journal onto the table.

I cannot leave until I get that chalice.

I turn and look around the large room again, really taking in that this is how people in this castle sleep. The room I saw in Ventraton was exquisite, but this is even on a grander scale.

This is what a leading country looks like on the inside.

Drawing the curtains back, light floods the room. A view of the castle's garden. I pull a chair over and unlatch the lock higher up on the hinge, and push the window open. The cool-near-wintering air greets my nose, the wind tickling my ears. I stick my head out, looking to the right of the garden, seeing a gazebo and patches of decadent flowers. Looking to the left, there are similar flowers, but there's a statue instead. It's hard to notice the details from this distance, but it looks familiar somehow. My chest begins to tighten and my eyes water.

I jump out of the window. My feet hit the soft dirt, crushing some flowers. I step onto the path and stick to my stride as I approach it. I can feel my heart beating. For a second, I worry it is beating so loud that one of the guards now watching me will think it's a weapon of some sort. I place my hand over my heart to try and conceal it.

The statue's features become more clear; a woman reaching towards the sky with one hand, the other like it should be holding something. Her ears are pointed, her hair braided into three strands. Her face looks peaceful, with that soft smile frozen on her lips.

I reach out and brush my hand against the smooth stone. "An angel," I whisper.

"Indeed, she was." I whip around, and see King Felguard admiring her, his brow still furrowed but jaw tightened.

Why did I just jump out of a window?

I drop my hand and bow my head.

What just happened? It felt just like when I first saw the Kindled Whip.

"Do you recognise her?" the King asks me, his voice strained.

I look up through my lashes and just barely meet his gaze. "Only from a dream," I admit.

Maybe that's what drew me. Master said magicae is in all things as it's what created all of Vitaterrium. "Even dreams can be influenced."

"That is Lady Xylia. The protector of this country."

I look back towards her.

This is Lady Xylia? Why would I dream of her? How did I picture her perfectly?

"She would have liked you. You remind me of an old friend of hers, someone she cared for deeply. I thought you might be his son, but that would be impossible," he confesses.

I glance back towards the King; he is now approaching the statue. Holding onto the hand that looks like it should be holding something. His hand seems to fit perfectly in hers.

Maybe he had it made that way. The King's love for his

should-have-been queen seems to weigh heavily on him. There is no doubt that the face he is adorning now is the same one he adorned when he saw the drawing of the chalice.

"King Felguard, did the chalice belong to Lady Xylia?" The Master didn't account for the fact that some of these items might mean something to some of the people who own them.

The King shakes his head. His shoulders are stiff, but he glances at me for a moment before furrowing his brow. "No, but it is connected to her. She is one of the few who were able to resist the chalice's magicae, so simply even talking of it reminds me of her."

So that is why he looked like that in the library, and excused me abruptly.

"I am very aware of the chalices' capabilities, so the intent you provided is not a true one. Whether you meant it to be intentional or not," the King says, placing a hand on my shoulder.

My body tenses and my fists clench under his grasp. I slowly turn my head to look into his emerald eyes.

I suspected he knew, but actually knowing he knew is much more terrifying.

"I'll give you one chance to remedy this situation and tell me the true intent Babylas Amara has for this chalice or claim ignorance." His grip on me tightens, eyes half-lidded and jaw now tightly clenched.

What am I supposed to do? Lie and hope it works or tell the truth and fail the Master.

Swallowing hard, I turn my gaze from him and onto the beautiful woman who has haunted my dreams since I was a child.

Lying is going to get me no where.

"To bring him back from the dead."

Making a promise might be my only choice.

"...What?" The King's words barely leave his lips.

I look back over to him and nod.

Please let this work.

"Or to cure illness. Depends if he is alive or dead by the time I obtain the apparatus from Aruna."

I hope I'm doing the right thing.

The King turns me to face him completely, a hand on either side of me. His eyes analyse every inch of my face before resting back into an intense gaze on mine.

"Then I will consider assisting you on one condition." He lifts his left hand from my shoulder to point towards Lady Xylia's statue. "You bring her back, too."

"Consider" is better than a no.

"Did your Master show proof that these apparatus really can bring someone back from the dead?"

I shake my head.

The King sighs, "Did Baby's really send you out with no plan or assurance?"

This doesn't sound great.

"Master believes in my abilities to complete this task," I mutter under my breath.

I wish I could say that with more confidence.

"The name Aruna does sound familiar," King Felguard mutters to himself. "You truly believe that bringing her back is possible?"

I nod and the King looks to his love.

CHAPTER TEN

BRINGING Lady Xylia back is a promise I will make King Felguard.

A promise I am hoping I can keep. There's a reason I've dreamt of her, right? Maybe this is it.

Since I jumped from the window and am not sure of what room I was originally escorted to, I look around a few corners and find Zain smiling at me. "Heh! I knew you would come looking for me, so I thought I..." his words trail off as he glances at the King standing close behind me. "Oh, hey, Uncle Kage."

And I knew he would be close around.

"Zain, I see you have met our guest." I look over my shoulder and see King Felguard giving his nephew a soft, closed-eyed smile.

"Yeah, just before you two met." Zain points between the two of us.

"Well, since you know everything that goes on in this castle, why don't you show us to Renatus's room." The King's tone perks up, his soft smile turning into a one-sided smirk.

"Of course I can." Zain sticks his chin high in the air and turns before starting a brisk pace down the halls of the castle.

I am still confused on how the King and the General's son are related.

Zain has a skip to his step as we make our way down the hall and around multiple corridors until a familiar entryway comes into view, the door slightly ajar.

Did I leave it ajar?

"And here we are, Your Majesty and guest." Zain spins around his arm, gesturing towards the door.

The King opens the door and looks around it, as if this is his first time seeing it. He and I walk in, my pack still on the table and window open.

"Based on our conversation, Renatus," King Felguard turns to me and says, "I will be needing to evaluate the situation. We will talk later. I'm sure Zain will keep you company and entertained."

I bow towards him, and he raises his hand before patting my shoulder and exiting the room.

Watching him leave, Zain enters and closes the door. "I don't think I have ever seen Uncle Kage that spirited. He normally wears this weird smile that never reaches his eyes. Kinda freaky."

That was spirited? Did losing Lady Xylia do that to him?

The King and I are going to have another discussion. He is probably going to want to know more about the process of bringing someone back, what I will need and how long it will all take. All questions I'm not sure I can really answer.

I'm sure the Master would not be pleased.

He knew I was lying, though. There wasn't much getting around it.

"I want to know more about you, Ren." Zain's smile is radiant, not just bright this time. "Making friends, and whatnot."

I've never had a friend.

"Okay."

Zain's eyes lighten, hearing me speak to him. He takes a seat at the table, and I follow suit.

Maybe I can get information too. There's so much I feel like I am missing.

"What brought you here? You had to talk to Uncle Kage; what about?" Zain sits back in his chair, resting his chin in one of his hands.

Well he doesn't beat around the bush.

"I am collecting things on behalf of my master. King Felguard has one of those things. I can't say much more." Zain's excited expression fades a bit. His eyes look me over before his expression changes back.

Maybe it was the mention of me having a master that did that. I don't want to lie to him; he seems like Em and the rest of the guards.

"So you are travelling around?" His head tilts to the side. I nod. "Where to?"

Walking over to my pack, I take out the map out of the journal and smooth it out onto the table. Zain leans on his arms, looking over the details of the cartography laid out in front of him.

"Kena, Xan, Berkin, Yral and Fosa?" He sits up straight. "You are really planning on travelling!"

I pull the map back and tuck it away where it belongs.

He seems excited by the thought, but it's terrifying. I will be on my own from here on out.

"Okay, well, since you told me something. Anything you want to know?" I nod, and he leans over, waiting for me to answer, but there are far too many questions I want to ask. "How about I start by telling you a bit about my parents?" Zain asks with a smile.

I nod again. *I am curious.*

"My mother, Madi, is one of the generals of the King's military and is one of the toughest people you'll ever meet. I've never seen her lose a fight, and even someone like Uncle Kage respects her."

She came across as intimidating when I first met her, but seeing her with her son, there was a strange kindness about her, too.

"Vasile, my father, is my best friend. He acts like he is still our age, but in reality he is old. Dad comes across as super oblivious and like a chatterbox, but he is actually really smart and observant. He can persuade almost anyone to do anything. Mom teases him about how much of a flirt he used to be and still can be." Zain laughs at his own words, making me laugh a bit, too. "I get that from him. Though I don't give just anyone my attention, I have to get this certain feeling. If that happens, I can't leave them alone until I know we are friends." He looks at me and smiles.

Guessing that's how he must feel about me, given he has been following me around since I arrived.

"They have this insane trust between them. Like no matter what, they know they will always love each other the most." His tone is much more sincere. His eyes look out the still open window. "I want to find something like that."

"You will," I mutter.

His gaze turns back to me. "How do you know?"

I look away.

It's not that I know, it's just that he seems like the type of person who will get what he wants one way or another.

"Hm, I like you, Ren." Zain slams his hands onto the table. "My turn!"

A knock at the door makes me jump. Zain stands and hurries to answer it. A Fel Watch steps in, locking eyes with me. I stand slowly.

What now?

"Your guards wanted me to inform you they will be staying

at the Smoky Nook Tavern." I sit back down and nod towards him. He nods back and exits the room, Zain closing the door.

"Guards?" he asks with a furrowed brow.

"The company I was sent here with," I explain, hoping I won't have to delve in deeper than that.

"So, they won't be travelling with you moving forward?" Zain asks. I nod my head in agreement to his statement. His brow stays furrowed as he returns to his seat next to me. "You are going to have one interesting story to tell."

If I survive it, but even then it's not a story I'd actually be able to tell.

"Guess that can count as my question..." he says with a slight pout to his lip.

"Lady Xylia?" I ask.

I need to know more. How she died, where she came from. I need to know why I've been dreaming of her since I was a child.

"Oh." Zain walks over to the bed, sitting on the edge. "I never met her. She died a sidereal year before I was even born. Though my father and mother have told me a lot about her, some stories of them growing up. She was an elf, or at least partially one. Crazy powerful and protected the Adamina Clan from anything that would try to hurt it."

The Adamina Clan sounds familiar, though I am not sure what an elf is. I think one of the books I read regarding the history of Limoria referred to them as an ancient race from one of the doorways.

"Uncle Codrin. He was my dad's best friend, and as he likes to put it, Aunt Xylia's husband, but Uncle Kage would strongly disagree with that statement as he was meant to wed her himself." He takes a breath and rolls his eyes a tad, from the probable fight or fights had about that comment. "He died in a fight against this scary sounding creature the night they all met Uncle Kage. The old king came after them, and so they fled the clan, went on this crazy adventure where my dad got kidnapped and tortured, but then Aunt Xylia saved him and killed the old king." Zain's hands act like he is pulling back the string of an arrow before "releasing" an imaginary arrow. "It gets kinda complicated, but there was—" Zain stops himself for a moment, biting his lip. "—some group after Aunt Xylia and her power. As much as Uncle Kage tried to protect her, they ended up taking her to Stran, where something really bad happened. Both my parents say they can't explain it, but she died saving the Felguard country. Her body was encased in stone, and the statue you and Uncle Kage were looking at earlier is actually her."

That was her actual body? What exactly happened in Stran? What group was after her?

"Everyone says that she was really beautiful and strong. Though everyone gets sad talking about her. She apparently lost a lot and went through some really terrible things, so when she ended up dying, a lot of people lost hope. Mom says that Uncle Kage was strong, though. He rebuilt the royal reputation, helped people return to Fosa and restored a lot of relationships with other countries. Also, I've got to see the work he has done with the M.G.A."

I raise a brow at him.

"Magicae's Guided Assembly," he clarifies.

That's a lot and also very little. Sounds like there should be a novel dedicated to her, to tell her story.

"Thank you," I say, joining him on the bed.

Her death is still a mystery and why it seems the people who experienced it are keeping it a secret is even stranger.

Maybe they don't even really know themselves.

"Why did you want to know about her?" Zain asks. His gaze is on his nicely polished black dress shoes.

I shrug my shoulders. Even if I don't want to lie to him, I

don't want to say anything that will upset the King. If he is secretive about her death, I am sure he won't want anyone knowing she could potentially be coming back until she is.

Also, admitting that I've dreamed of her seems like a strange thing to mention.

"Fine. Why don't you talk?"

"Nothing to say," I admit. There is little value to my words, so I'd rather never speak.

Only when necessary.

"I doubt that. You seem to watch everything so closely; you must see more than anyone else." His blue eyes meet mine. "Why don't I get us some lunch? It's getting late, and we should eat something."

I nod in agreement. Zain rises from his seat and leaves. Standing from the bed, I walk over to the table and grab my pack.

We are going to need a place to eat.

I set my pack at the foot of the bed and dust off the table.

AFTER EATING the sandwich Zain brought back, Zain decided that dragging me through the halls of the castle would be the best decision. He takes me around to see the gardens once more; the sun setting in the sky, turning a purplish colour.

I'm still not used to how different the sky is here in the Felguard Country.

We walk by the kitchen; it's massive. Multiple fire stoves, water pumps, large prep counters and every utensil you would ever need. Not to mention an ice locker filled with meat.

"You boys better hurry on out. It's going to get busy here.

There is going to be a shift change in guards and they are going to be hungry!" the chief says, waving us out with a knife and ladle in hand. He gives us a smile and closes the door.

That kitchen is incredible.

"This is the most excited I've seen you since you arrived, Renatus! Do you like cooking or something?" Zain says, nearly jumping on my back as we walk down the hall.

I nod and smile.

Cooking for the Master is something I have been missing.

Since being on the road, I have been eating canned food, dried meats and fruits, and tavern food. No time to stop for shopping or cooking in general.

"I want to try some of your cooking. I'm sure you are great at it!" My cheeks feel a little warm hearing him say that.

I don't know if my cooking is any good. The Master never complained, but that doesn't mean I'm any good.

"Let's head over to the dungeons next." Zain grabs my arm and begins leading me down the decorated corridors.

Some paintings depict different countries' landscapes in Limoria, potted plants and expensive-looking decorations lining each of them. We make our way around a corner where a slim staircase begins to descend deeper, below ground level. The carpeted flooring is replaced with a cut stone that matches the walls. Continuing deeper, there are lanterns hung just spaced out enough that every time the light seems like it is going to fade, the next one's light begins. The temperature drops a bit, a chill running down my spine.

After a few minutes, the stairs come to an end and open up to a lounge-like area. A couch, tables and Fel Watch all looking at us as they seem to be just passing time in this area.

"Hey there," Zain says with a wave.

One of the guards stands and walks over to us. "Zain. Your mom told us to keep you outta here."

"Come on, I won't tell her." He smiles, and the guard rolls his eyes.

"Fine, but if she finds out..."

"She won't! Relax." Zain slaps the guy's armoured arm and leads us down a corridor to the left.

It doesn't take us long to find the caged rooms, all lined up one after the other.

I wasn't expecting there to be people down here.

There are three cells currently occupied. One with a man mumbling something to himself, long white hair, beady eyes and wearing nothing but a nightshirt. Two cells down from his, there is a person wearing a cloak lying on the bed. The one after that has a woman with curly red hair and copper skin, wearing a simple blouse and trousers sitting in a chair.

The woman stands, seeing us. Her eyes widen as she looks me up and down.

"Codrin?" Her voice is a whisper.

The guard on duty stands and smacks the metal bars with his metal staff. She glares at him before looking back at me.

"You're losing your mind, Rose," the cloaked figure says, sitting up in the bed.

"Just ignore them." Zain leans over and whispers into my ear. "They have all been down here a long time."

Just how long? Her face reminds me of when Madi and Kage first looked at me. Some sort of recognition or remembrance crossing their faces.

The hooded figure pulls down their hood and rubs their bearded face. They have dark skin like mine, similar eyes, and curly black hair that falls to his shoulders. "Or maybe not."

"Looks just like him, right?" Rose asks.

"Both of you, shut up!" the guard says again, smacking the bars of both their cages. "You two, get out of here. You are stirring up trouble."

"What? You should have better control of your prisoners!" Zain shouts back.

"Let's go," I say, gripping onto Zain's shirt. He looks over to me, his brow furrowed and nods.

"Wait!" the cloaked man shouts, pressing himself against the bars. "Who are you?"

"I said... shut up!" The Fel Watch jams the metal staff into the man's stomach. It just barely fits through the space in between the bars.

Heading back the way we came, Zain remains silent and ignores the guard's joke about our brief visit before we ascend back up the stairs.

"Sorry about that; like I said, they have all been down there a long time."

"That keeps happening," I whisper. "People recognising me as someone else."

Zain continues walking, but looks over his shoulder back at me.

"You mentioned Codrin before." That's who the woman down there, Rose, said I looked like.

"Maybe you are related to Uncle Codrin somehow," Zain says in a soft tone. "Or maybe you just look kinda like him. He's been dead for quite awhile."

People will often try to look for comfort in times of loss. Maybe it's just their way of still mourning him? Seeing him in a stranger's face?

"We should head back to your room," Zain suggests.

I nod in agreement.

It takes quite a bit of time to make our way back. We turn a final corner and see a guard knocking on the door we are about to enter.

The Fel Watch sees us approach her, and she nods to us. "The King is ready for your audience." Her words are monotone and short, but the message is plenty clear. "I will escort you."

"I guess I will see you later!" Zain says with a smile.

THE LIBRARY DOORS are closed and it's just as intimidating as the first time I was standing in front of them today. That lump rising in my throat again. I take a step forward and knock on the large wooden doors.

"Come in," the King's voice sounds from inside the room.

Opening one of the doors, a soft firelight is flickering throughout the room. The large fireplace now has a flame roaring inside of it. The King's raven hair shines, almost reflecting the light of the flames.

His tired eyes fall onto my nervous ones. "Thank you for meeting with me. I thought we should discuss the details of exactly how you plan on resurrecting your master." He gestures to the chairs we had sat in earlier today. "Along with how it works, of course."

He speaks like the Master is already dead.

I nod and follow his gesture to sit.

How can I be vague but also forthright? I knew he would want to know this information, but I'm not sure how much I can really give him.

"First," he says, taking his seat next to me. "I am assuming you are going to be collecting more than just the chalice, since you mentioned something about apparatus from one of the mother's of Forged Magicae."

He must have freshened up on his history of Forged Magicae.

I nod.

"Where and what?" He leans back, crossing one leg over the other.

"Chalice, necklace, gauntlet, dagger and cloak. Kena, Xan, Berkin, Yral and Fosa. Both not necessarily in that order." I wish I had my master's journal for this.

Would be easier.

"Your master doesn't want anyone to know this, correct?" the King asks, raising a brow.

I nod.

"The reason for that is apparent. Everyone has someone they wish to bring back." He tilts his head to the side for a moment before lifting it back upright.

Or want to live forever.

"Your plan, or shall I say his plan, was for you to just walk in and demand items from their owners? I know Babylas well and think of him fondly, but I doubt many others do." He looks me up and down, which causes me to shift in my seat. "And why you?"

Master said that there's something he saw inside of me. His confidence in me is something I question myself.

The King stands and walks over to his desk. "You will need more support if you are to achieve this goal."

"Support?" I stand as well, following him over to the desk.

He nods, grabbing a quill and parchment. He begins scribbling words down, peering over his shoulder. I can see it reads about diplomatic research on behalf of the Felguard Country.

"This should be able to get you at least through the gates of the other cities you mentioned. Beyond that, your words and demeanour will have to do the rest." The King sets his quill down and turns back to me. "My advisor will have to sign off on this, but I will make sure you are more than equipped for your journey. Renatus, there is nothing I want more than Xylia."

His emerald eyes bare into me and the sincerity of his words makes my heart stop for a moment.

What is this feeling?

"I need to know... what are the consequences of this magicae?" he asks.

"The Master never told me."

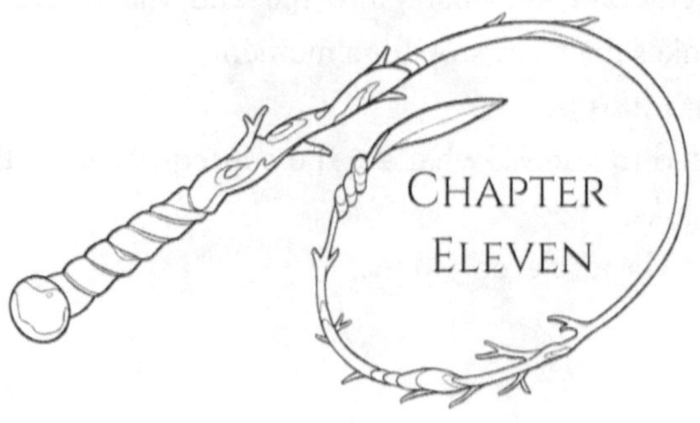

CHAPTER ELEVEN

"Please remain here as my guest as I need time to discuss the situation with my advisors," the King says as we exit the library and enter the hall. "Even though I'm King, I cannot give credence to just anyone. They will have questions, but I vow to keep the true purpose of these apparatus between us."

I nod to the King, taking a step through the door, but freeze when I see a blonde young man leaning up against the hallway wall.

"Hey, Ren!" Zain shouts, giving me an extremely wide smile. "Uncle Kage," he adds with a tilt to his head.

"Zain. Our guest might become concerned with your constant attention," King Felguard says with a dull smile barely lifting the corners of his lips.

"I guess so, but that'll be up for my friend Ren to decide," Zain retorts.

"Friend? It has not even been a full day, yet you are claiming to have strong ties." The King lightly pushes me forward so we both can leave the library. "Interesting." He closes the door behind him.

"Well, I am charming, handsome and a pure joy to be around." Zain's shoulders raise, hands raised on either side of him. The arrogance is very present in his smug smile.

The King chuckles and shakes his head. "We can call it a difference of opinion."

The three of us begin to walk down the hall, Zain going on about some trouper that has been travelling throughout Limoria, and her next stop would be here in Fosa.

"Mazu, you said?" the King asks Zain to clarify.

"Yeah, Mazu. She's apparently known for her storytelling and mystical tales of goddesses and devils." Zain confirms, skipping down the hall ahead of us.

"I remember meeting her once." King Felguard's words are soft and his gaze is somewhere in the distance, like he is remembering the moment he is referencing.

He's good at hiding what he is really feeling in moments like this one. There are hints, but it could be read in many ways. Maybe hiding is the burden of being a king.

As we arrive at the door of my temporary room, I open the door and nearly scream as I see a tall man with curly hair and light-coloured clothes, looking through the Master's journal.

What is he doing!?

"Vasile. Come to greet our visitor?" the King asks calmly.

The man, Vasile, turns his head and looks to the King before his eyes land on me. They widen despite his brow furrowing. His lip trembles for a moment before he shakes his head. Vasile steadies his breath while he brings his hand up as a fist to his mouth and clears his throat.

There are tears in his eyes.

"Well, at least now I know I am not imagining things," the King says in a brighter tune.

I feel like I'm missing some context.

Vasile laughs and nods. "Madi came running to Xylia's Respite just to let me know of our young guest and told me to come to his room to see for myself." He walks over to me and extends his hand. He is just as tall as I am, so his eyes are level to mine. I take his hand and shake it.

"Quiet little guy! We will need to break you out of your shell."

Zain mentioned his father's name was Vasile. They have the same smile.

"Would the both of you mind showing him around some more tomorrow? I will be preoccupied until dinner." The King's request is immediately met with two beaming smiles from both Zain and Vasile.

"You got it, Kage. What's your name again?" Vasile places both his hands on my shoulders.

"His name is Renatus," the King says on my behalf.

Thank you.

"Ren! Got it." Vasile smiles widely.

Father like son.

"It is growing late into the evening. I know a new guest can be quite exciting, but let us all rest, and tomorrow, you can begin whatever entertainment you already have brewing inside that head of yours," the King says, a smirk resting on his lips.

"Guess you are right." Vasile pats my back, a little too hard. He grabs his son, who waves goodnight as he is walking backwards from his father's grip.

I wave back and give him a small smile before closing the door behind all of them.

This place is strange, terrifying, interesting, and despite it being a castle, it seems people have made it their home.

The large bed looms over me now that I am alone for the night.

Can't believe they are allowing me to sleep in here.

It was likely that I would stay in Fosa for at least a night or two while trying to obtain an audience, and also obtaining the chalice, but I did not expect to be welcomed into the castle so readily nor see the King almost the moment I arrived at the castle. Everyone here has been more than welcoming; the guards are kind, and even friends of royalty like Zain, have tried befriending me.

Everything that has happened so far is beyond what I expected, Master.

Telling King Felguard the truth, in a sense, is by far my biggest surprise. The Master seemed it easy to come in and ask for the chalice, but I doubt he thought it would hold meaning to the King. I was not aware that Lady Xylia was the one I had been seeing, and now that I know, it only leaves me with more questions. The strangest part of it all is they seem to recognise me as her former lover. She died shortly after I was born, so that is completely impossible.

Codrin. Who was he?

There are a lot of questions rattling around inside my head. Questions that I don't have any claim to ask but want to anyway.

These are the decisions I get to make.

It's unlike the knowledge I have come to learn about; it's personal and not necessarily beneficial. Though getting answers about why I have dreamed of Lady Xylia nearly my whole life would be beneficial. Maybe the dream would stop, and so would her tears.

Readying myself for bed, I tentatively crawl under the thick covers on the bed. They are extremely soft, and the mattress is plush.

Strange.

I miss the stiffness of my old cot.

A LOUD KNOCK sounds at the door. I close the Master's journal, as I was making sure everything was where I had left it before Vasile looked through it. Wandering over to the door and opening it, a wild Zain appears with a large tray. I move out of his way, and he walks over and sets the tray down on the table, taking a seat. There are juices, cooked meats, fruits and bread all prepped nicely on the tray.

Zain grabs one of the plates on it and fills it up before looking at me. "You gonna sit?"

Wait, this is for us?

I nod and take a seat.

This is much more than the sandwich I ate yesterday.

"One of the servants was planning on serving you, but I made sure to take the job. I thought we could have breakfast together before my father drags you around," Zain mutters through the bread that is in his mouth.

He is very strange.

I take a few pieces of meat, fruit and a slice of bread and place it all on my own plate.

"Juice?" Zain asks, pouring some into a cup. "It's made from the lymnori berries that grow in the Vermilion Forest."

Pouring myself a small cup, I can smell the concentrated sweet smell of the dark red liquid. It has a slightly bitter after-taste that compliments the almost candy-like flavour.

We finish our breakfast in a silence that I am grateful for.

"Dad said he would meet us at the gate to Aunt Xylia's place." Zain stands and wipes his face with a napkin.

"Xylia's place?"

As in where she used to live?

"I think my father mentioned it yesterday. Xylia's Respite. It's where the Adamina Clan used to be before the old king ordered it to be burned down. The trees regrew so Uncle Kage rebuilt it," Zain explains, tugging me up and out of the room by my arm.

I am confused. He mentioned the Adamina Clan yesterday, but I cannot remember exactly the purpose of the clan or where it was located. He said trees, right?

We walk down a few different halls until we are back at the entrance General Madi and I walked through when I first got here.

Her place must be outside the castle grounds.

A familiar figure comes into view; the bubbly father of Zain is standing near the castle's entrance.

"Ren!" Vasile says, a bright smile plastered across his face.

There is someone else there, though. Her navy-coloured hood falls back and reveals her bobbed brunette hair, a small scar on her chin and a beauty mark under her right eye.

"I thought we were meeting you at the gate?" Zain asks, looking between his father and the woman standing next to him.

"Yeah, but I convinced Shaw to take us instead of walking all the way down there," Vasile coos, putting his arm around her shoulders.

Shaw rolls her eyes and shoves Vasile off. "You convinced me of nothing. You are my superior, and the King makes me listen to you."

Zain laughs and punches his dad's arm. Vasile makes a pouty face, but it quickly fades into the shining smile he and Zain share.

"Well, either way, let's head out!" the older blonde says, riling up the younger one.

Shaw waves her hand, signalling me to step closer as I am behind the group by a few feet.

"This is gonna be fun," Zain whispers into my ear before my vision suddenly goes black.

I blink, and suddenly I am standing on a red-planked deck, the sounds of leaves rustling all around me, a faint breeze blowing my hair into my face. My gaze travels from my feet to see the tops of trees straight in front of me. A wooden railing keeps me from falling over the edge. The trunk of the tree in view is the largest I've ever seen, a deep red colour to match its leaves. My shoulders are turned for me to face the other way and I see wooden buildings built right on top of the deck we are standing on. Carts being dragged by livestock, people walking around talking and laughing with each other.

How did that just happen? Where are we? This is like the door Master had in the tower.

I look to Shaw, who is staring blankly out at the rural life in front of us.

"How high?" I whisper. The air feels thinner, like it was in Ventraton. The sun seems that much closer too.

"It's a few kilometres down to the forest's floor," Vasile says.

My hand grips my chest that is pounding, a few droplets of water hitting the backside of my it.

Why am I crying?

"This is the old Adamina Clan. Even though it was disbanded, some folks still refer to it as the Adamina Clan," Zain says, stepping out ahead of me once again.

This place is incredible.

"It's a glorified clubhouse now. Exclusive to some of the old members, hunters and the Fel Watch who help take care of the place..." Vasile's words trail off. I look at him and see a funny look on his face as he is staring at me. "It was rebuilt in Xylia's honour and was to be the wedding gift to Xylia from Kage, but she died before they could marry or for her to even see it."

He built her an entire village in the trees? Or rebuilt. Either way, that seems extensive, even for a king.

"This used to be our home, before our world changed," Vasile explains, now joining Zain up ahead.

Their home? So she used to live here. Did she live here with Codrin too?

"I'll be returning," Shaw says, and in an instant, she is gone.

I look at Vasile and Zain, who seem completely unphased by her disappearance.

Teleportation.

"Well, how about we show you the place?" Vasile asks, arms stretched out wide and spinning in a circle.

I am not sure of his age, but Zain was correct in describing his father. I would assume just by personality that he is younger than me.

As I timidly follow them around the wooden grounds that make up Xylia's Respite, I can see that diligent care went into crafting it. Beautiful carvings decorate the frames of the buildings, each one traditional to the Felguard Country's history.

Like that woman's outfit back in Jod.

Most of everything is a tinted red, likely from being made of the same wood as the trees that surround us or from exposure to the dust I see gathered in corners.

A place like this seems so tranquil.

"The Vermilion Forest is unlike any forest in all of Vitaterrium. It's a renewable source and is how the Felguard Country originally made the majority of its wealth. You cut down one trunk, and it grows right back the next day." Vasile gestures towards the trunk larger than the buildings we are walking around. "Only Xylia's magicae was able to destroy sections of the forest."

The Master mentioned something like that when I was studying some herbology. The Vermilion Forest was a mysterious source of magicae but records only show it being this expansive and large just after the Ancestry War.

My shoulder caves into the shove it just received. Zain's looking at me with the same smile Vasile has. He interlocks our arms and pulls me alongside him as we follow after Vasile. He points towards a decent-sized home. A dark cherry wooden exterior and its trimming painted yellow. It has an open porch with a set of chairs facing to the east. The door is painted yellow to match the trimming. I hear a woman's familiar laugh, though looking around, I do not see anyone near us.

"This was Xylia's and Codrin's old place," Vasile explains, stepping up onto the porch and opening the door.

Despite Zain's movement forward, my feet lock into place.

It's that same feeling. The feeling to just jump and run towards something like I did with the Kindled Whip and with Xylia's statue. I want to run inside and see something, but I'm not sure what that something is exactly.

"You look just like him," Vasile's whisper carries itself towards me, and I look up to him. "That expression on your face. Codrin was always the one to worry; he was always right to do so. Knew how to read people and situations." Vasile smiles despite tears welling up in his eyes. "Who are you, Renatus?"

I don't want to cause them any confusion.

"I am not Codrin. I am the servant of Babylas Amara. Born in Draco eighteen sidereal years ago. Purchased at eight sidereal years old and have been living in Ventraton since." I didn't mean the words to come out so flat, but I also just want this feeling in my chest to go away, along with the look on his face.

Vasile nods and laughs, covering his eyes with his hand. "Right. I'm sorry."

"Dad..." Zain whispers, unlinking my arms and rushing up to comfort his father.

"I'm alright. I know it's impossible. You were born near the time he died. He never had any youngins of his own, and I was just happy to see my friend's face again. Even if it wasn't really his." Vasile's words sound broken, lips trembling and nose sniffling. "I'm sorry." I hear him barely whisper.

I didn't mean to make him cry.

"Codrin seems to be very loved by all of you. It's very clear that despite his death, he is still present at this very moment. Living in those who remember him."

I doubt I am the right person to try to comfort him, but I want to try. A part of me wants to cry too. Being here in this place, far from everything I know. In a way, that tower was family, and I am mourning in silence. It's the only thing I can do.

"We should head back. We have been wandering around for a few sunshifts." Vasile puts on an even bigger smile than the one he was wearing before, tears still running down his face. He jumps down from the porch and pats my shoulder as he passes me.

Zain and I follow after him. He rubs his face with his sleeve a few times, looking upwards towards the sky that is visible through the foliage. Looking at Zain, he is watching his feet.

I must have said the wrong thing.

Heading back to where we originated from, we continue past that. There are a few red armoured guards standing by a large black gate built right at the edge of the fencing that acts as the only border from walking right off the wooden deck we are all standing on.

"Fosa is just through that gate," Vasile says, turning his head back slightly before looking forwards again.

"You're not gonna fall off. Well, probably. Shaw enchanted

it to work like her magicae," Zain says; his grin turning mischievous.

I sigh and close my eyes for a brief moment.

It's just like the Master's door, it's just like the Master's door. Please be like the Master's door.

The guards nod towards Vasile, who gives them a wave. They open the gate inward, towards us, and gesture with their spears to walk through. Because there is nothing on the other side, it looks like they are inviting us to jump off to our deaths.

"Guest's first," Vasile says with a dulled smile.

I shake my head and grab onto Zain's shoulder. Vasile widens his eyes, as does Zain. They both burst out laughing, and I furrow my brow.

I don't find this funny at all.

"All right, buddy," Zain says, trying to control the chuckles still escaping his lips. "We can go together." He grabs my hand that is resting on his shoulder and squeezes it tight. We walk forward, and I take a deep breath as we near the deck's edge.

As my foot crosses the gate's border, my vision goes black again before a noisy street comes in both earshot and sight. We are in the merchant district in Fosa. I look at Zain, who is still holding onto my hand and he is still laughing.

"You are so wimpy! Are you really travelling the realm by yourself?" I roll my eyes at Zain's comment and begin walking towards the castle. "Wait! I didn't mean it!"

We all make our way back. Vasile keeps behind us all the way until we arrive at the castle's main entrance.

"I am going to head out and find my wife. You boys have some fun around here until dinner," Vasile says, ruffling both Zain's and my hair.

Zain and I head back to the room I have been lent for the time being.

"Sorry about my dad. He misses his friends a lot. Growing

up, all he would do is tell me stories about Uncle Codrin and Aunt Xylia. Even though I never met them, it's almost like I did."

I nod, hearing the tension in Zain's voice.

I'm sure, even though he said seeing me made him happy, it was actually extremely hard.

"I should say that I refer to them as my uncle and aunt because neither of my parents have any siblings, but their friends are the closest thing to that for them. Uncle Kage is the only one I've actually spent time with, but he's a king, so he's always busy," Zain explains, waving his hands around in the air as he talks.

That explains a lot of my questions. I'm glad Zain likes to talk, even though I don't reciprocate.

I open the door to the large room and close it behind as Zain struts his way to the table with my pack resting against it. I grab my master's journal containing maps and other notes before he gets a chance to.

It wasn't good that Vasile was looking through it. I am hoping we interrupted before he even really looked. I should be more careful with this.

My grip tightens on the book.

What if the King looked through it while I was gone? I mean, he asked Vasile to show me around and he happened to take me out of the castle. Far away from my belongings.

"You alright, Ren?" Zain grips my shoulder and shakes me a bit.

I nod and swallow the paranoia.

Chapter Twelve

"It's about that time," Zain mumbles. I glance up from my book to see him looking out the window. The dagger he has been playing with has now stilled. "We should probably start getting ready for dinner."

It's the second day I've been here, and he hasn't really left me alone. Only when I sleep or relieve myself do I get to be alone. Did someone ask him to keep an eye on me?

"Can I wash up?" Showing up to dinner with the King, filthy from my travels, seems beyond rude.

Plus, some alone time wouldn't be awful.

Zain nods and jumps up. "This way, my friend! There is a guest bath." I close my book, walking over to my pack to grab some spare clothes. "It's just around the corner here."

We take a right out of the door before turning left around the corner Zain spoke of. There's a set of large doors with dark blue decorated handles. Zain pushes them open to reveal a massive room with mirrors on either side. A cushioned sofa against the far wall and hooks on the other side of the sliding door on the right of us.

"You can put your clothes on the loveseat there and the bath is through that door. You just have to pump the water." I nod, acknowledging his words.

He closes the doors behind him and leaves me alone in this giant prep room.

It's like they are expecting multiple people to get ready here at the same time.

I strip out of my dirty and overworn clothes and place them neatly folded next to my clean ones. I open the sliding door and see a few extremely large barrel tubs. A pump next to each of them.

Oh. They really are expecting multiple people to be in here at a time.

I walk over to the one on the left and begin pumping the handle. It takes a few to start it up before the water starts pouring out. Steam begins to fill the air as hot water comes out.

It's heated water. They must have a furnace system that boils the water before pumping it.

The only warm bath I've ever had was when I first arrived at the Master's tower. I had to boil the water myself, though. It was a short bath, just necessary from the rough conditions I had come from. My family was poor, and taking a bath meant having the time to relax. We were always working on something or for something. I would help my mother sew and keep the house in good shape.

The door slides open, making me jump straight into the extremely hot water, the temperature almost making me hop right back out.

I feel like I am going to boil alive in this.

"Ren! We thought we would join you!" Vasile shouts, he walks in completely naked.

I avert my eyes to the water I am currently sitting in.

"I thought we could all bathe together for some bonding time," Zain chips in, probably naked too.

Why.

The sounds of metal squeaks as Vasile begins to pump his

own water. I sink further into the water, a sigh leaving my lips before my mouth dips below the waterline. I close my eyes and try to focus on the heat from the bath and not the noises of the two naked men roaming around the room.

"Don't be like that, Ren!" The water shifts, and my eyes shoot open to see Zain climbing into the tub with me.

I sit up and turn my head towards the wall.

He didn't need to climb into mine. I just want this to be over already.

Water splashes against my face, and I look at the smiling Zain sitting directly across from me. "You need to learn how to just go with things!"

"Zain, not everyone can live as carefree as you," Vasile says.

"Wel, I learned it from you!"

Vasile and Zain go on to talk about some things that have been going on around the castle. How a festival winning cow has gone missing, things disappearing every time a certain noble happens to stay at the castle and how that very unliked aristocrat had his portrait ruined by the artist who had replaced his face with that of a pig.

The King was right; Zain really does know everything that's going on.

We all climb out of the tub, fingers and toes wrinkled slightly. Drying off and changing into my clothes, I avoid looking at either of them. A part of me wonders if they are just here to make sure I don't run. They most likely read the Master's journal, and if that is the case, they might try to beat me in collecting Aruna's apparatus.

I can't let that happen.

"Ready?" Vasile asks, patting my back.

Briefly making eye contact with him, I nod.

They escort me down the different corridors until the hall opens up into a room with a tall ceiling where an enormous rectangular redwood table sits in the centre. There are large fireplaces on both sides, which already have a fire started in them. Giant bouquets of flowers in each corner, all resting in golden vases with navy blue detailing the Felguard Country's crest. A shield with two swords crossing each other inside of that, the swords blades in the shape of leaves.

With King Felguard came a new era. Despite him being born a Torrin, he changed his name and made the country's new crest the royal one as well.

Master mentioned that it was the first time he respected the Felguard's ruler.

There are several Fel Watch standing around the room, all of them looking at us. A few of them wave back as Vasile waves to them.

Security comes across as intense due to the sheer number of Fel Watch, but they haven't even taken my whip or searched through my belongings. Is that the protocol or is it because of the letter the King of Ventraton gave me?

"You can sit next to the head of the table, Ren," Vasile says, pulling out my chair for me. I widen my eyes and stare at the chair next to that one. "I'll be right next to you."

I give him a tight smile and sit down. Zain takes a seat across from me, leaning back in his chair enough to make it tilt.

"You always look so nervous." Zain chuckles.

"Zain, sit upright," General Madi says as she enters from the south opening of the room. Zain stops tilting his chair and rolls his eyes. "Lunamatrum have mercy." She sits next to Vasile. He leans over, whispering something into her ear, making her smile. She turns her head, kissing him.

I look away and to Zain, who is watching his parents with a disgusted look on his face, mouth soured and brows furrowed. The sound of metal shifting and clanging draws all of our attention. The Fel Watch are standing at attention; the King is entering the dining hall. He raises his hand, excusing the guards back to their on-duty stances.

"Thank you for joining us, Renatus," the King says, smiling at me. A long brunette-haired woman walks in as well with a fawn-coloured lanky male practically hiding behind her. "Laura and Fenny will be joining us as well. They are some of the best weapon specialists in all of Limoria."

I'm getting to meet a lot of impressive people today. I don't think I was ready for this.

"You give us too much credit," Laura says, a wide grin spread across her face.

"It was Xylia who truly believed that statement; I just happened to agree with her," the King clarifies, taking his seat at the head of the table and next to me.

Laura's smile fades a bit as she sits next to Zain, who is looking at his uncle. Fenny silently takes his seat next to Laura, and a part of the wall opens up, revealing a kitchen just inside of it. Multiple servants carrying trays come out and place a decadent plate filled with leafy greens, beets and onions in front of each of us. Another servant fills our glasses with a dark reddish liquid.

I've never been served like this before. Maybe when I was too young to do it myself, but that's from a time I do not remember.

All the servants, but one, leave through the hidden door in which they came. It closes behind them. The lone servant stands off to the side behind the King's seat.

"Renatus, do you not like your food?" the King asks before taking a bite of his salad. I look around and notice everyone has already begun eating. "I can have something else prepared for you."

King Felguard raises his hand, but I quickly shake my head and grab my utensils to begin eating. A chuckle rises out of the

King, and I see a curious brow raised; his emerald orbs watching me.

"Renatus, what did you think about Xylia's Respite?" Madi asks.

I look over and see a frown resting where I thought a smile would be.

I'm not sure why I feel like she should be smiling.

"It was... enchanting." The words are mumbled as I feel everyone's eyes on me.

Xylia's Respite was truly extraordinary. I've never seen a place like it before, but it is the feelings I got while I was there that leave me more confused than anything.

"Before the Xylia's Respite, the Adamina Clan used to be a lot bigger," she says, now with a smile on her face.

"And livelier!" Vasile adds.

I wish I could have seen that.

"It was quite a threatening presence to the old king," King Felguard admits. "He was worried that one day the Adamina Clan would overthrow him."

"Pretty much did happen that way," Laura chimes in, salad still being chewed in her mouth.

"Maybe not the entire clan was present, but it was in spirit," Vasile clarifies.

"Absolutely. Hearing that Xylia took that final shot meant everything to us. Our Maresal was protecting us once again." Madi looks next to her at the empty chair sitting on the opposite side of the King.

"She was very strong," Fenny mumbles, not glancing up from his plate.

It's fascinating hearing them talk about the past like this. Not just biassed retellings from the Master, but the people who actually lived it, that knew her.

Our plates are taken from us by the servant left behind

before the others come out and serve us a plate of potatoes and a large steak.

This is way too much for one meal.

"Renatus, when we finish this meal, I would like to speak with you in the library once more," the King says under his breath in my direction. He cuts into his steak, placing a piece into his mouth before he even glances at me.

I nod.

"Hey Ren, why don't you tell us a little more about you," Vasile suggests, smiling at me. "I saw in your room some stuff about Forged Magicae."

So he read enough to recognise what it was.

"He is actually the servant of Babylas Amara. He is a very prominent figure in Forged Magicae's history," the King explains on my behalf, then turns to me. "My assumption, though, is that you were also his mentee. Correct?"

"Yes. Though I still have a lot to learn," I admit.

A lot more.

"I would love to see it," Vasile says.

"Didn't Uncle Codrin used to study it?" Zain asks through stuffed cheeks; his plate already empty.

Vasile nods. "It was an interest, but he never actually used it. Whittling and woodworking were his true passion." He glances at the King for a moment before returning to his plate. "Besides Xylia, of course."

The King sets his utensils down and waves the servant over. They quickly leave the room.

Madi clears her throat. "Anyway, back to you, Renatus. Besides Forged Magicae, what else do you enjoy doing?"

I widen my eyes, hearing her question.

Enjoy doing?

I look at my somewhat eaten plate of food.

"He mentioned that he liked to cook," Zain chimes in. I meet his gaze, and he gives me a wink.

"Zain, you should let people speak for themselves," General Madi scolds.

"Cooking means I get to make the decision about what is to be eaten. I enjoy making the decisions I can, I guess," I mumble.

I glance around the table, and everyone's mouths hang open a little, besides Fenny's, who is still looking down and chewing his food.

The servant comes through the door and hands the King something bundled in cloth. He stands from the table.

"Excuse me. I am feeling a bit under the weather. Renatus, why don't you spend the remainder of the night with Laura and Fenny, instead. We can have our chat in the morning."

I stand to bow towards King Felguard as he leaves the table, taking his glass with him. The servant quickly clears his plate and pushes in his chair.

"Ow," Vasile hisses. I turn my head and see it is directed at his wife.

"You know better," she hisses back.

"Well. If you are spending the rest of the day with us, then we better not over stuff ourselves." Laura says, wiping her mouth and standing from the table. Fenny immediately does the same.

"I'll see you tomorrow morning," Zain says with a tight smile.

I nod towards him and leave, following behind the two weapon specialists I just met. Glancing over my shoulder, I see the family of three having a discussion, and no one is smiling.

Zain warned about mentioning Xylia around King Felguard. I see why.

WE ENTER A LARGE CIRCULAR ROOM, weapons decorating the walls, the majority of the room being taken up by a platform in the centre and blood stains covering a lot of the surfaces in here.

This is not my kind of place.

"So, the King mentioned that you are going to be working for him on some mission. Asked me to train you a bit in case things get dangerous," Laura says, walking over to the wall, grabbing a two-handed blade from the wall mount. "Wasn't expecting to train tonight but..."

I swallow hard.

He is claiming this is his mission now? Did he forget the purpose as to why I am actually collecting the apparatus, or is this just what he told them to get them on board?

Fenny takes a seat on a chair that is pushed up against the wall near a row of bows and a large basket full of arrows. I look over to Laura, who is now stepping onto the platform. She looks down at me and smiles, pointing the blade of her sword to the stairs that lead up to the platform.

I grab my whip that is still hilted at my waist.

Is she expecting me to just use it on her?

"You aren't going to hurt me, kid, so don't worry too much about it," Laura says, swinging her sword in a circle with a twist of her wrist.

Reaching the top of the platform, I walk around its edge, watching her watch me.

"Anytime now." She rolls her eyes.

I don't want to hurt anybody. The last time I used this whip, I made Seodi bleed, and I wasn't even trying to.

"Fine." Laura sighs. "Then I'm coming for you!" Her calm demeanour immediately changes as her words roar out of her. She begins to charge towards me.

I run to the other side, but she is just following right behind me. Quickly turning, I flick the whip at her. She stops moving as the whip wraps around her hand and sword. I can see that the blade didn't cut her, but the twig-like tail simply trapped Laura's hands.

"There we go, very nice precision!" she says, relaxing her stance, telling me that she isn't going to attack.

I recall the whip, concentrating hard on the blade not hurting her. It unfurls and shrivels back to its normal size.

"Handy to have some magicae on your side too," she says with a wink. "I can tell you are hesitant to instigate. Is there a reason for that?"

"I don't want to hurt anyone," I mutter.

"You need to speak up. You sound just like Fenny," she says with a furrowed brow. "You are gonna need a stronger voice if you are going to be travelling around."

I nod, hoping to move on from this conversation.

Laura sighs and places her fists on her hip, one of them still gripping the two-handed sword.

She is terrifyingly strong.

Laura smiles towards me. "It's admirable, not wanting to hurt someone. It's unrealistic in the same sense, though. Not every situation will result in violence, but when it does, you need to be able to trust yourself to not take it too far." She tilts her head, her eyes softening. "Hurting someone and killing someone are two different things in the world we currently live in. Maybe one day it won't be so life or death, but right now, if you don't act appropriately, you'll be dead at their feet instead of them wounded enough for you to get away. Not everyone will be admirable like you."

Hurting someone and killing someone. I really don't want to do either, but I understand what Laura is saying. I need to trust myself to know the right situation first.

Zain even said it; I always look worried, and it's because I am always worried. Especially out here, where nothing is known or common. Everything here is new and terrifying and interesting.

Master said to keep my curiosity, and I am, but not as curious as I am scared.

"I was like that too," Fenny mutters. I didn't even notice him standing and stepping up onto the platform. "I just needed to understand what was worth fighting for."

"What do you fight for?" I ask in a whisper.

He points with his thumb to Laura, who looks to him shocked. "She is my greatest ally. Saved my life plenty of times. It was worth it to repay the favour."

Friendship and a debt.

"Look at you being a mentor!" Laura says with a slight chuckle.

Fenny looks away from both of us and to a wall. "Just putting in my experience to help out."

"Mhmm," she says, raising an eyebrow. "Let's do what we just did a few more times, and then I'll let you off the hook for the night."

I nod.

Maybe if I can make sure that I won't really hurt someone, I'd feel better about this conversation.

CHAPTER
THIRTEEN

It's snowing.

The windows are slightly frosted, and little white flakes are drifting their way down to the ground. I close the Master's journal and admire the garden that still appears lush despite being littered with dots of ivory.

I bet Ventraton is covered in snow already.

The winters I've experienced there were always beautiful. Every inch of the city was decorated with fluff. The lanterns in the distance would reflect off the snow and make it look as if the sky was on ground level and the people in the distance were walking on top of it.

"Hey, buddy!" Zain bursts through the door. I drop the journal and jump from the chair I was sitting on. "Woah there." He throws his hands up in innocence.

"You startled me," I mutter, picking up the journal.

"I came to retrieve you! Uncle Kage says he's ready to meet with you now," he explains.

He could have knocked and not nearly killed me from fright.

I grip the Master's journal and gesture for Zain to lead the way. We walk down the halls, and Zain explains the dream he had just last night. Something to do with him and me frolicking

141

through a tall grass field holding hands as we skip. I roll my eyes and focus on where we are going versus his ongoing rambling.

I knock on the library door as we arrive.

"Come in," King Felguard states. I open the doors and walk in, waving goodbye to Zain, who just gives me a smile.

The King is sitting at his desk, flipping through a book, a familiar-looking chalice resting just to the side of it. His long flowing hair is tied back into a ponytail, the hair resting on his shoulder, a few strands falling in front of his face.

"Renatus, thank you for coming to speak with me." He stands and closes the book. He glances down to the hand that is holding the Master's journal. "My advisors signed the paper."

King Felguard picks up a parchment rolled up nicely and tied with strips of leather and places it next to the chalice.

This is it. The first apparatus.

"The roads are a dangerous place, and knowing that I am signing the country's name to the person having to face it, I am going to be assisting you in every way I can afford to." He steps around the desk so he is in front of it. The King leans back against it, sitting on the edge. "You met one of the M.G.A. members earlier, Shaw. She can only teleport to where she has been before, or at least has a very good idea of where she is going. I will have her teleport you to Kena, where the necklace is located."

He did read the journal.

"You have to understand that you have presented something of immense value to me, Renatus. If you fail, I have every intention of finishing the job." His eyes narrow, his lips pursed.

A chill rushes through my body and my hands clam up.

This is not just him being honest; this is his warning to me that he is only giving me one shot to do this before he takes them for himself.

"I understand," I mutter through gritted teeth.

Master, I really hope I can bring multiple people back. Otherwise, we might both have just made an enemy of King Felguard and with his country.

"Good. How are your provisions? Do you need more rations, gold, armour?" he asks and stands from the desk now and looks me up and down.

My worn trousers and shirt are probably not to the King's standard.

I could go buy clothing, I just didn't think it was necessary. These do the job.

"We can go to the vault and find something to fit you. You and Vasile look about the same size," the King says, waving his hands, moving past the subject.

"I have gold and rations. I can buy the armour too," I mumble, looking away.

The only thing I need from him is the chalice.

"I'll provide the armour, Renatus." He sighs and takes a few steps closer. "The chalice will remain here with me, however. You can call it my insurance policy. I'd rather not have every single item in the same place where someone can just take it from you if they please."

"You said—"

The King cuts me off, "I said I would let you bring back your master, not own the one apparatus I have in my possession."

Clenching my jaw, I narrow my brow. "Fine," I mutter.

Having all of Aruna's apparatus on me doesn't make a lot of sense. Especially since I know there are people after them, too.

"We should get moving on this. I have delayed your travels long enough. We can get you to Kena as soon as this afternoon."

I nod and relax.

The doors open. Turning my head, I see Zain walking in looking at the King. "I am leaving too. He is going to need someone who can talk his way into anywhere." My eyes open wide at his proclamation.

"You have no idea what is actually transpiring here, Zain. Renatus will have to rise to the occasion and do what is necessary to get the task completed," King Felguard says sternly, shaking his head towards his nephew.

Just like the Master said, do what is necessary.

"Expect that I do. I overheard your conversation in the garden, and just now, too. I want to help bring Aunt Xylia back. My father and mother would be so happy to see her again, and Renatus is going to need someone to watch his back." Zain's words come out as a plea, his voice steady, though. He grips his floral-patterned shirt with his fist and takes a deep breath.

Vasile was right. He really does know everything that goes on in this castle. Does he really want to help me and Lady Xylia? Or is there another reason behind this?

King Felguard sighs, pinching the brim of his nose. "Your parents should have disciplined you more."

"Uncle, please," Zain whispers.

"Fine. Though if Madi or Vasile ask me to stop you, I will not aid you in escaping the capital afterwards," the King says with a soft smile.

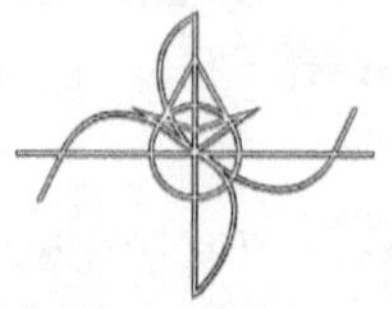

WE HEAD down to the old family's vault, almost opposite to where Zain and I went to see the dungeons. Zain grabs my hands and squeezes it as we walk down the stairs.

As much as I want to say that he is just presumptuous in assuming friendship, I don't mind having him around.

Reaching the basement level, the ground is carpeted, a

simple navy blue rug with yellow outlining. The room is circular, and ahead of us, instead of the lounge the dungeons have, there is a large steel door with a complex mechanism on the outside of it.

"Turn around boys," the King orders, stepping towards the vault's entrance. I pull out of Zain's grasp and turn around; he follows suit. There are a series of clicks and creaks before sounds of metal smacking against metal ring through the air. "Okay."

Turning back to face the vault and the King, I see the enormous door now wide open. Just glancing in, there is a large case in the centre containing some red armour with an engraved symbol of an upside down tree with a pointed root shooting upwards towards the sky. We all walk in, and the room expands larger than the room we were just in. Every wall has cases filled with necklaces, swords, books, musical instruments, bows, armour, cloaks and more than what I can process at this moment.

"Woah, Dad was right. You are a hoarder," Zain mumbles under his breath.

I hear a smack and see Zain rubbing the back of his head. "I heard that," the King says with a forced smile. "Don't act like you haven't seen this before." He shakes his head before turning around. "These are all items possessed with magicae. Though the armour here along with the blue book hiding behind it are only momentos."

"You mean they belonged to Aunt Xylia," Zain says; I'm sure making an assumption.

King Felguard nods, eyes intent on the items in front of us. "There is armour over on that wall." The King points over to green leather that has gold adornments outlining the leafed pattern embossed on the chest plate. I walk over to the case and delicately open the glass door. "If it doesn't fit, grow into it."

I take it off the hooks and untie the leather straps holding it upright.

This looks way too nice for me to wear.

"Zain, pick whatever weapon you feel your best at. I'll let you know if it's something you can handle Magicae wise," he mumbles, not turning from Xylia's case.

"Sweet!" Zain says, running around the room, almost immediately running to a dual set of swords.

I take the sweater I am currently wearing and pull it over my head. I place the chest plate on, tying the side straps tight so the armour fits snugly. Swinging my arms around, the chest piece doesn't pinch or rub in any way that is uncomfortable.

"Looks like that fits nicely," the King says from behind me. Looking over my shoulder, I see him double checking how I tied it.

"You look... really good," Zain says with widened eyes and a slight smile. "Why do you normally wear such baggy clothes?"

A chuckle escapes my lips, seeing his brow furrowed with such quandary shining in his eyes. Though as he hears my amusement, his features relax and his eyes soften.

"Take this dagger as well." King Felguard reaches over, opening one of the cases and pulling out a black steel dagger and its black sheath. He tosses it over, and it fumbles for a second before I have it firmly in my grasp. Flipping it over, there are small engravings I recognise. Sigils that signify that this particular weapon utilises magicae that is imbued with the element of Earth. "When it hits its target, shards of hardened rock spike out from the blade."

Incredible. Not something I plan to use, though.

"Are you sure I can use these?" I whisper, meeting the emerald eyes of the King.

He nods and smiles before turning to Zain. "You, those

swords will conduct lightning when you rub them together. It'll make your target feel an intense shock. Don't hurt yourself." King Felguard gives him a wink before turning to leave.

We follow suit; Zain leaves to pack his things and grab his own armour.

Is he really going to leave his life behind like this? The comforts of living in a castle, his parents, his uncle?

"Zain can be... overwhelming at times, but he is a strong fighter and knows how to charm someone with witty conversation. I am honestly glad he is joining you." The King grips my shoulder as we continue our walk to the room I have been staying in. "You would have struggled."

Blunt. I can appreciate that because he is not wrong.

The Fel Watch we pass on the way to my room all salute the King but he always dismisses them with a nod.

I wonder what their thoughts are on King Felguard. Is it as the Master said, that Xylia should have been Queen and Kage set aside?

"King Felguard?" I stop in my tracks, eyes glued to my feet.

"Yes, Renatus?"

That familiar lump in my throat rises, threatening to keep me from speaking.

A part of me needs to know. If his intentions are what he says them to be.

"Are you really doing this out of love for Lady Xylia... or is it because you blame yourself?" My eyes travel upwards to see a taken aback King standing before me. His eyes wide and brow stitched closely together. The King's mouth is hung open for a moment but then closes it. "Vasile and Madi speak of her fondly, and there is some bittersweetness to their voices, but they enjoy remembering her. You look pained every time someone says her name."

King Felguard storms up to me, grabbing me by my throat.

"That is quite enough!" he shouts, spit hitting my face. Clanging armour and shouts come up from both ends of the corridor. "You did not know her. I did. I was there the night she died. I saw her last moments. No one can grieve as I do. No one has any right to her. Xylia has always been and will always be mine!" He throws me back.

Coughs erupt out of me as air begins to fill my lungs again. Arms grab me, and I feel cold steel pressed against the back of my neck. "Your Majesty, are you hurt?" The Fel Watch holding me asks.

I should have never asked.

"I am quite alright. Release him. We were simply having an argument," he spits out.

I am quickly released; the ground hitting my knees instantly.

I have no right to speak.

The guards leave us, and we stay there silently. I watch the floor, terrified to look at the King again.

I am nothing but a servant.

"If this works, and I can—we can bring her back, I will spend the rest of my life serving her, Renatus," he whispers. "I am a terrible king because I will never forgive myself for not being able to stop her. For not stopping her from saving this country and possibly all of Vitaterrium. She lost her life because she is the true ruler of the Felguard Country, and I am simply the placeholder."

My gaze travels up to see his hand extended down towards me. I take it and the King helps me stand. "So you are doing it because of both." My eyes meet his.

The King's lips quiver before he bites it and nods. "Yes."

We walk the remainder of the way in silence. I pack the few books I have left out on the table into my bag. I make the slept-in bed, shut the curtains, look around the nicest room I have ever stayed in one last time and close the door behind me as I leave.

These three days have been the strangest of my life.

Even the day I learned Forged Magicae for the first time cannot stand in comparison to staying in a castle and meeting the colourful group of people who live inside of it. And now, I'm responsible for bringing back the "true" ruler of the Felguard country, who also happens to be someone I have dreamt of nearly my entire life.

Very strange.

As King Felguard and I arrive at the front entrance of the castle, I see a cowering Zain hiding behind his father as his mother has both hands balled into fists and resting on her hips.

"You spoiled brat! There are responsibilities you have here, ones you have been avoiding!" General Madi shouts.

"Love, I remember a time where the two of us in our youth ventured off and travelled for a bit. Without the blessing of either of our ladies." Vasile reaches out and grabs his wife's hands from her hips, pulling them to his chest along with his. "He's actually older than when we were. I think it's time he figures out some life lessons on his own."

"He is supposed to be shadowing me. Learning what I do." She sighs.

"I will, Mom," Zain says, stepping out from behind his dad. "This is something I have to do, though. There's this—"

"—feeling," she finishes his sentence, smiling at him. "You are so much like your father. He wrote that in a letter to me once. That he had to leave because he had that same feeling."

"I was right about it, too." Vasile leans in and kisses General Madi softly.

"He has my blessing," King Felguard interjects, grabbing the attention of all three of them.

A part of me cannot understand why Zain would want to

leave this. The love he is surrounded by, but another part of me is so grateful. I won't be alone.

Zain smiles brightly at us and runs up, wrapping his arm around my neck. A smirk plays on my lips, seeing the smiling faces of his parents as they look at the two of us.

"Madi, do you mind getting these two horses? Shaw should be by the stables already, waiting. I made her aware earlier on." Madi nods, understanding the King's words.

"Yeah, you really do spoil him," she mutters, turning away from all of us and heading out the door.

"Renatus." I look towards King Felguard. "Keep our last conversation between us."

I nod, and he gives me a short smile.

"Hey, Renatus," Vasile says, walking up to his son and me. "Take care of him. He can come off as extremely brave, besides standing up to his mother, of course, but he needs support too."

"I understand. I will." Vasile shakes my hand, and Zain punches his dad's shoulder.

The entrance door opens and Shaw pokes her head and expressionless face in. "Can we go already?" she asks with a pleading sigh.

We all exit the castle; Madi and two horses trailing behind her. One is all black, and the other is brown with a white spot on its rear end. The Fel Watch litter the front garden, some standing on guard while others are walking patrols. Some chat off to the side, but nearly all of them turn as they notice the King exiting the castle.

"Hop on the horses," Shaw says, pointing over to them.

Zain separates from me and runs over to the all black one. We hook our packs onto the horses with the leather straps attached to their saddles. Madi gives Zain a kiss on his forehead before walking up to me.

"You both are gonna make it back." She gives me a stern

look before smiling and ruffling my hair. I grin back at her before putting my foot into the stirrup and climb onto my stead.

"Ready?" Shaw asks, looking at both of us.

I glance over to Zain, who is gazing at me. We smile at each other and nod.

"I am counting on you, Renatus." The King's words reach my ears before my vision goes black.

CHAPTER FOURTEEN

THE FAMILIAR SMELL of the sea greets my nose as a grassy pasture comes into view. The horses rear back and cry out; I'm sure startled by the sudden movement and change of scenery.

"Woah, buddy! It's alright, shh," Zain says, trying to sooth his mount as he pats the creature's neck.

I reach down and do the same motion, but also rub the horse's shoulder.

"Alright. Head a mile west from here and you'll find Kena. It's too dangerous for me to teleport you there directly so this is as far as I go," Shaw says, pointing again but this time in the direction of where our target city is. "Bye."

And she's gone.

"Well, this is it, Ren! The beginning of our journey." He gives me a thumbs up. "Race ya!" Zain snaps his reins, and he and his black steed take off ahead of me and mine.

We are now over a full mooncycle away from Fosa, in an instant.

A lump rises in my throat, but my gaze on Zain makes it easy to swallow. I take after him, but at a much slower pace. The road is worn down gravel that is alongside what I assume is the Jako River. The soft trickle paired with the rhythmic motions of the horse's trot could put me to sleep if I let it. Some small animals fly overhead and scurry in their river bank homes as we pass them, or I should say, as Zain does as he is far ahead of me. A little dot in my farsight.

It's so peaceful, I feel bad for disrupting it.

As Zain leaves my line of sight completely, new shapes appear. Large spiked buildings and structures residing in front of me.

The city of Kena.

One of the sister cities, the reason the Allen High Territory and the Allen Territory separated hundreds of sidereal years ago.

Zain is waiting for me just a few feet before the entry line starts. There is a giant tower just to the right of it, overlooking the wide river. It has its main viewing deck pointed towards Clair, this city's twin. The deck has sharp edges and dagger-like points all around its roof, and white-coloured stone covered in greenery as its base.

"Took you long enough," Zain whines as he rights his horse to begin walking next to mine.

We approach the large archway made of a darker stone, and much shorter to its neighbouring structure. There are five or so guards standing on-duty stationed on top of the archway and several at its entrance.

I turn as much as I can and grab the letter King Felguard has prepared for me. The line is filled with travellers, merchants and other migrants or visitors from the looks of it. We wait our turn until the guards finally wave us forward.

"Reason for entrance?" they ask lamely, hand extended, expecting some form of documentation. I hand over the letter.

"We are doing some research here," Zain says, nearly matching his tone and expression.

The guards look over at him for a moment before looking back at me. "Alright, then. Mounts need to be checked into the stables just ahead and to the left. They will give you a ticket." They hand me back the letter. "Don't lose said ticket."

I nod in understanding, and we continue onward through the archway. As we pass under, an iron gate is hiding behind a lip. Once through, there is a massive building to the left where the guard mentioned the stables would be. The majority is made out of a pale-coloured wood, the same stone as the arch as this building's foundation. Zain and I dismount and tie the reins of the horse to a wooden pole just outside the main entrance to the main office of this establishment.

"They must house every animal that comes through in this stable," Zain whispers as we step in through the solid oak doors. The interior is lit by a candle chandelier hanging from the ceiling. There must be nearly a hundred candles positioned on it. "Would hate to have that job," Zain whispers over his shoulder to me.

I wouldn't want the job of cleaning up after the animals, but I guess we each have our own limits.

We walk up to the front desk where an orc is currently standing; her moss-coloured hair is long and braided back into a bun. She is wearing a large purple cable-knit sweater, the stone counter coming up to her waist. She is talking to a dwarvish man with long, black hair and a straw hat. Overalls and old worn work boots. We stand in line behind him and again, wait our turn.

"Next," she mutters, not even looking up from whatever is on the desk. "How many?"

"Two," Zain answers plainly.

Everyone seems disinterested. It is so unlike Ventraton, Jod and Fosa.

I wonder what makes them all so unsatisfied.

"Take these, do not lose them. Blue tags get attached to your animals." She hands Zain two tickets and two blue tags before glancing up at us for the first time. Her tusks curl up and inward where it pokes her upper lip. "Welcome to Kena." She flashes a smile for a second before looking back down. "Next."

I glance behind me and see that an older couple is standing right behind us. I grab Zain's arm and tug him to the side as I myself step out of the way. We make our way back to our horses and each attach one of the blue tags to their saddles.

I guess we just leave them here.

Unloading our packs and placing them onto our backs, we say goodbye to our mounts and begin to make our way into the city. The gravel path slowly turns into a cobblestone one, white bricks matching the tower we saw as we passed the entrance gate. The city is a downward slope that eventually leads to the port. We can see all the way to the sea from the start of the city here. Everything has matching white-toned stone and bricks, some overgrown by plant life, while others seem to be maintained and even painted. Most shutters and doors are painted a deep sea blue and windows' stained glass of different depictions. Some are illustrations of the ocean, others of families, one is even a picture of some sort of sea monster.

"Ren, look over there!" Zain says, tugging on the sleeve of my chest plate.

As I take a gander in the direction he is pointing, I see a large white building with a rounded top that is painted blue. There is a figure of a woman standing on the tallest pillar in the centre of the building's roof.

"That's a church for **Haldoris**," I mutter, looking at the beautiful figure with a serpent-like tail wrapped around her legs.

She also goes by Seasire. Known as the ruler of the oceans of the Vitaterrium.

"Do you think that's what she really looks like?" Zain asks as we continue walking. "I mean, when I was learning about the pantheon, they each had beautiful women drawn out on the page but has anyone even seen them?" I let him ask and rant about the goddess who created the Vitaterrium as a nesting ground for all the planes that the different doorways lead to.

I remember learning about the pantheon as well back when I had my tutors. They would talk about how each doorway was a plane that belonged to each individual goddess. Each one has its own form of magicae that was birthed from the original goddess, the **Awemother**. This magicae that was used to create the Vitaterrium's plane is why we have elements, and why Forged Magicae is even able to exist. Despite the doorways being closed for nearly six hundred sidereal years, the magicae from the goddesses still remain, even if it is now just an echo of what it once was.

After wandering around for some time, we stop at the Agapi Mou Inn. It's a small place; its stone walls are now being maintained and supported by wooden beams on both the outside and inside. There is a couple kissing behind the front counter but separate as they hear our footsteps approach them, or should I say, Zain's. My feet are glued to the doorway after walking in on that.

"Do you have any rooms open?" Zain asks, smiling at the both of them. Their faces drop after they glance between the two of us.

"Yeah, here." The shorter woman of the two mutters, handing Zain a key. "It'll be five silver a night. It includes both breakfast and dinner."

"Thank you. Sorry I had to interrupt," Zain says, giving them a wink. The ladies chuckle and continue where they left off. He turns towards me and waves me to follow him.

I rush to his side, seeing the numbered key in his hand. "Number ten."

We walk up the stairs that are just right of the counter. There is a small sign on the second floor stating that rooms one through four are on this floor. As we head to the third floor, the sign says room five through eight. Now, as we ascend to the fourth floor, it states that both the ninth and tenth room reside on it.

Though there were no more stairs so that should be obvious.

The ninth and tenth rooms are across the hall from each other, and our room is on the right. Zain opens the door, revealing a quaint little room with a twin size mattress in the centre of the far wall just under a single-paned window. There is a small wooden table on either side and a leather and wood crafted chest at the foot of the bed.

There is really only one bed.

Zain walks past me and fully into the room, setting his pack down on the left side of the bed. "You gonna just stand there?" He chuckles and plops down, stretching out his back as he spreads out on the bed.

"I've never..." I whisper, watching him make himself comfortable as he turns onto his side and props his head up with one of his arms as his elbow rests on the bed.

Zain furrows one brow while raising the other. "Shared a bed?" I nod. Zain bursts into laughter almost immediately. "I don't bite, kick or wet myself, Ren. As long as you don't, we will be just fine." He pats the right side of the bed with a smirk playing on his lips.

I chuckle a bit and set my pack down next to the edge of the bed before I take a seat. Zain sits up, scooching over to be next to me.

"Ren," Zain whispers, as I pull out the Master's journal. I begin flipping to the loose pages that showcase the apparatus, though Zain's halt in sentence causes me to look his way. His eyes are trained on the floor and he's biting his lower lip.

"Yes?" I ask, drawing him out from somewhere in his own mind. He lets up on his lip and looks at me.

He shakes his head and looks down at the page I landed on.

"So, this is the necklace we are looking for?" Zain asks, clarifying the image he is looking at. Two strings of pearls with a large sapphire in the shape of a teardrop in the centre of the lower strand.

What was that about?

"Correct. The Copious Riviere. Master said it belongs to a Madam Andromeda. She lives on the shore of the Jako River just before the portside of Kena," I mutter, tucking the page back into the Master's journal.

He really was listening in on what King Felguard and I were talking about.

"Great, so we just ask around for where she lives and we can figure out what we wanna do then. I'm sure we can get a feel about her personality by how people talk about her as we ask around," Zain says, standing up from the bed. "Or maybe we don't need to ask anyone at all..."

"What?" I stammer.

Zain grabs a piece of parchment that is nailed to a board hanging on the door. He brings it over to me, and it's a list of things to do in the city. One being a suggestion to go see the late Madam Andromeda's collection of rare items and art that is currently being displayed in Kena's Historical Vault. They made an entire wing just dedicated to her things.

She died. She died and all of her rarities, most likely including the necklace, are all locked behind glass for the public's viewing.

"Stealing, it is." Zain sighs.

I close my eyes and sigh, too.

I don't see how we have much choice.

Zain walks over to the window and places his hands on either side, leaning against the frame. I tuck the Master's journal back into my pack before standing up myself and walking over to stand next to him. He pushes off and stands up straight.

"You probably think I'm a bit strange," Zain mutters, a bit of a laugh forcing its way out. "The way I just inserted myself in like I did. Eavesdropping on private conversations, forcing you to have me tag along."

When he puts it that way, it does sound very strange.

"Thank you for coming," I mutter.

Zain turns his head and looks at me, a bit bewildered. "Really?"

I nod. He smiles and looks back out the window. "Why did you want to come?" I ask, my curiosity demanding an answer

My mind has a hard time rationalising why someone would want to leave a place where they are loved, fed, and cared for like he is.

"There's a few reasons..." he mutters. "You, for one." He glances over his shoulder briefly. "You are so timid, quiet, so curious about everything. I couldn't stop myself from wanting to know more, see your reactions to all the things that only you would find fascinating." A smile tugs at my lips, and I look down to the ground. "I've travelled with my father, mother, and Uncle Kage around the realm. Meeting Kings, Queens, ambassadors and the people of Limoria, seeing what working in the business of royalty means, but I will have the rest of my life to see the world like that. I want to see the world through my own gaze, even if it is for just this once."

My gaze focuses back on him.

His life's purpose.

"I know I'll have to take up that mantle one day, but I..." His grip tightening on the window.

"I understand," I mutter.

"Thank you, Ren." He turns around and wraps me up in his arms. I freeze, not sure what I should be doing. Zain laughs and pulls back, shaking my shoulders a bit. "Don't be so stiff; it's just a hug!"

THERE IS A BETTER way to do this, I'm sure of it. The only thing I am not sure about is exactly how it could be better.

"Alright, well, I am ready," Zain says with a satisfied grin on his face. He had gone down to the general store and bought some paints and clay, which all led to the painted-grey Zain before me with clay-made tusks and ears.

This entire thing is his plan. I've never stolen anything, but Zain said that he would steal things from the Torrin's family vault when he was a kid. His mother was right to call him spoiled; that would be a life sentence for anyone else.

"Come on, you know I look good." He winks at me.

It's not that he looks bad, in fact I am quite impressed with him. As long as no one takes too close of a look, he could pass as a scrawny orc.

The large domed building just to the left of where the port ends is where the second apparatus is. This is my third time walking this same path. The snow we saw in Fosa has reached Kena, and as long as we don't have to make a run for it, I am happy to have it. I listen to the soft crunch of the snow underneath my boots. My high green collared cloak covers my neck and mouth so I can stay plenty warm on my walk over. If everything goes smoothly, then we will be able to get this done and over with, and this will be my last time approaching Kena's Historical Vault. The first time was just finding it and making sure the necklace was actually here, but the second time was to map out the place and figure out the best way to take it. I made sure to shred and toss the map we actually made after we both had the place memorised. There are three floors, four exits, fifty-three display cases, twenty attendants and two historians. Well, at least, that's what it was just yesterday.

I hope Zain is doing alright.

Arriving at the familiar stained glass doors, a few youngins come running out laughing with their exhausted-looking parents.

"No running!" the mother shouts.

"Don't throw snow at your brother," the dad scolds.

They pay me no mind as I walk by and enter the building. I wipe my snow-covered boots off on a rug they have placed at the entrance; a gnomish girl stares at me from behind the counter.

"Back again, sir?" she asks with a slight smile and tint of red to her otherwise pale cheeks.

I nod and return her smile before approaching her. Using my hand, I brush the snow from my brown locks back with the water that was left behind.

"It must be really coming down. There is hardly anyone here." She glances past me and to the door I just came through. Her lavender eyes turn back and land on mine. "Not enough to keep you away, though." Her eyes soften and she giggles to herself. She tucks a few strands of her peach-coloured hair behind her slightly pointed ear. "I am Blossom, by the way."

This is my third time meeting her, so I guess her giving me her name is not out of nowhere.

"Renatus." I return the greeting.

Her eyes widen, as does her smile. "Well, Renatus, what section are you planning on viewing today?"

Shrugging at her question makes her giggle again. Blossom hands me a pass, and I make my way into the exhibit showcasing original stone work and tools from when Kena was built.

Most cities have something like this, dedicated to the history, but this is the first one I have ever actually been in, and I am going to be stealing from it. I am grateful Blossom has some strange notion that I am coming to see her because coming to a place such as this three days in a row is strange.

"She has such a crush on you," Zain says, poking me repeatedly. "Can't say I blame her though, you are quite dreamy."

I roll my eyes and continue looking at the different paintings hanging on the walls in this room. Some are landscapes of the ocean and grassland views; one is of a world that has floating rocks and ocean waves in the shape of a human.

"Come on, you gotta put yourself out there," Zain says, slinking his arm around my waist and leaning in close to my ear. "Flirting can be fun."

I chuckle and shove him a bit, and he releases his grip with a pout.

We continue looking over the different art work until we see the couple that was occupying the room we were really wanting to look at leave. Making our way into the room adjacent to this one, we are greeted by a man who nods towards us. He is one of the attendants who makes sure we don't touch anything.

"Look at that!" Zain says, running over to one of the cases. "It's so decadent." I catch up to him and see the heeled woman's shoes he is admiring.

Every inch of the shoes is covered in jewels. Rubys,

diamonds and pearls from what it looks like. It's too lavish, in my opinion, and too high a chance of ruining something so expensive. I walk past Zain and find the necklace we will be attempting to steal tomorrow. The locks are poorly made, and jamming something like a dagger in between the mechanics will likely cause the hinge to break.

Blossom was right; there is hardly anyone here. I exit the last of the first floor exhibits and head up the red-carpeted stairs where the **Copious Riviere** is currently residing. Rounding the corner, there are two attendants standing next to one another, talking. One of them rolls their eyes as I enter, but continues their conversation.

After three days of being here, it just seems this is the way people are here.

Glancing past the necklace as I walk by and into the next room where Madam Andromeda's painting collection is. A slim grey orc has their hood up and is staring at a painting of a man who is standing at the edge of a pier. I let my legs give out and collapse to the floor, making sure not to hit my head.

"Hey, are you alright?" a disguised Zain asks in a husky low voice. I close my eyes and remain still. His footsteps run in the direction I just came from before multiple footsteps approach me.

"Sir," I feel someone shaking me, but I keep my eyes closed and don't react to their timid shoves. "Seasire be with us, he's not even responding!"

"I'll go get help!" I quickly open my eyes and pretend to jerk awake. "He's up."

"Are you injured?" I feel hands roam my back as if looking for an obvious wound. "Can you sit up?" Nodding yes to their question, I feel both attendants help assist me in sitting upright versus face first on the ground. "Do you need medical attention?"

"Just need a moment," I whisper. Both of them look at me attentively and keep their hands on my shoulders.

It seems everything is going to plan so far.

I just hope Zain was able to break the lock. I doubt I will be able to distract them much longer, not both of them.

Zain shifts in the bed, his face turning towards me. The moon is in full light tonight, and with it reflecting off the freshly fallen snow, it seems to be brighter. The whole room is illuminated in a soft blue glow. As I stare at the ceiling, there is no stain or flaking paint. It looks well kept and looked after. There are already stains on me, things that I have seen and heard that have forever marked me, changed me from the servant boy who was forced from his master's tower.

I shift so I am facing Zain's sleeping form. This bed is not as nice as the bed I had in Fosa, thankfully. There is some stiffness to it, which Zain made sure to complain about when he first laid down for the night, but here he is in a sleeping bliss. His mouth is slightly open in a natural frown, his brows creased just a little bit, and chest rising and falling in a rhythmic pace.

Do I look that peaceful when I sleep?

I sigh and close my eyes. I feel myself drop; my eyes bursting back open, but this time I am staring right at Lady Xylia.

She is crying again.

Her face is blurry, and no matter how hard I squint, I cannot see her any clearer. My heart hurts hearing her wail and having her bury her head in my chest. I want to hold her; I want to comfort her, but I can barely feel anything and the flames that are flickering around in my blurry vision feel cold.

I open my mouth, "My angel," leaves my lips, but no sound makes it audible.

A scream erupts from her, and I am swallowed by light.

"Renatus, wake up!" Zain shouts, shaking my shoulders.

I blink a few times, letting him come into focus.

He leans back onto my lap as he is straddling me. Zain brings up a hand and brushes his thumb on my sweaty temple. "Thought I'd show that bad dream that I'm the only one who can make you cry out like that," he whispers.

I furrow my brows.

When has he ever made me cry?

He chuckles, falling back to his side of the bed. Zain puts an arm around me and pulls me closer to him. "I forget how innocent you are."

Well, now I know I do not look as peaceful sleeping as Zain does.

"Thank you." I stand from the chair Blossom has lent to me as I "recover" from my faintness. She is no longer standing on the stool that is hidden under the desk, so now I can see her true height is just to my waist.

She's actually tall for a gnomish girl.

"Of course..." she whispers, patting my leg with her hand. "Do you need me to walk you home?" I shake my head, and she sticks out her bottom lip a bit before nodding. "Well, make it home safe."

I move around the front desk and head out the door.

Still snowing.

Little white flakes are falling down, and in the centre of my vision, I see Seodi standing there, smiling at me. I blink a few times, hoping I am just seeing things.

"Been awhile, handsome." Her tone is still that even pitch it was when we met back in Ventraton. "I've been watching you, and I must say. For someone who doesn't like talking, you sure do make a lot of friends." She steps closer, and I take one step back.

How is she here? She was arrested, right? Did she escape? Did they let her go? How did she know where I was?

Seodi rolls her eyes. "Calm down. I'm not here to play with you, at least not today."

I swallow hard and bite my lip. My body is shaking and brow sweating despite the frosty temperature.

Please go away.

"Well, maybe we can play a little bit." She closes the distance and reaches out to run her fingers through my hair. I quickly pull away from her, but her loose combing turns into a grip. She brings my face down to hers; I can feel her hot breath on my nose.

I need to run.

"Aw, you are still trying to act tough. I'll be more persuaded when you actually mean it." She kisses my cheek; it feels warm in comparison to the cold temperature.

I shove her away and I am grateful she lets go of her grasp versus her pulling out my hair.

Why does she do this?

"You can come out!" Her tone doesn't change, but her volume does as she shouts just over my shoulder.

I hear the crunch of snow and look over to see Zain no longer disguised, for the most part. There are still some spots of grey he must not have been able to wash off with the snow. His nose and cheeks are a vibrant red.

"Hello, handsome number two." Seodi waves him over. Zain reluctantly steps forward but puts himself a little in front of me. "You got good taste, Renatus."

"Who are you?" Zain growls the moment my name started to leave her lips.

She laughs and takes a step back with her hands up. "That's what 'meaning it' looks like." Seodi looks at me before turning her attention back to Zain. "The name is Seodi. I'm just checking in on Renatus. He is someone of... interest to my group and me."

"Well, I can tell you right now, he doesn't like you. So, to infernum with whatever interest you or your group has." Zain grabs my hand and starts walking in the direction of the inn we are staying at. "Do us a favour and stay away." Zain focuses his attention on the road ahead, but I glance behind.

Seodi is smiling. "There is more than one person who can teleport, Renatus."

Chapter Sixteen

"Who was that?" Zain asks, throwing his cloak on the chest residing at the foot of our temporary bed. "It was obvious you two knew each other, and whatever that was, was intense." He sits on top of the chest and begins taking off his wet boots.

I slip my boots off at the door, careful to step around the puddles Zain left behind on the floor and hang my cloak onto one of the hooks. "Someone who is after Aruna's apparatus."

Zain stands and walks over to me. "Could have mentioned that before."

"Thought it would be obvious," I admit. He had overheard King Felguard and I talking. I assumed he must have gathered that it's dangerous, not just because of gathering the items, but that other people were likely after them too.

Though that was never explicitly said.

"I apologise; I should have told you about Seodi," I mutter; his chocolate-coloured eyes examine me.

Zain leans in and kisses the same cheek Seodi did. His lips are soft but cold from being out in the winter air. "I saw her do that to you. Was it the first time?" I pull away from him and turn to face the window. "Renatus." He grabs my chin and makes me look at him. "Did you want her to do that?"

I shake my head. Zain rests his forehead against mine and sighs.

The night she and I met was terrifying. She made me uncomfortable in every way possible and knew it, too.

"Next time, come find me before you approach her. I won't let her touch you," Zain whispers before stepping back and grabbing his cloak.

Why does he do that? He is always right there where I cannot escape him. It's not that he makes me uncomfortable, but that he always gets his way when he gets close like that. Makes me talk, makes me just go along with whatever he wants.

He reaches into the pocket of his cloak and pulls out the Copious Riviere.

Right.

The sapphire is larger than a gold piece and it shimmers like the sun reflects off the ocean. I grip it tightly knowing I am one apparatus closer to completing the purpose the Master gave me.

Closer to going home.

"You were right; the lock broke with just a little force." Zain pats my shoulder. "With you distracting them like that, they didn't even notice the noise from it."

"We should get going before they do," I whisper to him. He gives me that bright smile of his and nods. "Good job, and thank you." Zain chuckles and rolls his eyes.

Packing doesn't take us long, as most of our belongings are already packed up. I make sure to carefully wrap the necklace up and put it in between clothing I have packed at the bottom of my bag. We adorn our leather armour and strap our weapons to our belts. His twin swords to his and my whip and dagger to mine.

I close the curtains and make the bed. "You know they are probably, hopefully, going to strip the bed and wash all of that anyway, right?" Zain tilts his head at me as he leans against the doorframe.

Shrugging him off, I open the door, shoving him to the side and exit the room. Zain follows after me. As we leave, only the taller woman is standing behind the counter, reading a book. I walk up to her and set the key down in front of the book.

"Thanks for staying with us," she mumbles without even glancing up.

We leave the inn and make our way up the hill and back to where the stables are. The slick roads slow our pace as we watch every step we are taking.

"Ah!" Zain shouts, a loud thud following. I turn and see him slowly sliding back down the hill. His arms are dragging and he is completely stretched out.

"Leave me, I have accepted my fate."

I carefully walk back down the hill and bend down to grab his hand. As I pull him up, my footing slips and I fall right down with him. I land on him, and we both laugh.

"My hero," Zain says, his face squished against my chest.

As we travel alongside the Jako River, headed towards Xan, located in the Ashen Territory, Zain tells me stories he has heard about Lady Xylia and his Uncle Codrin. How they used to run along the branches of the Vermilion Forest trees. Hunting terrifying creatures and sparring with each other.

Sounds like they lived a good life; I wonder what made all of that change. What decisions all led to them both dying and leaving Vasile behind?

"Do you think we could bring Uncle Codrin back too?"

Zain asks, looking back at me over his shoulder. The movement of his horse, swaying him back and forth.

I shake my head.

There is no point in giving him hope I cannot promise. I already feel extraordinarily guilty for not telling him I am not even sure if I can bring Lady Xylia back.

"Oh," he whispers. "Is there a reason why?" I turn my head away from him, trying to give him the idea that I don't want to talk about it.

The grasslands, while covered in snow, look like a white blanket. If it weren't for the frigid wind, it would seem extremely inviting to just lay down in it. At least the sun isn't out; I'd be worried we would go blind from the reflection of it. Living so high above altitude, it was sometimes dangerous to go outside after it snowed as the sun would be shining through what clouds were left from the snowfall.

"Ren!" Zain shouts.

I follow his pointed finger to a man sitting out on the frozen river. A fishing pole in hand.

We ride a bit closer; he tilts his head towards us. He is thoroughly bundled up, only really his amber eyes peeking out. Must be trying to catch something to eat. My stomach growls, realising we haven't eaten anything since early this morning. I turn and grab some jerky from my pack.

"Did you wanna stop and eat something?" Zain asks, noticing me munching on my fried meat.

I shake my head. We haven't even reached the southern leading path yet, and we have been riding nearly half a mooncycle.

I want to keep moving. As much as I enjoy the snow, Zain is getting quite tired of being out here.

Our first night sleeping out in the snow, I think, has scared him of ever coming around to the idea of actually liking it.

Zain's chattering teeth are keeping me awake. "I'm going to freeze to death," he whimpers.

Our tent keeps us out of the actual snow, but the cold still finds its way in. We are laying in our respective bedrolls though. I crawl out of mine and move it closer to his side of the tent. Grabbing my dagger, I carefully rip the seam in the side of mine and tuck the bottom under his and crawl back in. I pull him and his bedroll into mine so I can wrap my arms around his shivering frame.

"This should be warmer. Sharing body heat," I mumble into his hair.

He puts his cold hands against my clothed chest and nuzzles his face into my neck. "How are you so warm?" His teeth still chatter, but his body has stopped shaking as much.

I shrug my shoulders and start to rub his back, hoping to create friction to help warm him up.

"Is that...?" Zain says, his words disappearing into his train of thought. He clicks his tongue, whipping the reins and his horse picks up speed.

Where is he going?

My horse and I gallop after him, a large building coming into view ahead of us. A few buildings, actually.

Is this Lurnik?

I catch up to Zain, who has slowed his horse's pace to a trot. "We missed the southern pass."

"I don't care. Look, that's a tavern, and it probably has a room for us to stay," Zain snaps, his brows sewn together.

I bite my lip, trying to not smile or laugh at how serious he is about this.

Hopping down from our mounts, we walk them over to the tavern, tying them up to the post outside. "Hey! If you plan on staying the night, just take them around back right away." A young girl, maybe a little younger than us, shouts at us. She is wearing a large hat that has flaps to cover her ears.

We untie the horses and make our way around back; a little boy on a tall stool is brushing a mule. "Guests!" His tiny body does not match his loud voice. He hops down from his stool and reaches up to take the reins from our grasp. "I'll take good care of 'em!"

"Thanks, bud!" Zain says, ruffles the boy's hat, making the kid laugh.

I add a nod and short smile before we grab our packs and make our way back around to the front. The only sign on the building just indicates that it is a tavern.

I am curious if it was the starting signs of a town that drew Zain into a dash, or if he actually could tell from a distance that this was a tavern.

We open the door, the smell of cooked meats and ale hitting our noses, the heat of the hearth causing us to gravitate towards it immediately. A woman politely greets us from behind the bar. Zain quickly strips off his cloak, hat and scarf. I chuckle slightly before looking around at this mismatched furniture that is placed around inside. There are three other patrons in here, three older men, all of which have greying hair.

"You boys going to need some rooms?" the woman asks, seeing me staring in her direction. Her curly fawn-coloured hair falls around her shoulders, a few strands stuck to her brow.

I nod. She ducks underneath the counter, a few noises being produced from under there. The old man chuckles a bit before she pops up and runs around the counter to give me two keys. A one and a two. I can tell now that she is close, that she is sweating and a bit red in the face.

"Food, drinks?" she asks, looking between Zain and me.

"Both, please, and we left our two horses with a boy out back," Zain says, giving her that dazzling smile.

She holds up a finger, hurrying her way to the door before opening it just a crack. "Liam, Ashley!" she shouts out into the cold.

"Helena, you could ask us to help you out," one of the older men says, attempting to stand.

Helena quickly walks over and puts a hand on his shoulder, pushing him down gently before walking behind the counter once more. "Nonsense. The rush just ended and the kids and I promised to look after this place while Owen was away. Besides, you are a paying customer."

The door opens and little footsteps come racing in. The little boy we saw earlier, along with the girl, quickly disrobe out of their snow soaked outerwear and rush up to their mother who has stepped out from behind the counter hearing them enter. Without her hat, the little girl's hair resembles her mother's perfectly. While the boy's hair is curly, it is black in colour.

"I have to go make some food. Take care of the geezers and our new guests while I'm in the kitchen." She pinches both their cheeks and disappears behind a swinging door that is just off to the left of the bar.

They must be struggling to run this place on their own. She even has the kids working hard out in that weather. Maybe we shouldn't have asked for food.

Zain puts his hands on my shoulder, pushing me towards the bar. His cloak, hat and scarf are now bundled in a pile under his arm.

We take a seat at the counter; the little girl stands on her tiptoes to look at us. "What would you like?" she asks, putting a smile on her face.

"Two pints, please!" Zain holds up two fingers and grins back.

She nods and lowers herself so she can walk over to the tapped barrel being propped up by a stool that looks like it is being held together by strips of leather. She pours our glasses, only being able to carry one-at-a-time back over to where we are sitting.

As we sip on the ale that feels warm going down, which is no more pleasant than the first time I drank something similar, we overhear the men speaking. "I'm telling you, it's all being exaggerated," the gentleman with a mole resting next to his eye grumbles.

"You weren't out in the field when it happened Earl, so hush. I was there, and they were saying that the end of times were coming if we all didn't do something," the shortest and widest of the group retorts, stating his story.

The third one hums. "Regardless of what they said, the money they were offering was what made them really go. I doubt many actually believed in what they were spouting."

"Exactly, which means it was exaggerated! Thank you, Paul," Earl exclaims, nodding his head.

Zain leans over me. "Sorry to intrude, but what are you talking about?"

The three men's heads turn towards us.

Earl puts up a fist. "These infernum young folk came through town a few mooncycles ago. Talking about magicae and history and such."

"Claimed that they were the revolution and had our salvation in mind. Isn't that right, Greg?" Paul adds with another hum.

"Not just that, but that the world would end if we didn't act now. Spewing that Limoria's leaders were all lying about the events long in the past," Greg says, a little bit of fear residing in his eyes. "Nearly all the young folk who could fight left with them."

"Gold speaks loud to a poor place like this," Earl mumbles before taking a drink of his pint.

Lying about the events long in the past? Salvation and a new revolution. The only conflicts I know that made waves in the long past is the Ancestry War, besides the feuding that happened when the main powers were put in place, but nothing major besides that happened in historical memory, anyway.

"This is the first I'm hearing of anything like that," Zain says, sitting upright on his stool. "Did they give you a name?"

"Said they were part of a large group. Went by the name... Dolmo, or Dinky, something like that," Earl says.

"Domi Nostre?" Zain asks, a waver in his voice.

"Domi! Yeah, that was it," Greg chimes. "That's what they said."

That's the name of the group Master mentioned back in Ventraton.

Helena steps out from the back with two plates in her hands. "Sorry for the wait!" She places them down in front of Zain and me.

So it's definitely a real group, not just a lie from the Master. Are they the ones Seodi keeps mentioning? She made it sound like a small operation, but they were here and apparently recruiting for this apparent end of time.

Zain and I eat our cooked meat and eggs in silence, just listening to the old men debate about when the next snowfall would be. Helena stays busy running around, fixing something poorly or cleaning something behind the counter. Ashley and Liam run off after their mother whispers something to them.

"We should get some sleep," Zain says, finishing his third pint.

I nod, finishing my first one.

"Oh, rooms are just around the corner there," Helena rambles off, seeing us stand from our stools.

I give her a wave of thanks and a grin before we head in that direction.

Separate beds for the first time since we started our journey. I wanted to ask him about the Domi Nostre, but it can wait until morning.

I hand the number one key to Zain and keep the number two one for myself. He looks down at his hand and then at mine, and then back to his again. Zain lets out a scoff, opens his room's door and then quickly slams it behind him.

Okay then. Guess he didn't notice her giving us two keys?

I open my door and walk in. There is a lantern already lit and the curtains are drawn. The bed is in the left-hand corner and a pitcher with a washing bowl in the other corner. I set my pack at the foot of the bed before hanging my cloak and setting my boots by the door.

There has never been a time, maybe when the Master was training me, that I have been this tired.

As much as I love snow, sleeping in it constantly, on top of having the same terrible dream every night, has worn me down more than I would care to admit. Zain was complaining so much that if I even muttered or thought about how right he was, it would have made it worse for the both of us.

One of us had to keep it together.

I walk over to the washing bowl, pouring some water in before splashing my face. The sound of the droplets dripping back into the bowl is soothing as I lean on my hands that are placed either side of it. Missing the southern passage means we will be on the road that much longer. Which means I am making the Master wait that much longer.

Would the Master have scolded me for being so careless?

The part of me that is hopeful imagines that Master is sitting comfortably in the Ventraton Castle, eating well, reading and is not in any pain. Though the reality of it, the Master was on a downward slope and likely is on his last leg, if not already dead.

My lip trembles a bit.

Am I doing any of this right?

It's my fault the tower was destroyed. I was careless and got caught up in Seodi's game. It's my fault that the King of Felguard is now holding out hope to see his love again and expecting the same of me as the Master is. It's my fault that I am distracting Zain from his own life purpose, even if he is grateful for the distraction.

I need to do better.

Standing upright, I dry my face with the shirt I'm wearing and begin to get ready for bed, but the door to my room opens slightly, and my feet freeze to the floorboards.

"He... hello?" I whisper.

Slicked back blonde hair peeks through the crack, his brown eyes squinted with his brows knit together. I let out my breath and relax my shoulders.

"Why did you ask for two rooms?" Zain asks, opening the door fully and stepping in. I arch a brown and shake my head. "Hey, words, please."

"I didn't," I mumble under my breath as I continue getting ready for bed.

The door closes, and I can hear footsteps approach me. Zain jumps onto the bed and crawls under the covers, him just staring at me. I take my shirt off and go to my pack to grab a clean one.

"Don't," Zain says. His hand grabs my arm and pulls me back a step. I look down at him and a tint of red is on his cheeks.

He is so confusing. It's like I have no idea what he is thinking at times like this, but at others, I can read his mind.

His eyes meet mine before he glances away again.

I don't understand, but okay.

Giving in to his strange demand, I crawl into bed next to

him. "Happy?" I ask, looking at him gazing at me as we are now only an inch away from each other.

He gives me his dazzling smile and nods, placing an arm around me, nuzzling his head into my neck.

Spoiled.

He's like this every night, constantly wanting affection. I don't mind it, but it's just something I am not used to. I've never had someone be affectionate with me like this.

It's actually kind of nice.

"One room," he whispers.

I nod. "Clearly."

We both chuckle. I look down at the hand resting on my chest and tentatively bring up my hand to rest it on top of his.

Zain inhales and I can feel him tense, making me quickly withdraw. I clear my throat and turn my head to look at the wall. "Zain."

"I didn't mind it there, Ren," he says, shifting a bit.

I look back down at his hand and then back to the wall.

We both lay there until the exhaustion takes us.

Zain finishes the soup in his bowl; a loud slurp rings through my ears, making my eye twitch a bit. I set my spoon down and look at his grin as he looks around the tavern.

"All done?" Ashley asks.

I nod, and she quickly grabs the bowls from us and scurries off.

"Ren, you should really smile." I slowly turn my head back towards Zain. "People would fall in love with you just like that!" He snaps his fingers.

I chuckle a bit, that smile he is referring to making a slight appearance.

He doesn't understand that my features are nothing to show-case. There is no point in doing so.

Reaching into my pouch, looking over the empty front room, pulling out a few gold coins and placing them onto the table. Zain pats my shoulder as we stand and make our way out of the establishment. The door opens with a chime, and Liam is already waiting for us. He is sitting on the tie post, petting my horse's face.

"Hey kid! They look well taken care of!" My back jerks a bit as Zain reaches into my pack.

A ting emanates from his hand as he flicks a gold coin over to Liam, who nearly falls off the post trying to catch it. His eyes widen, hands quickly squeezing together tightly after comprehending what he was given.

I was trying to be nonchalant about the fact we have more money than we should.

Let us hope they don't try to come after it.

"Thank you, sirs!" Liam exclaims loudly, jumping down from the post and running over to us, hugging both of our legs.

Zain ruffles Liam's hair as he separates from us. "You deserve it working so hard for your family with your dad gone. I hope he comes back soon." Zain's smile fades a bit and he clears his throat.

"He's super strong, so I know he is coming back!" Zain nods and steps around the kid, heading towards his horse.

I watch him climb atop his mount, his eyes focussed off of Liam. I look back down towards the kid and see him admiring the gold coin. "You keep that safe," I mutter, before joining Zain.

As we urge our horses forward, back onto the snowy path, I

can tell Zain's mind is still somewhere else since he isn't rambling like he normally does.

"Hey," I say, receiving a delayed reaction from him.

He looks back over his shoulder twice, double taking that I actually said something. "Yeah?"

I sigh and raise my brows. "This Domi Nostrae group, the recruitment, that boy's father joining them. What is bothering you?"

The waver in his voice last night when he said their name. The way he acted about Liam's father being recruited. It obviously means something to him.

Zain shakes his head. "Have you heard of them?"

"Master mentioned them, said that they were the ones who attacked us the night I fled Ventraton."

Zain halts his horse; it cries out from the shock of the rapid halt, and jumps down. I signal my horse to halt while he wades through the snow over to me. I'm prepared to get down, but Zain yanks me down instead. Falling backwards into the snow isn't painful, but it is shocking. Zain straddles me, grabbing my collar and pulling my face up to his.

What did I say?

"What the infernum, Renatus!" he shouts. "You never mentioned that. Not once!"

"I-I—"

"Is that who that girl is? Are you with them?"

I shake my head, my mouth open and my eyes wide.

"We are out here alone; she knows where we are and you have us just casually travelling across the realm with items they desire?" He shoves me down, his whole body is trembling.

"Zain," I whimper as the snow begins to soak through my cloak.

His eyes soften. "Ren." He stands up, offering me a hand, but I don't take it. I stand on my own and sniffle, taking a few steps back. Zain's eyes furrow and he bites his inner cheek. "They aren't good people, Ren. My dad told me," he pauses, looking to the ground, "that they are the ones who killed Xylia. The ones who destroyed Stran. Killed an entire city, reduced the ruins of the old kingdom to a pile of dust. A group who infiltrated the capital without notifying any of the Fel Watch or staff."

"I—" I start, but I swallow my sentence.

I didn't know that.

Zain runs his hands through his hair. "I'm scared," he chokes out. "They are the people I am most scared of, because they are the ones who are going to ruin everything." He looks to me but my gaze falls onto the snow.

Terrified is how I'm feeling right now. Master mentioned danger, the threat of having to hurt or possibly kill someone. He never went into explanation though, and now I see why.

Master knew I would be too scared if I had a grasp on the real severity of who it was after, not just the apparatus, but me.

Seodi has to be one of them.

"I'm sorry." Zain's hands caress my arm. I slowly meet his stare. "I shouldn't have reacted like that. I mean, it's not your fault. Not many people know about what really happened in Stran and with Aunt Xylia's death."

Master should have told me more; I knew I wasn't ready. Not for this.

"Ren." Zain moves his hands to my face and draws me in so our foreheads rests against one another. "Please speak to me."

I bite my lip and close my eyes.

I'm not sure I have anything of use to say.

"Tell me something, anything. Doesn't have to be about them. Could be about your favourite colour, or animal. Perhaps you spotted something curious at the tavern, or heard someone say something funny."

Why?

"Ren."

Why does he care about what I have to say?

"Green," I mutter.

Zain pulls back slowly, his hands remaining on my face. "Green?"

"My favourite colour," I answer.

He chuckles and nods. "It's a good colour. Suits you too."

"That girl, Seodi. I didn't know for sure. I wasn't even sure the Domi Nostrae were real until you said their name; didn't know how dangerous either."

"I should have asked you to expand after you said that people were after the apparatus. Jealousy was blinding me. I'm sorry."

Jealousy?

"You said sorry already," I kid, giving him a half smile.

He scoffs, returning my smile. "Yeah, well, I mean it."

Zain strokes my cheeks with his thumb before dropping his hands, my face growing cold without their presence.

"Did I hurt you at all?" he asks, circling me, brushing off stuck on snow as he goes.

Shaking my head, he lets out a sigh of relief.

"I'm sorr—" I hold up my hand, cutting him off. He nods and takes a deep breath. "Let's get going."

THE SOUND of crunching snow strikes me awake. Soft rumbling that is normally coming from Zain is somewhere outside the tent. The dark interior of the tent offers little assistance in figuring things out quickly. I reach out and feel a warm body laying next to me. My hand rises and falls with his breathing, but it gives me little comfort, as that means something unknown is standing on the other side of the hide that makes up our tent's structure.

Please be something friendly.

I gently start to push on Zain, hoping to wake him gently enough where he doesn't make too much noise. He turns towards me, my hand following his movements. I can feel his hand intertwined with mine as he brings it up to his face.

Seems I just made him more comfortable. Great.

A roar erupts from where the soft rumbling has been. I rip my hand away from Zain's, but he doesn't seem to mind since we are both now sitting up, slightly gripping onto each other.

"What the infernum was that?" Zain whispers, his words trembling along with his body.

I wish I knew.

Zain pulls away for a moment, and I hear the soft ring of a sword being unsheathed, quickly followed by something hitting my lap, startling me to jump. My hand quickly covers my own mouth to not let out a yip of surprise.

He could have warned me.

I reach down and grasp the familiar shape of the dagger King Felguard provided me. My stomach immediately starts to turn.

We don't even know what it is yet.

"I'm going to untie the flap," Zain whispers. Movement in our currently wound up blankets lets me know he really is going to do it.

A part of me wants to grab him, pull him back and just wait this thing out.

Though it didn't seem like this thing was moving.

The soft rumbling is audible again as the moonlight begins to peek in through the crack of where the flap has opened. The shadowed outline of Zain and his sword squatting right in front of me. Zain must realise what is disrupting our rest because before I can even peek outside at what it is, he opens up the flap completely, letting the moonlight burst into the tent at full force and showing me exactly what is "threatening" us. Two small little balls of fur are huddled up against a large one. Nearly all black, besides a tuft of yellow sticking up from their heads.

Beardadils.

Normally, they are extremely deadly beasts that are territorial and protective of their packs. Their tufts of yellow are actually concealing pores filled with a poisonous pollen-like substance that they can shoot out at will. Normally, yet it seems this mother beardadil and cubs seem to be alone as I scan the white tundra-looking landscape.

Oh.

Bright red glistens in the moonlight. A long trail from far beyond my vision leads to the creatures in front of us. I put my hands on Zain's shoulders and pull him back a bit so I can examine them. The Mother roars out once more as I approach, but as she turns her head our eyes meet, a docile and tired look residing in them. Gently, I place my hands on her stomach where there is darkened red fur.

Her stomach is cut open.

I glance back at Zain, his sword set to the side. He kneels down next to me and places a hand on my back. "Ren, something or someone had to have done this."

I nod in agreement.

Not only that, but her organs are hanging out.

I have no way of saving her from this. One of the cubs lifts their heads, examining Zain and I.

Their mother fought the pain and agony to get them somewhere safe.

"Zain," I whisper, not turning my head to look at him.

"Yeah, I know." He sighs. "What should we do about the cubs? They won't make it very far without help."

I stare at the beady black eyes of this tiny little living thing in front of me. It yawns and the rumbling sound I heard earlier starts again.

She chose us to try to care for her cubs.

Zain leans back and grabs his sword.

We will make sure they are safe.

He feels around to make sure he is certain of where the creature's heart is.

You did a good job of being their mother.

I grab both of the cubs by their scruffs and lift them over their mother and into my lap, their heads pressed against my chests.

There will be no more pain.

Zain thrusts his sword into the mother beardadil, and I snap my head to look in another direction. One last roar shakes the air around us, my heart sinking to my stomach.

CHAPTER SEVENTEEN

CONTINUING OUR TRAVELS FURTHER SOUTHEAST, the wet snowy plains of the Allen Territory quickly turn into the misty volcanic mountainscape of the Ashen Lands. The fear of the Domi Nostrae has subsided for the time being, after many talks of the lack of action we have seen so far on their end. Zain and Bran have figured out their comfortable riding position. Bran likes standing on his hind legs and gripping Zain's shoulders. I can't help but laugh every time I look over at the two of them, both mindlessly happy. Only difference between them is Bran generally keeps his tongue dangling out of his mouth.

Gwen is much more refined.

She stays curled up on my lap, her front paws nearly wrapping around my waist. I scratch the top of her head, avoiding the yellow tuft.

"I saw that," Zain mocks, and I roll my eyes.

He needs to stop this.

"Mister 'let's not name them because we are not keeping them'." His attempt at trying to make me feel guilty for not wanting to travel with yet another animal. They are not even animals that a city would likely allow in; I'm not even sure if a stable would take them in.

Gwen is adorable though and very well behaved. I'm sure they would make an exception for her.

Zain came up with both their names after the two main characters in a story he read. *Mystique in the Promise Land,* I think is what he called it.

The dust and steam that reside here make it hard to see, but the Ashen Land's volcano stands tall, not even able to see the top.

Master warned me about this place.

During the lunamatrums' season, the hot air rising up from the ashen land and the cold winds and snow that should be falling on top of it create tyrants of wind that send whatever is in their way up to the stars.

Explains the steam too.

"This place really is just... ash," Zain mutters, looking around at the endless landscape of nothing. No fauna, no flora, nothing but a towering mound far ahead of us.

I am unsure of how far our mounts will make it if there is no water. We bought some small barrels with water from the Jako River, but they have already drunk the majority of it since we arrived in the Ashen Land.

Let's hope they can make it to one of the outposts.

When I was a youngin, one of my tutors taught me about the history of this land. How there was once an all-ruling king that reigned over the Realm of Limoria. The Ashen Land was once the most vibrant and filled with life. A large lake that acted as an enormous moat for Limoria's capital. Races from all the doorways would migrate their way through it, parties held nearly every day, and life was a celebration. Limoria was at its most prosperous in both history and present times. That was until the **Ignisium Doorway** burst open underneath the island, where the palace and the capital resided. From there, not much is known of how, but a volcano emerged from the lake's depths, erupting and destroying the ecosystem and the life that lived in its radius.

I thought everyone's descriptions were dramatised since Meka prison resides here, but it truly is infernum.

"Renatus?" Zain says, his horse coming up right behind mine. He points a finger out towards a small mass ahead of us. "Is that a person?"

We quickly pick up the pace and rush over to the tanned, broad-shouldered woman lying unconscious. She is covered in dust and has some blood splattered across her chest. I hop down from my horse, Gwen hopping down with me. Walking over, I adjust the stranger's form to lay her on her back.

A sharp pain emanates from my stomach, air no longer reaching my lungs. I glance down, and she's holding the handle of a familiar-looking dagger, the blade disappearing past my shirt.

I cough and flecks of blood land on her face, her hazel eyes glaring into me. Gwen growls and wedges herself between the two of us, like her tiny form is a threat enough for this person to run.

"Ren!" Zain shouts, taking a step forward.

"Move and I kill him!" she shouts, pushing me hard enough to pin me on my back, her now hovering over me.

Zain watches me with both a look of horror and anger. His fists balled and hands on his swords. My body begins to tremble from the pain radiating from where she is holding the dagger.

She needs to take it out before she kills me.

Gwen jumps on the woman's back, causing her to ease up a bit on the pressure she is putting on me. Zain takes the opportunity and dashes towards her.

"Zain, wait," I mutter.

The blade is ripped from my abdomen as Zain tackles her away from me. Gwen jumps away before Zain slams her back onto the hardened earth. He lands in a few hits, but he doesn't stay on top for long; she quickly manoeuvres her way on top of him. Her fist making contact with his face.

"Leave him be," I sputter out, my legs trying to find their fitting, but I collapse to the ground. "Stop it!" My voice breaks from the cry it released.

Bran latches onto her arm, and she cries out in pain before punching him off. "If you don't want them to die, tell them to back off!" she shouts.

Bran whimpers as his sister rushes over to him.

I have to do something.

"Just tell us what you want," I say.

She stops and looks back at me. Her hood falls back and showcases her shaved head, a reddish tint on the stubble that is still there. She stands, wiping the blood from her mouth, and walks back over to me. "Fine. Give me your water and money."

I look over to the unmoving Zain, only the soles of his boots really visible and the trembling beardadils huddled together.

You can do this, Renatus.

"I'll give you whatever you want. A horse, all the coins I possess, the little water we have left. I just ask that you leave me my pack, that dagger you are holding and a horse for me to get us somewhere safe." The words stumble out, my voice shaking.

Please. Listen.

She smiles and crouches down in front of me. "You think I am going to say yes to that?"

There is no blade on that dagger. Just like the one in the Master's journal. **Asiferrum** *or Fools Blade.*

"Hoping," I whimper. Slowly making my way up, I stand; she is only shoulder height to me. The pain in my stomach is no longer gut-wrenching, but now a subtle sting.

She laughs and tilts her head. "I'm Minka."

Zain's face is already looking swollen, blood trickling out of his nose and mouth. His chest is slowly rising and falling.

Good...

I close my eyes and take a steady breath in. "Renatus."

She walks over to the horses, petting Zain's mount's neck and whispering something to it. "Why my dagger and not the one attached to your belt?" she asks without glancing my way.

Can't really tell her the real reason.

"Figured it was useless to you. With no blade." I look back to Zain; Bran and Gwen are now investigating his unconscious form.

"Is that so?" she laughs. "The only way you are getting this dagger is if you are going to replace it with something better."

Pointing down to my belt, showcasing the whip and my own dagger, showing her this is what I have to offer.

Minka rolls her eyes. "No, you idiot. I have something in mind. I just need help getting it."

Oh.

"I normally wouldn't want to partner with someone so..." her judging gaze looks me up and down, "scrawny, but I need someone to keep an eye out. Also, be my bait, in case I get caught." She points to me, and then Zain.

More stealing, and she plans to pin it on Zain and me.

Walking over to my unconscious companion, I softly shake him, taking in his beaten face. It makes me feel angry and sick seeing him like this. I brush my thumb lightly across his cheek, his eyes fluttering open before he winces.

"That hurts." He groans, putting his hand over mine to stop my thumb, but pins my hand to his face. He gives me a smile before his eyes widen and he sits upright. His hands quickly reach towards my abdomen, searching for the wound that should be there.

"Zain, I'm okay," I whisper and smile at him.

"How?" Zain whispers.

"I'll tell you later," I answer in the same hushed tone.

His lip trembles and he pulls me into his chest, his arms wrapped around my shoulders.

"Are you okay?" He nods to my question and squeezes me tighter.

He isn't okay.

Pulling back, breaking his grip on me, I look over his face again. There is going to be a lot of bruising, but it doesn't look like she broke anything. His teeth are all still there.

Looks like it'll just be a massive headache.

A guttural groan sounds from behind me. "You two love-birds done yet? Horses are gonna get thirsty." Minka slouches her shoulders, brow furrowed and a scowl resting on her face.

Lovebirds?

"Wait, what did I miss?" Zain asks, looking from Minka to myself.

Z AIN'S GRIP *around my waist is way too tight. Though I'm sure it's because his face hurts.*

His head is resting against my back, quiet grumblings reaching my ears every so often. To say that he is not happy about our circumstances would be putting it lightly. Having to help the person who punched him until he was unconscious has made their acquaintanceship pretty bitter. Bran and Gwen are not as happy as they were before, as they had to get strapped onto us. Gwen tied to my chest and Bran on Zain's back. They whimper and whine, but it's either this or they walk.

"We should make camp," Minka says, slowing her and her mount's pace with a tug on the reins.

"We should make camp," Zain says in a hushed, mocking tone. I roll my eyes and kick my leg over to hop down. I reach up and assist Zain down. "She just came in and took over," he grumbles.

She has something I need. She can take control if she wants it. I should catch Zain up on that.

Since travelling with her, though, it seems we have covered quite a bit of distance. Minka said that by midday tomorrow we should reach the first northern outpost.

Minka begins setting up Zain's tent, while I unpack ours after letting Gwen free from her binds. She immediately runs over and smells her newly freed brother.

"Zain," I whisper, stealing his attention away from the concentrated glare he was focussed on.

Waving him over puts a smirk on his face, and he scurries to my side. "Yeah?"

I caress his face with both my hands, to examine how bad the sweeping and bruising is but am halted as his face begins leaning in close to mine, but I pull away.

What is he doing?

His smirk fades and turns his face away from me. "I thought you had something on your face."

I blink a few times before shaking my head. "Okay," I mutter. "While she's distracted, I need to tell you about the dagger."

"I know. After you said that we were going to help her, I saw it. Observation is not something only you are good at." Zain sighs, turning his head to look up into the sky. The moon is in full force. It's been over two mooncycles since we left Fosa. It'll be at least five days before we even make it to Xan. "Necessity won't change my attitude towards anything." Zain turns away from me.

Apparently. It's understandable, though.

The only reason I didn't bleed out or have any injuries is because of the magicae enchantment that the dagger possesses. It mimics the pain a normal blade would deliver if stabbed or cut into someone, but no serious damage is done.

As long as you don't hold it there too long or get too close to the heart.

"Blondie, I know I punched you to oblivion earlier today," Minka says, tossing something to Zain. "No hard feelings, though. Wasn't personal." She gives him a wink and goes back to setting up her sleeping arrangements.

Zain looks over his shoulder at me and glares. I shrug and give him what I hope is a reassuring smile. He rolls his eyes and drops whatever she had thrown to him.

These two are going to be a handful.

We spend the rest of the night in silence; watching Bran and Gwen play with each other a safe enough distance from the small campfire we have going.

Thankfully.

Gwen yawns and rests her head on my thigh while Bran is laying in between my legs. Zain, after I treated his swollen eye and bruised nose, curled up at my side. He looks a lot more at ease now that he isn't bickering with Minka or angrily mumbling to himself. A few of his blonde strands drape over his face, covering his closed eyes. I brush them back, tucking them behind his ear.

She saw us as lovers? Or was that some tease to try to break the concentration we had on each other verus her?

I never thought about it. Being with someone. I belong to the Master, not much free time in the way of a servant. At least not one that manages the entire house by themselves.

Do I want something different than the way things were?

Biting down on my lip, I shake my head.

That is not a choice the Master offered me. The choice, he said, was how I choose to obtain Aruna's apparatus.

I'll have to say goodbye to Zain, allow him to live the life that he and his mother have mentioned. I will have to go back to the Master.

Get to go back to the Master.

An ache emanates from my chest as my brow furrows, my vision growing slightly blurry. My lips begin to quiver as a soft sob escapes them. I put my arm over my eyes, trying to hide my face from Zain as he stirs awake, hearing my pathetic attempt of being quiet.

"Ren?" he whispers. I feel him shift from my side, his hands now tugging at the arm, keeping me from seeing him. "Hey now…" One of his hands moves from my arm, and I feel it start to stroke my hair.

"Sorry," I breathe out, a small chuckle from him following suit.

His nose brushes against my ear, his warm breath sending a chill through my body; that ache seems to intensify. "Shh," he coos, trying to settle me down.

"I'm sorry I can't make this journey easier on you. You got hurt because of me." The shame and disappointment in myself coming out, and a feeling of a loss that hasn't happened yet.

"No, I'm sorry. This is not just tough on me. I've been complaining, angry, ungrateful for the journey you have allowed me to accompany you on. You have been strong and resilient, enduring it all for the both of us." His voice is so deep and soft. He finally pulls away my arm, the only thing between us. He sits up so I can look into those chocolate eyes of his. "You can cry and complain and get it out. I can be strong, too." He leans down, his soft lips brushing against my cheek.

My arms wrap around his shoulders, and I pull him down on top of me, burying my face in the nape of his neck. My quiet sob is now loud, the tears no longer just a watering but a salty mess soaking his shirt. "Please... don't get... hurt... again." The words coming out in brief pauses I get from my sobbing.

His muscles tense in my grasp for a moment before a sigh releases the tension. "Okay, I won't." He kisses my head. "As long as you don't scare me like that again." His words are muffled as his lips are still pressed against my hair.

THE SUN IS OUT, and the temperature is slightly warmer as we near the post Minka mentioned yesterday.

At least, that's what she told us.

Zain's chin rests on my shoulder as he rides behind me. His eyes are closed and a soft snore is escaping his lips. He didn't sleep much last night. I woke up once or twice and found him just laying there with his arm around me, eyes looking at the ceiling of the tent.

I don't think he is having as much fun as he thought he would be having.

Especially after our run in with Seodi awhile back, things have been a lot more serious. Not to mention the extreme weather we have had to deal with, and now we have a brute who is the wielder of one of the apparatus we are in search of.

He did get excited about seeing the lava pits, though.

As we begin to near the volcano, it's as if in two days it has doubled in size.

"It's just up ahead," Minka says, gesturing to a mound of dirt. "Not much, but it has water."

I nod, responding to her.

"You really don't like talking, huh," she mumbles without even glancing in my direction.

Not when there's nothing to say.

"Are we there yet?" Zain groans, lifting his chin, his arms stretching high above his head. "I am ready to get off this damn thing." He smacks his forehead lightly against my back.

I snort, shaking my head and rolling my eyes. He has been napping this entire time.

Gwen and Bran should be the ones protesting their form of transportation.

The distance to the post doesn't take us long to cover. As we arrive, the large mound is actually made out of dirt and mud from this region. Holes acting in the structure-like windows.

Minka hops off her horse, but holds up her hand to halt us following her action. "That's weird." Her words are soft and her brows are knit together as she looks around, pulling her hood down. "There are normally guards stationed outside."

I look around from atop my mount and notice dots of red filtering through the ashen dirt. Pointing in their direction, Minka's eyes widen. She quickly hops back onto her horse.

She seems scared.

"What's going on?" Zain asks, gripping onto my sides tightly. "Why does the tough, scary girl look worried?"

"Shut up, pretty boy. We need to leave now," Minka says, turning her horse around.

"Aw, so soon? You three just got here." A familiar voice calls out from inside the mound.

Seodi.

"Thought we could actually play this time, Renatus," she says, stepping out where we can see her.

I shake my head and begin reaching for my whip.

"Be careful now; wouldn't want to excite my friend there," she says, pointing causally behind us.

I slowly turn my head to see what she is pointing at, and a tall lanky man with eyes completely black in colour is standing there with an arrow drawn and already ready to fire.

How did we not see him?

The arrow is shot through the sky and pierces Minka straight in the back. She lets out a blood-curdling scream and before she can do anything, Seodi's companion is already at Minka's side, ripping her off of her horse.

Either he has Natural Magicae abilities or that was a movement spell.

She cries out in pain as he drags her towards Seodi, who is walking out to meet them.

I can feel Zain begin to shake. "Ren, we have to do something."

What can be done? They have Minka, which means they also have the dagger.

"Care to join us down here, boys? Or I can have my friend help you down," she says while the man begins to walk towards us. We quickly hop off. "Oh, and tie those things up; don't want them getting into trouble while we play."

I nod and let Bran and Gwen down from our bodies before tying them together. They whine in protest, but I ignore them.

Seodi chuckles her monotone laugh and looks down at Minka, who whimpers with her face down in the dirt. "You look very capable; too bad there isn't much use for a cripple out here, though."

Minka screams out again, this time not out of pain but anger. Seodi raises her hands and turns her attention towards us.

"You two look so cute, with him hiding behind you like

that." Seodi smiles, tilting her head. "It kinda pisses me off." Her smile fading.

The sound of crunching soil comes from behind us and her companion is now standing right behind us. I grab Zain's collar and throw him behind me. He catches himself from falling and draws his swords.

Seodi's companion grabs his dagger and dives for me, but Zain steps forward and blocks it. A flicker of white light courses through the blade and causes the man to drop his weapon and take a few steps back, jittering a bit. Despite his recoil, his bored expression hasn't changed.

"Oh, pretty boy has some fight!" Seodi shouts. I glance behind, leaving Zain to watch the threat in front of us. "Why do you always wear such a worried scowl?" she says, pointing at me as she steps closer.

"Back off!" Zain shouts, my head whipping in his direction. Both of his swords are pointed at the terrifying stranger in front of him, who is stepping closer.

Minka screams, but it's muffled. I glance back and see Seodi stepping on her head. "Stop!"

"Or what?" she says, putting more weight on her foot.

I clench my fists.

My satchel with the prepared spells is in my pack.

The clashing of metal draws me to it and I see Zain blocking a different dagger than before. Suddenly, hands twirl my hair and I feel a sharp object lightly pressed against my cheek.

"Stop ignoring me, Reantus, or I will have to do something bad," Seodi whispers in my ear.

Zain looks over and his eyes flare. He shoves the man back and swings towards Seodi, who jumps back and shoves me to the ground.

The man kicks Zain in the back, causing him to stumble

forward. Seodi quickly grabs Zain's head and brings it to connect with her knee. Blood spouts out and I try to rush to his side, but Seodi's companion grabs me and begins dragging me towards the post.

"Let go!" I scream as I flail against his grip.

"Ren..." Zain mutters, trying to get up, gripping his swords tighter.

Seodi stomps on his hands before ripping the swords away from him, throwing them a metre or so from where she is standing.

"Drop him there; I want him to watch." Her companion lets go of his grip but continues walking towards Minka and the post.

Watch? Watch what?

My eyes are trained on Zain, who is clenching his jaw, tears and blood streaming down his already bruised face.

Please don't.

Seodi grabs Zain by the hair, lifting him upward and placing her dagger to his throat.

CHAPTER EIGHTEEN

ZAIN and I ride silently along the southern route towards Yral. The snow makes its reappearance as we have passed the barren border of the Ashen Land. White tufts of snow sticking to our cloak, hair and horses. It's a lot less dense, and the temperature isn't as cold. Zain hasn't been complaining about it, but then again, I think he is just being careful about what he says at all.

I am too, well I'm actually not saying anything at all.

Focusing back on the white canvas in front of me, it reminds me of the ceiling that once lived above my cot in the tower.

I feel stained.

There is nothing I can do to make it pure again. Nothing I can do to restore the naïve, childlike hope I had. My confusion of both my desire and dread to return to the tower, to live as I had, is now no longer a worry. The boy I was a few weeks ago is not the boy riding this path at this moment. I am not the same boy the Master entrusted with the purpose given to me. There are now scars in places only I can see; red stains covering my hands and my mind.

Did I do the right thing?

I glance towards Zain, who sniffles, rubbing his red nose.

Yes. I did the right thing.

Zain's eyes meet mine and he tries to give me a smile, but it looks like it just nearly made him cry. "Hey, are you doing okay?" he asks in an uneven tone.

I open my mouth slightly but quickly shut it again, turning away.

"Ren, please," he begs.

I close my eyes tightly and take a deep breath.

Nothing I say is going to make this better.

He rides up next to me and reaches over to tug on my cloak. "I apologised for messing up. Can you please just acknowledge it, or even yell at me for it? Say something!"

I bite down on my lip hard enough to make it bleed.

You did nothing wrong.

"You're such an idiot, Renatus!" Zain takes off.

"Seodi!" I scream, her hand gripping Zain's hair tightly. She tilts his head back, exposing his neck. Gwen and Bran are wound together, their cries enough to make my blood run cold.

"I really like it when you say my name like that, Renatus." Her eyes are no longer dead, but crazed. "I want you to choose. The favour of the women holding onto the apparatus, or your newfound friend." Her pupils are almost nonexistent in this moment.

I run towards him. Towards the person who has been making me question everything. Making me rethink what it is I want. Making me want something.

"Ren, don't do this to yourself!" Zain's cry passes through my ears as I reach him. I shove Seodi off of him, a laugh emanating from her chest, seeing me wrap myself around him.

There is no choice but this one. I will figure out another way to get the apparatus.

Zain sobs into my shoulder, gripping the fabric on my back tightly.

Seodi nods her head towards the man with black eyes; Minka's screams violate every inch of my soul.

I killed someone.

"Ren," Zain says, tugging at my arm. "The horses are done drinking." I stand from the pond's bank and follow him a few paces until Gwen sees me and starts walking towards me. She rubs against my ankle and makes a rumbling noise like she did the night we first found them.

I pick up Gwen and place her on top of our mount, scratching under her chin. Zain intertwines his hand with mine. His reddened eyes speaking the words he has been saying ever since we left the Ashen Lands.

He wants me to speak.

I pull my hand away and climb on top of my mount. Zain looks off into the distance.

There is nothing to say.

Urging my horse forward, we continue down the trail. The sound of hooves stomping through muddied earth. The beginning of Fons showcasing itself beautifully in budding flowers and dew ridden fields and patches of grass. The sun makes our path look like it is encrusted with diamonds, the little droplets reflecting its light.

It should all be melted by the time we reach Yral, as it's generally warmer there.

"Ren." Zain pulls me away from my thoughts. I look over my shoulder at him and watch him raise his brow. "We are going to be okay, right?"

I know my distance has been bothering him. I pulled away from his grasp, and haven't spoken since leaving the post.

How could I allow myself to feel happy, be joyful... receive care from someone who I put at such a risk?

I don't deserve anything because in order to save him, I had to be the reason someone died.

"Ren?" His voice is shaky. "Please... tell me we are alright."

My chin quivers at hearing and seeing him like this.

It's all my fault.

He hasn't smiled that bright smile of his in so long, and it's because of me.

I turn away from him and bite down on my lip.

There is nothing I want more than to tell him that, of course, we are going to be alright, but right now that would feel like a lie. He's hurting, and that means we are not fine at all. I don't know how to make this better, or how to make him happy.

I snap my horse's reins and ride ahead, not wanting him to see the pain I myself am feeling.

Her lifeless body is just laying there. Eyes open, muscles limp. Seodi steps around Zain and me and skips her way over to Minka. She unsheathes the dagger and looks over it carefully.

"Sorry, Renatus, you were just taking too long. This brute was going to drag you around the Ashen Land and run you dry of coins. Figured I would just help you out with this one," Seodi says, walking back over to me, dropping the dagger at my feet.

"You really had to threaten me?" Zain shouts his question, trying to stand, but I pull him back down.

Seodi smiles and nods. "Part of the fun. I like seeing Renatus uncomfortable." She turns away from us. "Not to mention, it helps with my own motives."

What motives? I thought she wanted the apparatus, but now she is helping me obtain them. I don't understand any of this.

"I'm so sorry, Ren," Zain whimpers.

I shake my head and lace my fingers through his hair.

This is my fault. I knew she was following us and I know how crazy she is; I just didn't think she would attack anyone other than me.

Seodi's companion begins dragging Minka's body towards the post. I squeeze Zain before letting him go and running after him. Seodi doesn't even glance at me as I run past her. Her companion looks over his shoulder just before I shove him. He drops Minka's arms and stumbles to catch himself. He just stares at me.

"Careful, Azrail is quite vicious when provoked," Seodi says from behind me. I tense my jaw. "Just let him pass, Azrail. He should see for himself just how terrifying you can be."

Azrail steps to the side, lifting up one hand to gesture for me to enter the post. Glancing back towards Seodi, she just smiles.

I didn't shove him to see the post; I did it so he'd leave Minka alone.

"Oh, go on. You should know who your enemy is, Ren." She laughs and raises a brow.

Don't call me that.

The sea salt in the air is warm, unlike the air that was in Kena. The Seeker's Territory is known for its white sand beaches and academics. People from all over the world come here to study in their libraries and colleges. Specifically, Lona's University has one of the most expansive literary collections in all of Vitaterrium.

Master mentioned studying there when he was a youngin.

Yral is visible in the distance, and in a few sunshifts, we will arrive at our next destination. The weather is nice, clear skies and temperate now that we are nearing the mid Fons season.

I'm sure Zain is enjoying it.

Zain has stopped trying to get me to talk and has hardly talked at all himself. We wake up in silence, eat in silence, ride in silence, set camp up in silence. Bran and Gwen make more noise than either one of us at this point.

I miss him.

Looking over to him, he is gazing off to the left, towards the beach. The ocean waves wash over the sparkling sand. I turn my horse off the path, urging the horse to gallop towards the water.

"Ren?" Zain shouts, but I keep heading towards my destination.

A pile of bodies, twenty or so, are all stacked together. Some are armed soldiers, others look like travellers, there are even some youngins amongst them. Bile rises in my throat, and despite my attempt to swallow it, the little contents I've eaten today are now covering the dirt floor.

Seodi laughs, patting my back as I am hunched over. "See. Now you have some idea of how much you and those apparatus you are hunting mean to me and my group." She grabs my chin and makes me face her, wiping my mouth with her other hand. "If you don't stay focussed, if you make me wait longer than what I have to, I will kill that whiny castle brat you keep around." She shoves my face back, making me lose balance.

Why. Why doesn't she just kill me? Why doesn't Seodi just torture the information out of me? Why?

"Why?"

Seodi smiles, kneeling down in front of me. "Does the reason matter? Either way, it's happening to you." She rubs her thumb across my cheek before standing. "Oh, there is another party after you, by the way, and from what I've gathered, they have been sticking close by. A little tip from me to you." Seodi gives me a wink before exiting the post.

This is all my fault. I should have been more careful. Been more prepared.

I jump from my mount, Gwen following suit. I strip myself of my cloak, armour and tunic.

"Renatus, what the infernum has got into you?" Zain says now, hopping down from his horse, Bran stretching out, still riding on top.

I reach out to his cloak's clasp and undo it swiftly enough so he cannot stop me.

He furrows his brows and starts shaking his head. "What is going on?" I start unbuckling his chest plate, but his hands find mine and pry them off of him. "I can undress myself. Don't know why I'm doing it, though."

Zain strips off his own armour and tunic before looking at me.

The water is probably still chilled from the lunamatrums' blessing, and we will probably freeze, but we need this.

I grab his hand and run with him to the water. The moment our feet hit the chilled water, Zain tries pulling away. I turn around and wrap my arms around his waist, lifting him up and allowing myself to fall, bringing him down with me.

"Ren, wait!" Zain screeches before we plummet into the ocean's waves.

I just want to see him smile.

We come up for air, our lips quickly turning a shade of blue, our bodies shaking. Zain splashes some water at me, the salty flavour hitting my tongue.

"Why did you do that?" He stands and tries to rush out, but

I grab his wrist again and pull him so his back is pressed up against my chest.

"You can splash me again." The words chatter through my lips; Zain's back muscles tense from shaking.

"Ren, you... idiot." Zain turns, eyes squinted, brows furrowed and a bright smile shining at me.

He wraps his arms around my neck, tackling me back into the water.

His laugh is infectious and makes my burdened heart light.

I don't ever want to see him hurt, and I say that knowing that one day I will be the one to hurt him.

YRAL'S tall and glistening silver walls showcase very well the wealth the capital has. I'm sure that if the sun were to hit the walls just right, it would blind anyone looking at them.

Only two more to go. Once we obtain the cloak, the only thing left is the gauntlet.

"Ren." Zain extends his hand towards me. I take his hand in mine. "Let's enjoy ourselves here." He flashes me a smile, tilting his head. Some longer strands of his hair falling into his face.

His hair has grown a lot. His easily slicked back locks are now a curly mess framing his face.

I nod and return his smile. I release his hand to grab the letter necessary to enter the city. Even from the gates, you can see the tall spiralled towers of the castle. Its light blue pointed roofs and sandstone bricks match the ocean and sand it's built next to. I hand the guard my paper. They are dressed in loose fitting clothing, all a shade of off-white. He has silver rings, necklace, earrings and even the straps on his sandals appear to have some sort of silver band.

They must not feel very threatened. It doesn't look like any guards are wearing actual armour.

As we walk under the arched gateway, guards smile and

wave at us. Youngins are laughing and playing in the street, parents sitting off to the side at restaurants. We dismount, and an older gentleman approaches us. His long white hair tied back into a ponytail.

"Well, hello, sirs. Will you be needing a stall for your beasts?" He gestures to our horses, giving a second glance towards the beardadils resting on them.

"Most definitely," Zain says, smiling at him, reaching for our coin pouch.

The old man holds up his hands. "'Tis quite alright. The capital pays me for storing animals. You need not waste your coin here with me. Please enjoy yourselves and spend your gold on something you'd like."

I raise my brows, hearing him say that.

Yarl pays for all of its travellers' animal storing expenses?

"Oh wow! Thank you for helping us. Oh, and they don't bite," Zain says, petting Gwen and Bran goodbye. "Behave yourselves," he whispers to our furry friends before he takes my hand and pulls me away.

I wave goodbye to Gwen, who looks ready to run after me, but the stable hand grabs her.

They will be okay, right?

As we meander our way through the streets, our packs on our backs, it looks like the city's entrance is full of life. Bright colours hanging from strings that connect to each of the buildings. Merchants smile and offer samples of their desserts and drinks; Zain, of course, sampling each and every one of them.

"Slow down," I tease him as he is stuffing his face full of some crab sampler. He gives me a wink before we move on to the next stand.

Everyone here is smiling. It's nice.

With a tight grip on my wrist, Zain drags me around looking at the different stands, stalls and stores that line this area of the city. Each of them having prices quite a bit more than either Fosa or Ventraton would price similar items.

"Zain," I mutter his name, pulling his eyes away from the earrings he is admiring to look at me.

He rolls his eyes, as if reading my mind, letting out a sigh. "Yeah, yeah. Let's find a place to stay and blow all our coins." Zain waves me off and starts moving again.

After walking a few blocks, the crowds thinning a bit, a large inn with a giant sign of a pillow resting above its entryway beckons to us. We cross the street, making our way in.

Two women immediately greet us, both of them have their blonde hair tied back into a neat ponytail. "Welcome to your home away from home, gentlemen!" They gesture for us to walk further in.

Zain straightens his posture and smiles brightly. "Thank you for the warm welcome, beautifuls."

My turn to roll my eyes.

Another woman with blonde hair styled into a neat ponytail waves us over to the front desk. "Welcome, sirs. How can I help you today?"

"We are looking for a room," Zain answers, still wearing that smile.

The desk clerk looks between us. "And we are happy to provide you one!" She dips below the desk for a second before popping back up and giving us a silver key with a ten engraved on it. "I will have one of our ladies' escort you to your room."

Immediately, yet another similar-looking woman appears from just around the corner, waving at us.

Zain and I glance at one another, blinking a few times, him trying to stifle a laugh. We make our way over to the woman waiting. She leads us down the long hall, past a staircase and to the end of the hallway. A silver ten nailed to the door.

"Here you are, sirs. Dinner is served to your rooms at the

third moonshift." She holds out her hand, and Zain puts a gold coin in it.

My eyes widen, and I bite my lip to stop myself from gasping in shock.

A gold coin? Is that how much a room costs a night?

She gives us a bow and leaves. Zain turns and takes the key from my grasp.

"What?" Zain asks, unlocking the door and opening it. "She was expecting a tip."

That was a gold coin.

Entering the room, it looks like a small house and not just a room in some inn. There is a dining table, a cushioned sofa, a large bed, a private bathroom and a window on the far side of the room.

Only thing missing is a kitchen. This place must be extremely expensive.

"Finally, a decent place to sleep!" Zain shouts, kicking his boots off and running to the bed. He plops onto it and spreads out.

"Spoiled," I mumble, shaking my head at him.

Zain props himself on his elbows and gives me a one eyebrow raised look. "Hey, I know I'm spoiled. I could have anything I want at the snap of my fingers." Closing the door and locking it, Zain's hands wrap around me. With my back facing him, I feel his hands on my chest. "Well, almost anything."

I turn around in his grasp and look slightly down at him.

He's referring to connections. Why he follows people he gets a good impression of.

"You already have me, Zain." The words leave my mouth, and the most handsome smile spreads across his lips.

How does he do that?

Nothing.

We have searched every lead the Master had on the cloak. Every name, historical establishment; I even went as far as to show the sketch of it to a few people. They all directed us to a seamstress who could possibly mimic it.

Not likely, but I understand that they wouldn't know it.

We end up back in the room, which is costing us five gold coins a night.

Master would think I am a glutton.

Zain pats my back. "We will look again tomorrow, and the day after, and however many days it takes to find something." He takes a seat next to me at the table. He holds out his hand, which I take. "Maybe the library has something about it."

Nodding my hand, I squeeze his hand a bit tighter.

I appreciate him trying.

The longer this takes, the more I think about what Seodi said. The more I think about how the Master is doing. The more I think about what is going to happen when this ends.

Maybe, I don't want to find it.

"No!" I shout.

Zain nearly jumps out of his seat at my sudden outburst.

"Woah! Ren, what in the infernum was that for?" He pulls his hand away and stares at me wide eyed.

That thought startled me.

"Sorry. I just... had a bad thought." My words stitch Zain's brows together.

"What kind of bad thoughts?" His words are stern and his tone deep.

I shake my head before placing it inside my hands. "Just had a thought that I'm not who I actually am." The words come out as a whisper.

Zain sighs. "What does that mean?"

"I'm my master's servant." My words begin to shake. "Nothing... more... yet I'm yearning for things I have no right to."

An arm is wrapped around me, my hands being pried away from my face.

Zain's brown eyes are very intently looking into mine. "Don't you ever say that!" My self-doubt halts, his voice sending a shiver through me. "You are so much more than a servant. In fact, you don't even resemble the guy who showed up in Fosa. Renatus, you have changed, not just yourself, but you've changed me too." He rests his forehead against mine.

Have I really?

"Thank you, Zain."

No. I think he is the one who has changed me.

"So, where do you want to start looking next?" Zain asks.

"Library," I mutter.

Zain nods and stands to look out the window. "We should have enough time to look around for a bit before it gets too late. If you are up for some more looking yet today."

I nod, grab my master's journal, and we head back out.

Zain says he remembers seeing a sign that pointed towards where the nearest library would be. As we meander our way through the streets, it's hard not to notice that most people are wearing the same type of clothing and that, depending on their age, their hair styles seem to be the same too.

As great as this city seems on the outside, their prices are extremely hard, and individuality seems to be punishable.

"Hey, it's over there," Zain says, pointing to a tall spiralling building. The roof is, of course, blue, the walls white, which includes the outdoors staircase that wraps around the building.

We make our way to the silver engraved doors, opening them and seeing the rounded room filled top to bottom with books.

"Woah," Zain whispers; his mouth hangs open as he stares upwards.

I take a few steps in, spinning slowly as I gaze to the top of the tower, thin ledges with people walking ginger on it pick out their desired reads.

Someone clears their throat and I jump back a bit and realise I need to look down to meet their feathered form. "How can I help you today, sir?" their voice is higher pitched and a tad scratchy. Their body is covered in blue feathers, their beak yellow, and their eyes, which are surprisingly human-looking, are brown.

I think I read about this race. It started with a P but the name is escaping me. I remember reading that they are generally native to The Lonely Island but have spread out in the last few hundred sidereal years.

"Uh, we are looking for apparatus from a long time ago. Seeing if there is any inventory archive or something we can reference?" Zain answers, his mouth still hanging open.

They bring up their feathered hand to their chin and look away for a moment. "Do you know what type of apparatus? The maker or method of creation?"

"Ren?" Zain turns towards me.

I think I'd raise some red flags by saying Aruna's name. Besides what they look like, I'm not a hundred per cent sure what type of Magicae it contains or how it came to be.

"It would be older than five hundred sidereal years," I state, hoping what little information I'm offering can help.

"That's all you got?" they ask, and I nod, confirming.

"Well, our archives don't go back much further than that regarding apparatus. Most folk were born with Natural Magicae back then." The clicking of their talons on the marbled floor causes a shiver to run down my back. "There was little use for them."

We follow them up a set of stairs leading outside to the set of spiralling stairs we saw earlier. The view of Yral becoming more and more beautiful the higher we climb. The rooftops look like seashells glistening on a sunny day. Zain's hand intertwines with mine as we make our way up.

As we crest the last platform, they step in and we follow suit. "This is where we keep our oldest archives and readings," they mutter, stepping out onto the ledge and reading the titles on the shelves. "No, not this one."

The part of me that wants to start looking is halted by the straight drop. I lean over the edge slightly to glance down.

"A pancake," Zain whispers in my ear. I look at him with a raised brow. "That's what you would end up being if you fall from this height." He gives me a smirk, and I roll my eyes in return.

"Hm, maybe this one," they say, pulling a large title from its resting place. As they scurry over to us, we meander to the crescent-shaped table next to the entrance. They set it down delicately and open it slowly. "This is about some of the first apparatus ever created. Not the firsthand account, of course, but a researched opinion on the effects of having those types of items a part of our existence in that time."

I wonder what they meant by "of course".

"Is there something about a cloak in there?" Zain asks, peeking over their shoulder.

They glance his way, causing Zain to have a funny face backing out of their space. "Give me a minute," they grumble.

This is a longshot, and the likelihood of it giving us anything of substance is almost nonexistent, but it's better than just sitting around.

"Nothing about a cloak, talks about the fear of Magicae enslavement and the dangers that could occur from allowing just anyone to purchase or own them. Mass genoside being one of the highest concerns," they clarify as they continue to read.

Makes sense; just handing that power over to anyone is dangerous.

"Anything else?" I ask, making sure to give them plenty of space.

They hum, "Mentions Ayla and Aruna's teaching of item crafting and enchantment, but that is beyond my understanding, as I am not a Natural Magicae user."

That's interesting, but not what we are looking for.

I look to Zain and shake my head. "Thank you for showing us up here and trying to help us figure this out," he says on my behalf.

"'Tis my job," they say, closing the book. "Can you see yourselves out?"

We nod and wave our goodbyes.

MY EYES BOLT OPEN, feeling the force of something hit my side. I glance over and see Zain sitting in bed, eyes darting and breath uneven.

He must have hit me by accident.

Zain buries his face into his shaking hands. I furrow my brow and stir a bit, as to not startle him more with an abrupt touch.

I touch his back, rubbing soft circles from my laid out position. Zain lifts his head slightly, meeting my gaze. He gives me a sympathetic smile before pulling on my arm to get me to sit up with him.

Zain nuzzles his head into my chest the moment it is made available for him. I continue to rub his back lightly with one hand while the other scratches his head.

"Zain," I say, tugging on his hair lightly to get him to look up at me. He sits back, his eyes wide and face pale.

"Ren," he says, running a hand through his hair.

"What's wrong?" As the words leave my lips, tears start to drip from his eyes. He grabs my shirt and buries himself into my chest once more. I place one of my arms around him this time, squeezing him.

Must have been a really bad dream.

"Ren, we are at war."

War? The Felguard Country hasn't been at war for over a century. What country is even amusing the idea?

"I am to head back to Felguard Country immediately. Shaw is already on her way." Zain's words are breathy and blabbering between his sobs.

I don't want him to go back. I don't want him to leave me.

"Why would you need to go back?" I whisper, remembering quite well the conversation he and his mother had just before we left.

Zain shakes his head. "To... fight." His entire body is shaking now, his breaths sporadic.

"Shh," is all I can muster in this moment. I don't have any words of comfort because I don't know how someone could comfort anyone in this moment. The only things rumbling inside my head are the questions I want to ask and the begging of him not to go.

What if he gets hurt? How am I supposed to do this without him? We were just beginning to... understand each other.

"I don't want to go, Ren," Zain admits, wiping his wet face and reddened eyes.

"I know," I whisper, pushing back the hairs that keep falling in his face.

"I'm scared."

"I know."

"I didn't know this would ever happen."

"I know."

"What if... what if I—"

"No." Zain looks up, his mouth agape, hearing me cut off his sentence. "You will be fine." His lip trembles for a moment before he bites it, nodding his head.

My chest feels like it is burning seeing him like this, to be thinking the things he's thinking. If he can't think positively, then I will. He has been my light through this journey thus far. Now I need to be his.

"You are smart, cunning and strong," I say, grabbing both his cheeks.

"War won't be like this. I won't be with you."

"Zain, war doesn't mean the end of all things. It often means the beginning of something entirely different. That's what the books I have read taught me."

"Books can only capture so much, Ren."

"Then improvise with the rest. Just like I've seen you do."

Zain nods and slaps his face with both his hands. He turns away from me and looks out towards the windows in our rented room. The wind picks up for a moment; the glass rattling against its frame. As he watches the window, I am watching him. The moonlight that is creeping in on our moment illuminates his tousled hair, giving it the appearance of golden waves. He starts to laugh, even though it sounds strained, and looks back at me.

"You get winded after talking that much?" he asks with an amused, but still teary, look on his face.

I give him a smile and shake my head.

"Such a chatterbug! I couldn't get one word in. You even cut me off!" Zain exclaims, putting his arm around my shoulders. I laugh and put my arm around him.

We lay back down, being as silent as possible.

The world will be stained, water damaged. That's what war does. I couldn't say that, though.

I try to memorise this feeling. Him in my arms, his arms wrapped around me. The warmth of his body hugging me tightly.

This is worse than leaving the tower, then watching it get destroyed. Knowing that in a few moments we will have to separate, and he will be joining in on a fight I cannot join him in.

When I was travelling with Em and the rest of the group, I was surprised at how much I enjoyed their company. I thought that's what friendship was, but with Zain... my whole heart feels like it is going to be leaving with him. I didn't think it was possible for me to care, to want something so badly.

I was just a servant boy who had never made a choice in his life, who never wanted anything other than to stay with his master in that tower. Now, I am greedy. I want my friend to stay with me.

"How did you know?" Zain shifts, hearing me ask my question. "That we would end up friends?"

Zain chuckles a bit and repositions himself on top of me, his chin resting on my chest so he can still meet my gaze. "You are the one who called me spoiled just the other day." He pokes my nose. "I always get what I want."

"I'm serious."

His eyes soften, and he sits up in my lap. "There was just this feeling. I thought you were the most handsome guy I'd ever seen, a little rugged and poor looking, but handsome none-theless. Then talking to you, it made me just want to break you out of that shell of yours."

Nodding, I sit up so we are face to face. He wraps his arms around my shoulders.

"Friends, huh?" Zain smirks, his face leaning in closer to mine. "What if I wanted—"

Pounds at the door send a shock through both of us, and in a moment, we are both standing, looking at the door.

"Zain. You were supposed to meet me at the gate," Shaw grumbles through the wood.

How did she find us?

"They really weren't kidding..." Zain trails off into a laugh. "I mean, I knew I was great, but man, being in such demand is exhausting." He drags his feet to answer the door. "Samir should have mentioned you were bringing Raiden with you." Zain opens the door and a familiar Shaw is leaning against the frame, though a new face is standing slightly behind her.

"Hey Zain," the woman, I am assuming is Raiden, greets Zain with a tight smile. "Shaw dragged me along, said she had a feeling you wouldn't show."

"I would have!" Zain says, putting his hands on his hips looking at Shaw. She tilts her head slightly. "Eventually..." he admits.

Raiden laughs, and Shaw shakes her head. "We are in a hurry. Grab your stuff." Shaw enters, walking past Zain.

She gives me a nod, and I nod back.

"Who are we fighting, anyway?" Zain asks, walking over to his pack, pulling out clothes to get dressed.

Shaw sits on the bed while Raiden tentatively walks into the room, her nose a little scrunched. "Does it matter?" Shaw asks.

"Yes," I mutter.

Shaw doesn't acknowledge my response.

"What he said," Zain says, pointing to me for a brief second.

Shaw sighs and leans back on her hands. "I'm not at liberty to discuss that with current company."

Now she glances at me.

Zain puts a fresh tunic on, grabbing his armour. "That's supposed to mean what?"

"That the King doesn't want Renatus being distracted from his current mission." Shaw's words are dry.

That tells me it's a country that the King believes would distract me.

The Hunter's Territory and the Felguard Country are considered allies. I don't think it would be reasonable or possible for them to be the cause of this war.

"Ren." Zain draws my attention back to him. He buckles the last strap of his chest piece. He starts walking towards me but stops, looking at both of the women standing in our room. "Do you mind giving us a moment?"

"A minute, then we are going." Shaw points to Zain's pack. Raiden walks over and grabs it. They both leave, Raiden closing the door behind them.

Turning back to Zain, he has already closed the distance between us. His hands caress my cheeks and he pulls my head down towards his, our lips colliding together.

He just...

I pull away, grabbing his hands with mine. My wide eyes and now agape mouth must be the reason for the soft chuckle escaping his lips.

"I love you, Renatus."

Lovebirds, lovers, more than. That's the feeling he was talking about. Not friends, buddies, companions, but something more.

My instincts take over, my lips meeting with his once more. I wrap my arms around him, letting myself consume what I can.

I want him.

He accepts my affection, giving in to my greediness.

I love him.

We stay together, hoping time itself freezes us in this moment.

CHAPTER
TWENTY

"I love you, Renatus."

I lay in bed, the morning sun shining in. His words, his lips, have been running through my mind since the moment that door closed and he left to fight a war against an assailant I have yet to figure out. I turn over onto my side and stare at the table that we should be eating breakfast at right now. When the woman knocked this morning, I simply ignored her. Food just didn't sound appealing, but now my stomach is making me regret that decision. A groan escapes my lips as I ball my fists and cover my eyes.

I wanted to respond. To tell him my own feeling, but Shaw meant it when she said a minute. I didn't even say goodbye to Bran and Gwen. Zain mentioned he would be taking them back with him before Shaw slammed the door shut.

Rolling onto my back, I let my fists fall onto the bed we will no longer be sharing. The unstained Renatus who was given the Master's purpose would have had no problem letting Zain leave; a part of him didn't even want Zain to come. There was a time where I had thought it crazy that the people of Ventraton did not all know or care for each other due to how close they all are to one another, and now I know it as a fact. Having Zain so close allowed me to know him, care for him, and have to deal with all those pesky annoyances of his. Being close allowed me to fall in love with him. Eventually, Lady Xylia stopped appearing in my dreams as she had. She stopped crying and started to smile before she disappeared altogether.

If she does come back, I plan to ask her about that.

My body flings upwards and I sit, staring intently out the window.

What if Zain stops to care for me now that we are no longer by each other's side?

I fall back into a lying position.

What if my own feelings change?

Shaking my head, I roll back onto my side. There is a definite reason for our separation. He said those words for reassurance, to let me know that our care for one another is not going to end just because of us going down different paths.

He has his own purpose, just as I have mine.

I sit up and walk over to my pack to start getting dressed.

Even if it takes me years to find this cloak and gauntlet, I will find my way back to him.

As I pull the leather chest piece over my head and buckle the straps, my eyes trained on the ocean view waving to me through the paned glass, a knock sounds at the door. I walk over to the door, opening it. My blood runs cold as I see Seodi standing on the other side. I quickly try to slam the door shut, but she throws her body against it to keep me from doing so. I let go of the door and take a few steps back. She walks in and closes the door behind her.

"Hey, Renatus." She smirks at me with her lips only.

This is terrible. I'm alone and now she is here for another tormented intimidation session.

"Saw that your dear friend left this morning. Such a shame he couldn't stay longer," she says, eyeing me up and down. "More fun for us, I guess."

Stay away from me.

Gritting my teeth, I take a few more steps back, slowly. My eyes glance towards the Master's pack.

A part of me believes she has rifled through my things since before she seemed clueless about the apparatus, but now knows some intimate details. I could just make a run for it.

My eyes focus back on her; she is looking at me with her head tilted slightly to the side. "Aw Ren, you wouldn't run out on a lady now, would you? That would be very rude manners." She walks up to the pack I had just been blatantly staring at. "May I?" Seodi points to the bag.

Master would probably not like that, but I don't think she is really asking.

Without my reply, she walks over, opens the pack and starts to pull out the clothes the Master provided me, the sack of gold coins, and every other book and item from the pack before lastly pulling out the red dyed journal I have read over a hundred times. Every word memorised, and every sigil has been seared into my brain. Seodi flips through the pages until she comes across a loose-leaf paper with the Master's scribbles written on it.

The incantation I am meant to do once I've obtained the apparatus.

"Answer me this time," I say, taking a shaking step forward, "why me?"

Seodi groans and leans her head back slightly. "Renatus, you really should just drop this."

"I have a right to know!" Seodi's head snaps towards me, hearing me raise my voice.

She chuckles, taking the loose-leaf paper from the journal before slamming it shut and letting it fall from her hand to the floor. "I really don't think you want to know."

I want to run, not be stuck in this room with her.

I ball my fists, my palms are sweating.

She raises an eyebrow and tsks, "Poor Renatus."

There is no reason to trust the reason she provides anyway, but I just want something. Even if it's a lie.

Seodi extends and points towards me. "You are the reason I am here." My eyes widen before quickly narrowing. "Sure, the apparatus are a part of it, but when I was in Ventraton, I was also there to collect you." I'm about to ask "why" again before her pointed finger is held up to signal me to remain silent. "Let's finish this talk while we go collect the cloak."

I am not going anywhere with her.

She gestures to the door, but my eyes don't leave hers. She chuckles and lowers her hand, seeing that I'm not moving. Seodi stalks closer to me, I step backwards, mirroring her forwards ones. "Or we could stay in and catch up."

My back pushes up against the window. "Where is the cloak?"

SEODI CLINGS ONTO MY ARM, playing into her part as well as her knowledge of how uncomfortable she makes me. One of her hands occasionally reaches up, playing in my overgrown locks. Her lips brush my cheek and graze my ear, Seodi doing anything she pleases.

I'm gonna be sick.

Biting down on my lip seems to be the only thing keeping it from trembling. Every touch I just try to imagine if it were Zain instead.

"Isn't this nice, darling?" Seodi chimes, her head now resting on my shoulder.

Her speaking ruins the illusion that is making me not throw up.

I hum while nodding once. A soft chuckle escapes her lips, and she squeezes my arm a bit tighter.

Don't grimace, don't grimace.

Seodi tugs on my shirt a bit, the signal she mentioned earlier when we first left the inn. I look down at her and she lightly points her chin in the direction of a massive abode just past a decadent and looming silver gate decorated with a scenic picture of the sea. There are four guards standing in front of it.

A part of me wants us to get caught, just to get her away from me.

"Let's take this road," Seodi chimes, turning us slightly just past the guards and down a thin alleyway between the gate and the houses on this side.

One of the guards nods his head towards me; I swallow the lump in my throat and nod back.

Well, they seem to be buying Seodi caressing, while I'm stuck here being tormented.

Her arms fall from mine as she reaches into a pouch strapped to her waist, hidden under her cloak. "Stand behind me slightly," Seodi whispers. I can see prepared spells neatly organised lining the interior of her pouch before I slow my pace down so I can walk a few steps behind her, nearly hiding her from the guards.

Seodi is a Forged Magicae user?

She brings one of the bottles to her lips, a few words being mumbled through them. Her fists tighten and the bottle cracks, a colourful array of lights outlining her body. The outline shifts from her body and suddenly disappears. I look down and where there had been a broken bottle in Seodi's hand is now gone and her pouch zipped up as if it had never been touched.

What was the spell she just used?

I lean closer, my curiosity driving my brave motion, smelling the still magicae-charged air around us. The smell of pickled radish and rosemary. There are a few other things I can't quite decipher from this brief inhale, but it definitely has mixed components a Forged Magicae user would use when casting a spell.

Sneaking a glance quickly in the direction we came, the guards seem to be oblivious to whatever Seodi is up to. The sound of the gate rattling slightly makes me jump and stop in my footsteps, Seodi continuing her same pace forward.

"Oi!" a deep voice shouts behind me. I turn and see two of the guards rushing towards us.

I look towards Seodi who hasn't even so much as glanced this way. Turning back to face the guards, I put on a smile. They quickly reach me and start to look around, at the fence, my hands and down the alleyway where Seodi is now a lot further ahead.

"What's the lady's hurry?" one of the guards, wearing a large blue pendant, asks, his hand resting on the hilt of his sword.

"Did you see what hit the gate?" the other guard, with a blue sash tied around his waist, asks.

Glancing between the two, I swallow harshly and lick my suddenly dry lips. "Uh..." I wipe my hands on my trousers. "She is not happy with me at the moment." My lips turn up into a meek smile, my shoulders shrugging slightly and head tilting to the side. "Her stubbornness probably caused her to ignore the sound of something hitting the gate and your shout."

The guard with a blue pendant nods, his eyes softening a bit and his pouting out. "Now that I understand, mate."

"You didn't see what hit the gate then?" the sashed guard asks, and I shake my head now, causing him to nod and move closer to the gate, inspecting it himself.

His face is a few millimetres away from the silver grid when the wind picks up a bit, tunnelling through this small alleyway. The gate shakes once more, and the sashed guard jumps back, drawing his weapon.

The pendant guard bursts into a fit of laughter and pats his jarred colleague's shoulder. "Bit a wind makes you lose control of your bowels, good boy?"

The sashed guard clears his throat and sheaths his blade. "No, sir. Of course not. Just thought I saw something."

"Right." The pendant guard chuckles before facing me. "Sorry to bother." He tips his head towards me, lifting an imaginary helmet and points with his thumb, signalling to the other guard to start moving back to their station.

They leave my company, and I quickly turn around to see Seodi completely out of sight.

Maybe if I can just get back to the inn quick enough, I can head out and circle back to the cloak a little later now that I know where it is.

"Stay right there," Seodi hisses.

I spin around, not a single living form standing near me.

"Where are you?" I whisper back, stilling my body, but my eyes dart every which way

I don't trust her and now she is watching me from an origin I cannot discern.

I can hear her monotone giggle sound from just ahead of me and on the other side of the gate. "Aw, are you worried?"

Rolling my eyes is an involuntary action, but I simply take a few steps back and place my back against the wall of the structure just behind me.

The gate rattles again; my eyes turned toward the guards who only glanced my way this time. Soft footsteps approaching me before I feel hands touching my chest.

What in the infernum?

I'm suddenly pinned against this wall and an invisible force is in front of me.

"Just relax, Renatus. It's just me," she teases. The hands leave me and a soft tremor starts within me.

Just?

I clench my jaw and I dig my nails into the palms of my hands, trying to stop myself from shaking.

Why are things like this? Why is she so terrifying?

I turn towards the way we had been heading before she disappeared and I start to put one foot in front of the other. Happy not to see those dead eyes of hers watching me as I do so. Whatever spell she cast must shade her from people's vision.

Shame I won't be able to learn that one.

"Renatus, are you mad?" she giggles from somewhere near me. "It's just a little invisibility spell. Don't worry. My beautiful self will return for your gazing pleasure in a few more minutes."

My eyes roll without hesitation, but the motion startles me a bit.

Don't let her catch you doing that.

Seodi hums softly behind me; the sound of her feet hitting the pavement sounds like a skipping rhythm.

"Seodi," I growl, looking over my shoulder and now see auburn hair and golden dead eyes.

Her lips curl into a wide smile, a few wrinkles forming around her mouth. She swings her arms back so her hands are intertwined with each other behind her.

Seodi raises her eyebrows and leans forward, glancing under my hair and up into my glaring blue orbs. "Yes?"

I blink slowly and give a glance in the direction she had disappeared to before returning to meet her gaze. Her mouth makes an "O" shape, and she straightens her posture. Seodi offers me a smirk before moving past me and continuing her skipping down the road.

Following behind, no one seems to be paying either of us any mind. The thought people might get the impression that she and I are friends or something more makes my stomach flip.

Would Zain see this as a betrayal?

"Ren! This way," Seodi calls out to me, taking a few steps into the doorway of a cafe.

There is a sign in the shape of a circle with a hole in the centre, painted a pale yellow colour with some small blue and pink lines.

Luk's place.

There are two large windows on either side of a blue painted door that matches the others in this city. Pastries stacked in decorative mounds in both windows. The smell wafting out of the shop as Seodi holds it open is more inviting than her calling me in.

"Welcome!" a man near the same height as Seodi says as he pops out from under the counter. He wears a vibrant smile and piercing blue eyes. "I am Luk; just step on up whenever you are ready. I am just going to quickly add these to the display." Luk shuffles out from behind the counter; his slightly pointed ears have a green tint to them.

Didn't his teeth have a slight sharpness to them as well?

As Luk adds a few more pastries to the towers already present in the store windows, Seodi grabs my wrist and pulls me towards the small case connected to the front counter.

Donuts, croissants, muffins, cookies, chocolates, all things I've never really thought about eating.

"I'm not normally a sweets kind of person, but you have me all buttered up," Seodi says, nuzzling my cheek with her nose. I hold back the gag that threatens my lips.

"Have you decided?" Luk asks, walking around us to back around the corner.

Seodi nods and leans over to point at the pain au chocolat. "Two please."

Luk leans forward a bit to see where she points and gives us another smile. "Well, of course! Please have a seat and I will bring those right out."

"We will be sitting outside," Seodi says, yanking on my arm.

Following her out, we sit at one of two patio sets that are out here. The white and blue striped umbrellas keep the sun from shining down on us. Luk comes out fairly soon after we take our seats and warm chocolate-filled croissants are now sitting in front of us. Seodi pays the amount due and Luk quickly disappears back into the store.

"So," Seodi says as she takes a bite.

I raise an eyebrow and clench my fists.

There is nothing I want more than to just find this cloak and get away from her.

She chews for a bit before swallowing. "That house is pretty out in the open. Not a lot of sneaking can be done, besides the side of the house that is facing the gate." She wipes a bit of chocolate off from the corner of her mouth before sticking the finger in her mouth. "There is a first floor window we would just need to shimmy open." Seodi takes another bite.

She wasn't over there for long. I doubt she found where the cloak was. Unless it was right there in the window.

"We will just need to rummage around for the cloak," Seodi says, confirming my thoughts.

I let out a sigh and lean forward, placing my head into my hands.

I wonder what Zain is doing right now. If he is imagining me sitting eating a pain au chocolat with a homicidal sociopath.

A tap on my shoulder causes me to stand, knocking over my chair and taking a few steps back from. I take ragged breaths as Seodi's dead eyes watch me.

"Renatus, what about my presence is so bothersome?" Seodi asks, gesturing to my standing and panicked form.

Bothersome? She thinks I am simply bothered by her? I am revolted.

"Y-you shouldn't have," I whisper, tears threatening to spill. "Don't ever touch me."

Her eyes widen, and she looks down at my uneaten food before grabbing it from my plate. "Hm, I see. Do you want me to tell you why this is so important?" Seodi asks, taking a bite out of my croissant while she pulls out that loose-leaf paper again.

I already know what it does.

Seodi chuckles, "You know, the thing I love most about you, Ren, is that you are so easy to read. Every little emotion or thought that crosses your mind is right there," she points to me, "all over your face. It's like only you and I are privy to this little language of yours." Seodi stands up. She walks up to me, and I hold my breath. She shoves the piece of parchment onto my chest and begins walking back towards the inn. "It's not what you think it is, because if you actually knew, you would have used it already."

"Then what?" I ask, walking behind her.

"To awaken the **accursed punarjanmam**."

The what?

"I'm not surprised your master didn't tell you. I mean, then he would have to explain how he took you from the care of the Domi Nostrae," Seodi whispers as she unlocks and opens the door to my rented room.

I shouldn't believe a word she says. I have memories of my parents, faded, but they are still there.

She looks over her shoulder and smiles at me. "I'm not lying, Ren." We walk in and I storm over to the bed and sit down. Seodi shuts the door and sits on one of the chairs at the table. "I knew your caretakers from the Domi Nostrae, the ones you were stationed with in Draco." My eyes widen a bit, hearing her say that name. "They used to tell me about how handsome and intelligent you were." Her words leave my breath halting, and fists gripping the edges of the bed tightly.

My parents? How did she know them? They talk about me? When was this? Did they send her after me? Do they want the apparatus?

Seodi chuckles, biting down on her lower lip. I stand from my seat, my eyes scanning the floor as I try to remember the details of my life. "Sorry, maybe this is too much for you, but I'll keep going anyway." I hear Seodi stand from her seat. "Your mother, Dianatha, and your father, Elikai, well adoptive parents, took you from your birth mother's womb. Was such a blessing that she went into labour when travelling past one of our training facilities in Vlona." I feel her grip my shoulders and begin to massage them. "Of course the Domi Nostrae noticed what you were by the pretty little birthmark you have on the back of your neck, and just in case murdering your birth parents wasn't enough cover, we sent your adoptive parents and you to Draco to live a humble poor man's life until we had Aruna's apparatus."

This is all a lie.

Her hands move from my shoulders and into my hair. "Things were going smoothly, until one day, out of the blue, Babylas decided to betray us. Killed your caretakers and stole you away for himself." Her chest presses up against mine. "Quite honestly, the Domi Nostrae weren't sure what to do. They could have killed him, stolen you back, but then our high priestess figured that the day would come that Babylas himself would send someone out to collect the apparatus and could do all the finding for us." Her nose brushes against mine, her breath now on mine. "That time has come, and he sent you out so unaware, unprepared, ill-equipped for what you were really facing. Maybe he thought that quiet temperament would leave you a hermit. That you would go unnoticed." Her lips graze against mine. "I thought that he would have done a better job, you being his apprentice and all, but it looks like you really are just a quiet little servant boy, after all."

Grabbing the dagger from my belt, I grip the back of her head and spin us around, tackling her onto the bed. I push a bit off of her just enough so I can place the blade against her throat just like she had done to me. "I hate you." The words seethe out of me.

I want her to feel like how I felt when she tortured me in that healing ward. How I feel every time she touches me. I want her to be afraid.

CHAPTER TWENTY-ONE

"I think that's enough for tonight. You have a big day tomorrow," Mother says, closing the storybook she's been reading me.

She looks towards me. I smile, but she just sets the book down on the nightstand table. Mother stands and walks out of the room, closing the curtain that substitutes a door. Father said a door was for hiding things and removed it from its hinges.

"Night, Mother," I say, snuggling myself into the hemp blanket mother and I knit together.

Both Father and Mother keep talking about tomorrow. Maybe we are going to be celebrating something, just like we did my birthday last year.

I giggle thinking of the colourful feathers Mother strung together to make that necklace. I wore it so often the string snapped. Now the feathers rest inside a small chest Father whittled.

"If you keep that up, your mother is going to scold you," Father whispers to me, only his head peeking through the curtain. With seeing and hearing my father, I sit up, causing him to step fully into the room so he can gently push me back down into a lying position. "Shhh, I meant it. I just wanted to tuck you in." He pulls the blanket up to my nose, tickling it, causing it to scrunch and wiggle. Father leans down and kisses my forehead; some words whispered, but no sound reaches my ears.

The curtains shift open and Father quickly sits up, my head turning towards a distraught Mother standing in the doorway, holding open the curtains. "He needs rest. Leave him be," Mother hisses, and Father holds up his hands in defence.

"I called for him!" I lie to ease Mother's tension.

She stomps over to the bed; the curtains falling from their held position. "That's enough." She pulls Father off the cot I sleep on and tucks the blanket under my sides. "Sleep. Now," Mother scolds.

Mother stands upright from her bent position, grabbing Father's arm, and they leave me to rest.

It only felt like a moment from when I closed my eyes last night, but the birds are already singing their good mornings and the sun peeks through the glassless window. I sit up, adjusting my nightshirt to its correct position. My feet hit the cold wooden planks and I scramble past the bedroom curtain and see an empty kitchen and bed as I rush through the only other room in our house.

"Mother? Father?" I call out, silence being the only one to greet me.

Maybe they are outside.

My feet pound hard as I run out of the front door and see Hunk, our goat, gnawing on one of Father's handker-chiefs. "Give that back, Hunk!" I whine, walking over, grab-bing the bit of cloth not in his mouth and pull the eaten fabric out.

Father is not going to be happy Hunk ate another one. Maybe Father will actually cook him up this time.

I wrap my arms around Hunk. "I'll hide it. Maybe he won't notice."

The sound of horse hooves sound from down the road, stealing my attention from my dear friend. Each hoof shakes the ground as it nears closer. Its long, dark mane contrasts its stark white body. An old man is riding on top of it. He rides up until his eyes land on mine.

"Hello, child," he says, clearing his throat afterwards. "I come from town where I just spoke to your parents. They seemed to have been wanting to get rid of you for quite some time, and I have offered to take you off their hands."

What?

"Maman! Papa!" I scream, tears already streaming down my face. I quickly cling to Hunk, who has found something else to gnaw on.

"Hush, youngin. You are now my servant. I am your master. Stop crying over matters that no longer matter." His sharp tone stops my verbal crying. Uneven breaths, tears and nose sniffling still remain. This stranger sighs and holds out his hand, expecting me to take it.

I shake my head and start taking steps backwards.

Why aren't they here? Who is this old man? Why is he saying these things?

"Come!" he shouts, his voice shaking me to my core. "I can see why your parents wanted to rid themselves of you! You spoiled, unlearned child!"

"You're lying! You are just a mean old man!" I shout back, snot now running from my nose faster than I can stifle it. "Just leave me alone! My father will be back soon!"

The old man jumps down from his horse. Suddenly, a carriage I did not see or hear coming now pulls up behind his steed. He greets them with a wave before stepping towards me.

I scream and shout as I trip on my backward step, unable to escape his approach.

A cold hand makes contact with my cheek, silencing me completely. "Enough! I should have not had to pay the sum I did with such a noisy brat like you."

My eyes stare at the ground, still shocked from the contact of his hand to my skin.

Mother and Father don't want me anymore?

"Drink this and we can begin our journey to my tower," the old man says, putting a small vial of a blue liquid in front of my eyeline. "Drink!"

I quickly take the vial from him and swallow its bitter contents. Instantly, my vision begins to blur; two Hunks appear in front of me, gnawing Father's handkerchiefs. The old man producing two heads.

"Old man? I don't feel good," I whimper, my stomach feeling upset from the motion of my vision.

He chuckles and pats my head, ruffling my hair. "All a part of the process, Renatus."

"That's not my name," I mutter.

"It is now. I am Babylas Amara, and my gift to you on this day of jointment is your new name. Renatus Amara. Remember it well." He picks me up from the ground, carrying me to the carriage. I can hear the door open, but my eyelids are now too heavy to open.

"I can't say I don't like this side of you," she says with a strained voice from the pressure I am putting on her throat.

I press a little harder, a thin line of crimson streaming down her neck and onto the bed. "No more lies, Seodi!" I yell, my spit hitting her face. "I am done being tormented by you. There is no ownership, companionship, or even friendship between us."

"Oh yeah? Then just kill me, Ren. Do it. Take me off the

threat list." I can feel her push against my arm just enough for her to talk without struggling. "Do it!" she screams.

Something comes over me and hearing her scream makes me want to do it all the more. I scream back at her, my eyes not blinking or looking away, and I see in Seodi's something that looks an awful lot like fear.

What am I doing?

I push myself off of her, retracting the blade. She gasps for breath, but a smile is still resting on her face. I throw the dagger to the ground. It punctures the wood, stone like shards shoot out from the blade itself puncturing it some more.

This is not what I want.

Bringing up my hand, it's shaking, just like my whole body. "Get out." I hiss, not looking towards her.

The bed shifts under her moving weight, then her footsteps make their way out of the room. "Seodi," I whisper, hearing the door creak open.

I shiver, feeling her hands press down onto my shoulders. "Yeah?"

"After we get this cloak, I want you to tell me what the accursed punarjanmam is."

"Of course." There is no point in looking, I know she is smiling.

The door closes behind Seodi as she leaves me to let the tears of confusion roll down my face. So much information coming at me all at once.

Am I supposed to just believe her?

Shaking my head, I unstrap the chest plate, letting it fall to the floor before ripping off the shirt the Master gifted me. The torn fabric slips past my hips and joins the chest plate to rest on the wooden flooring. A whimper escapes my lips.

Bending down, I pick up my shirt before bawling it up and

throwing it at the wall. I bite down on my arm, hard, and scream.

The ceiling is crumbling around me.

"Who am I?" I mutter against my bleeding forearm.

Storming over to the table in the room, I grab the chair and throw it against the wall, breaking it into pieces just as my resolve has.

Seodi was right? Was everything she said my reality?

I grab the second chair and throw it, to share a similar fate with its match.

Those dreams, Vasile and Madi believe me to be someone else, maybe it's not so crazy. Am I him? Am I living another person's second chance? What about my parents? If they are not my blood, then who is?

All these questions I had no desire in learning cycles ago are now flooding my brain, and my heart desiring the answers. My feet carry me to the bed, where I bend over and start slamming my fists into the feathered mattress. The blood dripping from my forearm is staining the white cotton.

THE STREETS ARE much quieter at night. Only guards, maintaining their posts, are awake and watching. Seodi is leading the way as we duck in and out of alleyways, hide behind store boards left on the cobblestone roads, and run when a guard hears me stumbling behind Seodi. It is nearly impossible to see as the moon is not shining down onto us, and the little light that is visible is either through curtained windows or through the lanterns the guards carry with them on their belts.

My palms are clammy and stomach turning. Not over the fact we are going to break into someone's home, or that I am going to be stealing for the second time, or that I am working with a person who disgusts me. It is an accumulation of all three, the last fact being the biggest contributor.

But she knows the answers to the questions I have. As much as I want to run, to have her leave me be, I know I can't and that she won't.

I can feel the tears threatening to spill knowing that I am no longer, as Babylas once said, innocent. My ceiling has been reduced to crumble, just like the tower.

I have nothing but curiosity, or maybe it's hope, pushing me to move.

My eyes shift around from the surroundings of the night ridden city and the back of Seodi's head. The snail pace at which we are moving unfortunately gives me ample time to glance her way and notice that she glances back every so often herself. Most likely making sure I am keeping up with the pace she is setting and I'm sure to make sure I haven't bolted on her.

Gives me some comfort that she knows I don't like her.

The large gate that halted my entrance earlier today is now just up ahead. Seodi stops in her tracks and looks up at the building I was pressed up against earlier. Voices emerge from the left of us, the dim lantern light now growing brighter as the voices grow louder.

"We're going up," Seodi hisses, grabbing a bottle from her pouch, quickly activating the prepared spell.

She grabs my hands, and slowly her feet begin to lift from the ground. With our hands connected, my arms left above my head until the strain of being lifted hits me and my feet are no longer touching any sort of surface. The voices reach the corner of the alley we are currently levitating in. I look down and see that we are just barely higher than eyesight. I hold my breath and hold on to Seodi for dear life as two guards appear on the street. One of them, slimmer than most of the others guards, peers down the alleyway for a mere second before he continues his conversation with his colleague.

We continue to rise until Seodi positions us over the building's slated blue shingled roof. "You are so heavy," her words struggling to escape.

I smile.

As much as I do not want to be dropped, it is kind of funny seeing her actually struggle at something.

"Just a little more." She breathes as we now continue to move forward, slowly passing the gate.

I wonder if I combined this spell with the movement spell if this could be a quicker means of transportation. Though the more complex the spell, the harder it is to actually master.

Slowly, we make our way over the top of the target house. We begin to lower until our feet find purchase on the roof.

As Seodi lets go, I feel myself shift, my boot kicking loose one of the shingles. I wince, hearing the ting of it hit the gate and then the thud of it hitting the ground.

"Well, now that that's done." Seodi sighs. She tilts her head towards the western end of the house.

Carefully watching my step, I follow closely behind her to the edge of the house. My heart is pounding knowing I am going to be entering someone's house. Stealing from the museum was nerve-racking, but this feels completely wrong.

"Is there another way?" The question slips out as I peer over to the window Seodi told me would be the easiest one to get into.

Seodi punches my shoulder, my hand immediately covering the pummelled spot. "Renatus, this is not the time to let your morals ruin this perfectly good bonding moment between us."

Well, her saying this was a bonding moment has now made this whole thing a lot worse.

"These people aren't the type to just hand something over. The clock was bought off the undertrade. You knowing that they have it is enough of a threat for them to kill you," Seodi says, grabbing the edge of the roof. "Now, grab my ankles so I can unlock the window."

If that's true, then this is a lot more dangerous than I thought.

Grabbing Seodi's ankles and making sure I have good footing, she leans over the edge and leaves my sight. I hear small tinks and clicks until a soft creak lets me know she was successful. I feel her tug her feet away three times before I let go. Waiting for just a moment, I then follow, gripping onto the edge and lowering my feet down first. Seodi grabs them and leads them to the window ledge.

This is where being tall comes in handy.

I let go and step down inside the house.

No going back now.

Seodi points to the door down the hall before running a finger across her neck.

So not that door.

I nod, and she gives me a thumbs up before heading down the staircase. Scurrying over to the door directly to my right, I gently test the knob to see if it is locked. It turns with ease and so I quietly open it. Luckily, probably thanks to the servants most well-to-do folk have, the door's hinges are well oiled and don't creak. Sneaking into the moonlit room, I see a large desk in the back centre, bookcases lining either side of the room, and a cushioned seat in the corner behind the door with a small side table resting next to it.

Must be the study.

I close the door, not seeing any chests or clocks plainly

insight. I cross the long hallway I am in and over to the room residing next to the stairway, glancing down quickly to make sure I won't be spotted taking my time. I test the door again to see if it is locked, but it opens with ease. Glancing in, I nearly scream seeing three figures standing in front of the window, but they do not move or seem to notice my entrance. I then see a spinning wheel to the right of me, bookcases filled with fabrics, twine and yarn.

A sewing room.

I close the door behind me and walk over to the mannequins. One of them is wearing a long flowy dress that is reminiscent of the night sky, the other wearing a suit that looks the colour of gold, and the third a cloak that matches the sketch the Master provided me of the **Lovers Cor**. I strip the headless doll of the cloak and roll it up to fit into my satchel. Making my way back to the door, I peer out and see the hallway is still empty. I bolt to the window. Looking back, the door at the end of the hallway is open, but no one is standing inside of it. I quickly climb out and reach up to grab the roof's edge. I kick off the edge and pull myself up, crawling a little further up before laying down and panting as just getting up took every ounce of strength I have. I look around the roof and don't see Seodi anywhere.

I hope she made it out alright.

Taking a risk, I glance over the edge and don't see an expecting hand to pull up, but a head sticking out and looking down at the ground. I pull my head back and cover my mouth with my hand.

They definitely know we are here.

My body freezes, and my breath is shaky.

What am I supposed to do? I'm stuck up here without her.

"I said stop!" a man's voice bellows out from somewhere in front of the house.

That was not for me, they wouldn't be able to spot me.

I carefully stand and walk over to where I heard the commotion. Seodi is surrounded by a handful of guards. Her belt pack in the hands of one of them.

She doesn't have her spells. She's going to get caught unless I do something.

"You have nowhere to go. Let us take you in peacefully or it will be your head," the guard holding her pack says.

"I know the laws here; it'll be my head, regardless." Seodi reaches down and pulls a dagger from her boot.

I could just run. I have the cloak. I have no witness.

Clenching my fist, I bite down on my knuckle.

That would make me no better than her.

Reaching into my satchel, past the cloak, I pull out the air spell. It could wake up the whole city if I concentrate hard enough. I take out its contents, making the sigil in the air, before pouring the contents of the vial into my hand. I ball my fist and put the small gap to my lips before blowing the contents out of my hand, focusing on the point a few metres in front of Seodi. The grains of salt crackle into small flashes of green before a bright light comes crashing down from the sky, striking the ground where I had intended it to go.

Hopefully that's enough of a distraction.

With lightning, there is always a loud bang that rings through the air. The glass from the windows on the house rattle. The light fades, and Seodi is gone.

I should take my leave as well.

I make my way over to the side of the house where the gate is.

This is going to hurt.

Taking in a few deep breaths, I jump. Just barely making it over the fence, my body crashes onto the cobblestone alley. The air escapes my lungs and pain radiates through my left ankle. I bring up my arm and start screaming into the fabric covering it.

I have to get up. I have to move.

Tears of pain trickle down my face and I bite my lip as grunts escape while I try to stand. I stumble through the alleyway into the next one. I take out a piece of cloth from my satchel and shove it into my mouth to muffle any whimpers that find their way out.

Such a bad idea. Did I really just jump from a roof?

Zain would be first worried and then immediately bully me non-stop for doing something so stupid.

I push the ache for him away for the moment and make my way to the main road. I look left and right, not seeing any guards. Limping from store door to store door, I test each one of them until one opens with ease. I reach up and grab the chime that is ready to alert everyone here that I've entered and squeeze through. Gently, I close it and move to the side, just out of view of anyone passing by.

I'm lucky all the guards are probably still distracted by the commotion at that house.

Rolling up the cuff of my trousers, I take a sigh of relief not seeing a protruding bone or broken open skin. It's swollen though and not in good shape. I lean back against the wall and wipe my sweaty brow.

Note to self: never do that again.

I will need to go see a healer in the morning unless Seodi knows anything about healing.

I wonder if she got away.

Closing my eyes, I focus on my breathing, trying to calm myself down. I can't stay here, but I need things to quiet down a bit before I head back out. I reach into my satchel and pull out the spell the Master scribbled out for me. The one Seodi says is to awaken the accursed punarjanmam. There is no reason to trust her, but the only way for me to really know is doing it. Master never said that I could only use it once, and that seems important enough of a detail that he would have shared it with me.

It's just a few words. Just a few materials.

I reach into my satchel and grab the herbology kit the Master gifted me. I unlatch the lid and pull out a strand of corn husk, ginger, ground yerba santa and the small vial of water. I place all the dry ingredients in my mouth before swallowing it down with the water.

What do I want?

Focusing on the centre of my torso, I mutter the incantation, "**Mors et nativitas unum sumus.**"

CHAPTER TWENTY-TWO

I am floating in an endless landscape of black, but turning, I see her smiling at me.

Xylia.

She is crying again. Her face is viable as a clear blue sky is on a sunny day. Xylia smiles and opens her arms and I go running. Embracing her as she embraces me. We slowly separate and I am in a red stained wooden cabin. Green light pouring in from the window and Xylia in a red tinted suit of armour.

"Now go back to bed." She chuckles, shoving my chest away a bit.

I smile and grab her hand, pulling her in closer. "Don't go." My plea causes her brow to furrow and break our eye contact.

"Codrin. Not yet." She rips her hand away from me and I bite my lip.

It will never be time. Her love for this clan supersedes her love for me.

I take a few steps back before turning to sit on the edge of the bed. She sighs and joins me, placing her hand over mine. Glancing towards her, I can see she is struggling to tell me something, to explain her thoughts. Nothing about her face or gesture could prove or suggest my knowledge, though.

I just know.

"Vasile has been itching to join the hunters. He keeps failing the whole listening part of the test portion, though." I flip my hand over to intertwine our fingers. "Maybe he will listen to you."

Xylia laughs and shakes her head. "I'm not even sure if the terrifying thought of the Ashen Lands could get him to listen to someone other than those idiotic impulses of his."

"Yeah, he is not the best at staying on task." I join in on her laughter by adding my own half hearted chuckle. "But he's our dearest friend."

She inhales sharply and bites her cheek. "Think we could change that?" Xylia kids.

"Unfortunately, we signed on with him for life. I think he plans to be buried in between us when we all go."

I look behind us, as the wind picks up, shaking the foliage from the enormous trees of the Vermilion forest. I turn back and see Lidia and her short brown hair as she is holding a cloth to her face.

"I can't believe he did that!" She yells, kicking a bucket. I stand from the bar stool I am sitting on and rush over to her. I grab her hand that is holding the cloth and try to pull it away. She rips herself away from me. "You won't love me anymore."

I narrow my gaze and storm over to her, pushing her until she is pinned between me and the empty tavern wall. "That is impossible." My lips are only inches from hers. I push off the wall and take my shirt off, showing her the multitude of scars covering my body. "Can you still love me?"

Lidia nods, her lip quivering. "Always," she whispers with a shaky breath.

I rush back to her, our lips colliding.

As we pull apart, Elmric smiles and laughs before putting a hand up to cover his tusked mouth. "I never took you for the assertive type, Ordell."

I laugh and nod, taking a few steps back. "I'm not sure what overcame me. I just really wanted to do that."

"Well, I would be lying if I said I hadn't thought about doing that every day since I met you." Elmric rubs his hand on his bald orcish head. "Promise me it won't be the last time."

"I'm okay making that promise," I say, a big smile plastered on my face.

Glancing towards my feet, I curl my toes in glee before I look up and see a raven-haired woman standing on the edge of the sister peaks. "Ayla. You are damning Aruna by doing this," I mutter, the gushing water from the Jako River that was newly formed only a day prior nearly drowns me out.

"You have no idea what you speak of," she says, turning around, shoving a piece of parchment into my hands. "I warned her, and I will not lose her over some pathetic whim."

Glancing down at the parchment I was handed, it goes into the details of how the apparatus are used together.

I ONCE BELIEVED I was naïve, unaware of so much. A child still learning about everything that moves, breathes, and exists here in Vitaterrium, but as the spell's components slide down my throat and the words escape my lip, there seems to be little that is now left unknown.

The seasons come and go, my face never altering despite my death and rebirth and death and rebirth and death and rebirth – the cycle going on and on. It's as if each separate life and the one I am living now are trying to fit together like a puzzle that is only missing one piece. I am watching their experience from both inside and outside their minds.

Every item I touched, laugh shared, story told, moments passed are showing themselves to me. Key moments of my lives over the last five hundred sidereal years.

CHAPTER TWENTY-THREE

"**Where in the infernum were you?**" Seodi says, opening the door to my room. I stumble in and collapse onto the floor just a metre in.

She sighs and squats down next to me. I place an arm over my eyes, still overwhelmed by the pain, and more so the information rolling around in my mind. She grabs my ankle and I kick at her with my non-injured leg. She quickly lifts her hands up in defence, not aware of the situation.

"I just jumped off a roof," I mumble.

"Yeah, and I had a lightning bolt nearly singe off my eyebrows. We all have our problems." I tilt my head up at her as she slowly lifts the cuffs of my trousers up. "Ouch," she says, raising her eyebrows.

Seodi stands and walks over to my pack. She pulls out the healing balm I once used on Zain, as well as some cloth. She sets the items down before walking away again to one of the chairs. Seodi grabs it by the legs before smashing it onto the floor, pieces of wood flying everywhere.

"Seodi," I hiss.

She pays me no mind, grabbing two pieces roughly the same size. "Gotta get you walking somehow," she mutters.

Guess she has a point.

Seodi takes her time dressing my ankle, making it good enough for me to limp around without grimacing from the pain. Even though I know she is doing this to help me, or maybe herself, it is hard for me not to flinch every time I feel her touch me.

"You didn't answer my question," she says. I sit up and scoot away from her a bit before leaning against the wall and tilting my head. "Where were you?"

I shrug.

She was right. My master lied, hid the truth. If she was telling the truth about the incantation, maybe all of it was the truth.

A chill runs through my body, releasing now that I am not sure of my path forward. My life was based on a devotion to someone who put me in the position of a servant. Collection Aruna's Apparatus has lost its original purpose.

Xylia is the only reason I have a purpose for them still.

I furrow my brow and tilt my head upwards towards the ceiling. There is a chance to bring Xylia back, the person only nineteen sidereal years ago I was planning my life with. The cabin is far from judgmental eyes and Rose's influence.

Rose is in the dungeon of the castle.

I grab my head and shake it a bit.

Engel was in the dungeon. My brother. Why would he be there? I can't believe I didn't recognise him. No. I didn't know him then. I know now.

I slowly begin to tug on my hair.

Zain. What happens when Xylia comes back? What am I supposed to do?

"Renatus, if you don't stop doing, that I will tie your hands to your side," Seodi says, walking up, smacking my head. "You did it, didn't you?"

I slowly look up to meet her gaze.

She doesn't need confirmation.

I push off the wall and stumble a bit as I try to stand.

The Adamina Clan was destroyed and rebuilt. The apparatus were meant to strip someone of their immortal life. I knew Aruna and Ayla. I lived in Idyllia and died when the doorway opened.

Seodi grabs my shoulders and leads me to the bed. "Ren, you gotta block it out. Focus on where you are right now. Everything you are seeing is in the past. You have your own life right now."

Milla and Kinny, my kids. I held them as they died. I told them their favourite story as they fell into eternal sleep.

Tears begin to stream down my face.

That dream, with Xylia. That's how I died, how I was taken away from her and placed into the life I am living now.

"The life I'm living now," I shakily mutter.

"Yes. The life you are living right now has nothing to do with what happened a long time ago," Seodi says, sitting down next to me.

"But it does," I say, looking over at her. "Xylia was the love of my life. Zain is the son of my best friend. I met Kage the night I died in the Vermilion Forest. My clan leader and brother are in the dungeon of Fosa. It is all relevant. Even the instructions to the apparatus are engraved in my memory."

Seodi stands, rushing over to my pack once more, pulling out the Master's – Babylas's – journal along with a piece of charcoal. "You should write it down. Memories can fade in and out over time. If you don't do it, the instructions could be lost forever."

I nod, taking the journal and charcoal from her. I sketch out the very journal page Ayla provided me.

She takes the journal as I finish, looking it over with raised brows.

"How do you know so much about what is happening?" I ask in a hushed tone.

Her eyes close, and she looks away from me. "From experience. You are not the only accursed punarjanmam." She looks back towards me. "My brother is one, and he let the past take over his present. That's why when you came along, I was assigned to watch over you."

"Why do you torment me, punish me?" I add. Her eyes widen a bit. "You are still mad at your brother for leaving you behind instead of the past."

Seodi punches me in the face, and I grab my now bleeding nose. I tilt my head back to limit the amount of blood dripping out.

"Mind your mouth and get ready to go," Seodi growls, reaching into her pocket and pulling out a marble with a familiar sigil engraved into it.

Seodi and I appear in the middle of a field, damp grass glueing themselves to my boots and trousers. I glance around until my eyes fall on the familiar ever-so-towering walls that protect the capital of the Felguard Country.

Fosa.

Turning back to face Seodi, she is smiling with her arms crossed across her chest. "Renatus, I need you to know that this is not personal against you." Something hard smacks against my head, the blow knocking me straight to the ground. I am able to catch myself by grabbing onto Seodi, who throws me to the ground the moment I do. I roll onto my back and see a familiar black-eyed man standing over me.

Azrail.

He motions with his finger that he wants me to flip over. Remembering the terrifying massacre, I do as instructed. I roll onto my stomach. My arms are tugged and creak a bit as he rips my pack off of me.

"I am going to be needing these," Seodi says, opening the pack and taking out the cloak and Babylas's journal. "I'm not going to lie, when I first came by your room in Yral and searched your bag, I was pretty impressed with that fact you thought to send off all the other apparatus with Zain when he left." I figured she noticed after she emptied my bag when she first grabbed the journal out of it.

Especially since I always pack away the journal at the top.

"You made a big mistake in that same instance, though, thinking that the apparatus would really be safe with the King of the Felguard Country around," Seodi says, stepping around me so she can look me in the eyes. "You have no idea who that imposter king really is, what he's done to obtain the throne he sits on." I glance from Seodi to Azrail and then back.

The night of my death... Codrin flashes to the forefront of my mind. "I can imagine quite a bit."

"Not just a bit. He used to buy beasts from the Domi Nostrae. Killed his own family, used Xylia as the sword his own father had intended her to be originally. Imprisoned people just because he didn't like them." I watch Seodi fester, her eyes darkening. "He didn't even tell you that on the day you arrived, the news of your master's death was sent out by carrier **locquins**. He chose not to tell you."

The jumbling of information stops for a moment hearing her words.

The Master is dead. Babylas is dead.

I knew that he would likely pass during my travels and I thought my world would feel more broken or stained hearing of his passing, but he is not my master. He is a man who gave me the power to see the truth, and nothing more.

"The King is evil," she mutters.

He is not innocent, that is for sure, but that's not what she actually cares about.

"Who did he take from you?" I ask.

Her eyes widen and then narrow. She storms up to me, grabbing my collar. "He stole him away and threw him in a dungeon to rot!"

There were only three people in the dungeon.

"They all seemed content, the people I saw down there." Seodi throws me back into the ground. I let out a moan of pain and try to take a deep breath to calm myself.

"Doubtful; my father has never been one to be content," she hisses.

The old man that was down there?

"I am not going to let him spend the rest of his life down there." Her voice shakes a bit.

Seems she hasn't had the most stable family dynamic.

"So, what is your plan?"

"Your little boyfriend is going to be the one to bring us the apparatus," she confesses.

I shake my head. "Zain would never just hand them over."

"Well, let's hope for your sake he cares more about you than his country."

After a few moonshifts of walking and limping, we arrive at the gate. Seodi has hold of the parchment the King gave me in one hand while the other is wrapped around my arm. The moment she made it clear that I would be the bait, she threatened to hunt Zain down and kill him out of spite if I tried to run away and warn him.

A part of me hopes Zain doesn't care for me at all, so I do not put him in harm's way.

Seodi holds the dagger against my back. I bite my lips as it's pierces me slightly as our steps are uneven.

She's smart, though, hiding it under my cloak like she is.

Azrail went ahead to hand off the ransom letter for Zain, taking my pack with him, but Seodi allowed me to keep my satchel. We are apparently going somewhere just a little further out of the east gate that leads into the Vermilion Forest. The threat of monstrous creatures gives her the purpose of allowing me to have my prepared spells.

Of course, within reason, she is keeping a close eye on every movement I make.

Someone bumps into me, knocking Seodi and me apart. "Watch it!" Seodi snaps, scrambling to hide her dagger and get back to my side.

"Heh, sorry! Guess I really have had one too many," a familiar burly bearded man says, patting my shoulder.

I look at Seodi, whose face is paler than normal and has a rare look of fear in her eyes.

"Darius," she whispers.

"Little sis! Look at you trying to show your stuff. I'm still the master in this scenario and it shows," he says with a laugh.

The accursed punarjanmam.

"You are the master of no one. You are nothing but a traitor!" She bares her teeth, her chin trembling slightly.

From what time do I recognise him?

"Hm, well, I made my own little dojo. So, I am a master, just looking for my first student yet — oh hey!" he says, shaking me slightly. "Why don't you join! It'll be fun. I'm a pretty laid-back guy as long as we are all on the same page."

"Ren, do not listen to him. He is a pathological liar," Seodi says, reaching out and grabbing my arm.

Darius tsks and shakes his head, their relation starting to shine just a tad through their same-coloured golden eyes.

I met him in Jod with Em and the Ventraton guards.

"Hm, you both are making great points," I mutter, glancing between them. "This seems like a family matter, though." I give them a forced smile and take a few steps back before turning from them completely, slipping from Seodi's grasp.

Darius laughs, which stops me in my tracks. "Kids got some spunk, S." I look back over my shoulder and see their bodies facing me. "Too bad it's not enough in this kind of situation, though." He tilts his head.

Seodi shoves Darius slightly and storms up to me, but before she can grab me, Darius reaches forward himself, grabbing Seodi by her hair, pulling her back. He spins her towards him so he can grab her by the throat, lifting her up from the ground. She kicks her legs, but he just smiles at her, unphased by her desperate defence.

"You've really changed Renatus; makes me think that your eyes have been opened to the real truth."

I doubt my lying is going to be convincing enough to really stop him, but telling the truth won't do me any good either.

My eyes are trained on Seodi's paling face and agape mouth. "Not sure what you mean."

Even if it's not convincing, it's a lot easier to lie to him than a king.

Seodi falls to the ground, gasping for air. My gaze moves from her and onto her brother, who steps towards me now, grabbing me by my hair and pulling me in so close that our noses are touching. "Let's cut to the chase, kid. I want the apparatus from Aruna. I know Seodi sent that freak off to bait them out of that fancy vault the King's got. I also know they plan on telling him to meet you at the edge of the city near the eastern gate." He pushes me off, and I collapse to the ground. "We're going to go ahead and let Seodi catch her breath, and hope she realises that staying away is probably in her best interest."

He sighs and that docile smile he wears comes back. "I'm excited to meet that boy you've been running around with."

"Zain is only dropping them off," I say clearly, standing up.

Darius chuckles and nods. "Yeah, and if you do anything to stop that from happening, I will make that cute little scene Seodi put together in the Ashen Lands look like youngins play after I show what I can do to that handsome face of his."

I swallow hard and ball my fists.

No one is touching him.

"Got it?"

"Got it."

Darius nods and glances down at his sister. "It was nice catching up with you, sis! We should grab a drink next time." He pulls a tobacco roll out of his pocket and brings it to his lips. Darius puts the ring on his thumb to the end of it, mumbling something under his breath before a small flame ignites it. White smoke comes tumbling out as he exhales.

His eyes meet mine, and they widen. He reaches back into his pocket and offers me one.

What is wrong with this guy?

I shake my head, refusing his offer.

"Alrighty then, let's go!" He points with his nose in the direction Seodi was leading me.

I glance down towards Seodi for just a moment, but can register her hunched over form, her eyes glued onto the cobblestone path she's kneeling on. All that work she's put in, the pain she's put me through, the lives she took to obtain what she was after, is all thrown away, just like that.

Darius' stride takes him ahead of me, and I stop in my tracks, limping back towards her, leaning down to her level. "I really thought you were stronger than that." Pulling back, I see a few drops drip from her face.

I really don't want to go with him, but I really don't have a choice about it.

We begin down the path, Darius ahead of me.

He smokes his tobacco roll, smoke floating its way out of his lungs with every exhale. The smell is sharp, and I cough every once in a while if I inhale too much of it. As the dim light at the bud's tip burns away the paper and tobacco, Darius sighs and flicks the small piece off into the street.

Fosa is silent, no lights to illuminate the dark path we are headed towards.

"How long do you think it'll take your guy to sneak the apparatus away?" Darius asks, lighting another tobacco roll.

He glances over his shoulder, raising his brow, expecting an answer, but I just shrug my shoulders.

I honestly don't know. He mentioned stealing from them before, but I bet that was before Kage had the cure to death stowed away in there.

"Why don't we just pass the time, like the pals we are." Darius chuckles. I scoff and shake my head. "Come on. We can either enjoy the time we have together, or I can make it extremely miserable."

Darius slows down his pace a bit so we can walk alongside one another, the tobacco smell intensifying. "Tell me about this other kid we are meeting up with."

No, I really don't want to talk to him about Zain. How about the times he was right there in front of me instead?

"Why didn't you just introduce yourself as who you are?" I ask under my breath.

Darius hums for a moment. "I probably would have if we had chatted a bit longer at the Regnant Night, but you were terrified at the prospect of talking with a complete stranger." He exhales some smoke after a deep inhale. "I would have definitely cued you in if you had stopped and talked with me when you passed me fishing on the Jako River."

That was him?

"Alas, you passed me by, chewing on jerky." Darius shakes his head. "I had thought to break into your room after that and show you who I really am, but the two of you just looked so comfortable cuddling like you were." He tilts his head slightly to look into my eyes.

"So you did break into my room." I growl, upset at the thought he could have hurt Zain in that moment.

"Guess I did! But hey, I left, so no harm, no foul." He chuckles, bumping me with his elbow a few times.

What am I going to do? What can I do? I can't afford to allow Darius to get the apparatus, but I also can't put Zain in danger.

Darius sighs, "Always in that head of yours." He knocks on my head. "Gotta learn how to think, out loud!" Darius shouts out the last word.

I hope he wakes everyone up.

"Hey!" The familiar voice of Zain fills my heart with dread, tears immediately threatening to spill.

I need more time.

"Well, look at that!" Darius cheers

He cares about me, but his care is going to get him killed.

"I'm not worth this," I whisper.

Darius glances at me. "What was that? You should look more happy to see your lover."

"Zain!" The scream rips from my throat as I begin to run towards him. His pace halts, the bag dropping from his grasp.

"That's more like it!" Darius shouts after me.

"Run, you idiot!" I scream, panic in my voice. Reaching into my satchel, I grab the only vial I think will help in this moment.

He shouldn't have come. I'm not worth the risk of losing the apparatus. I'm not worth threatening the safety of the realm.

"Ren!" He opens his arms to me. "Did you call me an idi—" I cut his sentence short, colliding into him.

The brute force of my grasp in combination with our legs entangling is enough to take us both down to the ground, Zain taking the majority of the impact. My ankle throbs from the full on sprint, but I push past it. My heart is racing a kilometre a minute. I scramble, bringing my hand up to caress his face, those deep brown eyes nearly consuming me whole.

"I'm sorry." My lips graze his briefly before the vial in my other hand breaks, activating the terramotus spell. My intent is for the ground to take him far enough away from here.

"Ren?" he asks as the earth and cobblestone begin to shift underneath him and pull him out from under me. His hand grabs onto my arm, but I rip away from his grasp. "Renatus!" he screams out, his hand extended towards me.

I'm sorry. I hope I can explain later.

Zain disappears out of view.

Grabbing the bag still left by my side, I stand.

This is it. He would have chased down Zain if he still had these. This is going to have to be a fight, and a fight I win.

I turn to see Darius smiling. "I'm glad you thought this through. Better only one of you having to die versus the both of you." He shrugs his shoulders, "but it didn't really matter to me."

I will not allow him to have the apparatus.

Darius holds out his hand, expecting me to just hand them over to him.

"You and I should know better than most, that no one is meant to live forever," I say, my words coming out steady despite my shaking.

He lets out a boisterous laugh, grabbing his stomach and

wiping away a tear that is not there. "Says the boy who has only had his mind open for a day." His laughing halts instantly. "You really don't get it, do you?"

"I could never understand a mind as poisoned as yours, killing for no other reason but for himself," I say, glancing down briefly to make sure I am grabbing the right vial from my satchel.

Darius shakes his head. "We have all this knowledge, from hundreds of years sitting inside of us, Ren. When we die, it's like our memory is wiped until we can find it again, but there's a cure for that." He runs his hands through his hair. "If we never die, we will never have to forget. The children, the love, the power that our knowledge possesses. We can keep it all, use it to bend the will of Vitaterrium to our will!"

I'll pass.

Darius holds up his left hand, a soft glow emanating from the gauntlet he adorns. It only takes me blinking before we are standing in an empty space. I turn around, glancing at my surroundings.

Well, this makes things a little harder.

Chapter Twenty-Four

I break the vial. "Memento." My body feels light as air and it's my signal to run. I dart to the only exit I feel some hope of getting back to the Capital, that is before a wall of vines erupts from the earth block just as I reach it. I turn around and see Darius holding onto a gem strung around his neck.

"That was cute, but running isn't an option for you. You wanna fight? Then show me what you're made of." He raises a hand, gesturing to me to come at him.

I drop the bag.

It was worth a try to at least get some backup.

Reaching into my satchel, I feel for a soft pouch. Opening it with one hand, I reach in to grab one of the vials. These are spells I was hoping I would never need, and if I did, it was in situations like when I saved Seodi.

Time to see just how good of a student I really am.

The vial in hand has a piece of paper glued onto it, and when broken, with a focus on where to send it, a fire erupts in my hand. I flick my wrist and it sores through the sky, doubling, tripling, quadrupling in size before hitting the spot where Darius is standing. All within a half a second.

It's not strong enough to kill him, but it'll hurt.

Laughter sounds from the right of me a few metres away. Darius is leaning against the crumbling wall.

Or maybe not hurt at all.

"You were quick, but you are so obvious with your movements. The key to being great at combat is moving without your enemy noticing. I learned that lesson after dying in the Ancestry War," he says, standing from his relaxed position.

My feet sink into the cobblestone and soil I am standing on, then my waist. I grab the same earth movement spell I used to.

The ground begins to rumble and shake as our intentions for it contradict one another, but his spell effect wears off before mine does. A tower of dirt lifts me into the sky, away from any direct contact with him.

"Very nice!" he shouts up to me, and instead of replying, I send a bolt of lightning crashing through the ceiling, this time striking him. That echoing roar sounds throughout this old building.

Darius is down on one knee, that shackle filling the air as the roar dissipates. "Now that! That is what I was looking for." He stands, taking a few steps to stabilise himself.

I wasn't expecting to hurt him beyond repair, but at least do enough damage for him not to just stand right on up afterwards.

He pulls out a small disc from his satchel and twirls his wrist as if warming up. Darius spins around and lets go of the disk. It soars through the air, directing at me. I duck, letting it pass me by, but just as it does, an explosion nearly sends me flying off my mud platform. I grab onto the edge and pull myself back up, a burning sensation on my back.

"That was a little something I stole from the Domi Nostrae before I left. Pretty cool, right?" Darius asks, not needing me to agree to that question.

"Do you always talk this much?" I ask as I send another ball of fire hurtling towards him.

He dives to the side, a bit of his leg getting caught this time. "Nice one. Seems you are picking the pace up a—"

I don't let him finish. I concentrate my focus on earth, just in front of him, and send a boulder from the ground crashing into him. Darius shouts as he is thrown through the wall, causing it to crumble and fall. My heart feels like it stops for a moment seeing the impact he made.

Did I just?

My mouth runs dry until I feel something wrap around my waist and pull me from my tower. My body hits into the ground, my already wounded leg cracks. I let out a scream.

"You know, for someone who was trained by one of the greatest Forged Magicae users, you sure do mess up a lot." He chuckles with a wide grin resting on his face. He jumps from the rubble he is standing in and shakes off the dirt on his cloak. "It's alright, grasshopper. You won't be alive much longer, anyway." He grips the gem on his necklace and mutters something under his breath.

Vines shoot from out of the ground, restraining my arm. I try to pull away, but the vines react like quicksand and I'm pulled down to my knees. I reach for the dagger resting on my hip, but Darius grips my wrist. His eyes are wide, but his pupils are barely visible.

"I need you to stay still," he growls as he shoves me to the ground, using one foot to pin my free arm down.

Grunts leave my mouth as I try to pry myself free.

I'm going to die.

"I know you aren't big on talking and all, but any last words?"

I failed.

I close my eyes. Remembering everything I've got to experience since leaving Master and that tower. I met so many people I would have never known otherwise. I found confidence in my abilities, even if I am not strong enough to win the battle I am in now. I spoke more than I ever have because I felt I had something to say.

There are only two things I can regret. Not saying goodbye to Zain, and that I couldn't save Xylia.

I feel something sharp pierce my abdomen, all the air in my lungs leaving me in an instant. I open my eyes and see Darius smiling down at me.

"Silent until the end. Man, you are so cool." He chuckles and pulls the dagger out of me. I gasp as the pain spreads through my chest.

My vision blurs and I can hear that faint screaming again, like in those dreams. The flames are still licking around the ceiling from one of my earlier spells.

Xylia? Whose is screaming?

Darius turns his gaze from mine and scowls. He stands and moves out of my field of vision. Heat radiates around me, but I cannot see what is causing it. Someone is fighting. I can hear the clashing of metal and shouted incantations. My eyes begin to lull and my body begging for rest, but I want to help.

"Seodi, come to congratulate me on my success?" Darius asks Seodi, assuming she is actually there beyond my field of vision.

"Not even close," Seodi says before I feel a vibration from the ground I am laying on.

Heat from fire and the sound of gushing water fight each other just above my head.

I want to stop, Darius.

"You've been practising!" Darius laughs and Seodi just grunts before a loud bang rings through the air.

I need to do something, anything.

Reaching into my pack, I feel for the hardened mud wrapped carefully with his matching vial. I pull it out and turn my gaze towards the sounds of fighting. I can feel my eyes widen seeing Seodi there fighting with Darius. I can hardly focus, but they both have looks of determination. Brows stitched, sweating and both bleeding.

Unwrapping the prepared spell, I lay the mud on the ground next to me, trying not to move my torso. I uncork the vial and pour its contents into the mud and reach back into my bag for my flint. I focus on my intent, on what the spell was made to do and who I want it to do it to.

The thought of taking someone's life was something I swore I wouldn't do. That was not the way I wanted to do things, but of course the Master was right.

I remember his words, "I'm sure the thought of killing someone doesn't please you, but one day it might be necessary. You will know when that time comes and kill."

The spell's contents ignite with the spark of the flint. I simply point towards Darius.

I know the spell doesn't require it, but "Evaporate."

Dark smoke shoots from the tip of my finger and before Darius can look, it envelopes him. His eyes widen, his dagger falling to the ground, his hands grabbing at his throat as he struggles to breathe in. He is lifted up and slowly his body begins to evaporate into the smoke that surrounds him.

"Holy Lunamartum," Seodi mutters as she looks on to the place Darius was just a second ago. She shakes her head and rushes towards me, pulling something out of her pack. She opens up my shirt and looks to be examining the stab wound Darius left me. "He was about to win," she chokes out. I notice now the blood dripping down her forehead, her hair chard at the ends, her armour in pieces.

He wasn't holding back.

She opens the jar in her hands and begins spreading the

contents on my wound. I wince and gasp as I feel her fingers enter the wound.

"I am only doing this because you saved me." She sets the jar down and places her hands flat against my opened abdomen and whispers something under her breath. Her eyes shut tightly. A light glow illuminates the area around us and I feel a warmth spreading throughout my body.

She cuts open the fabric of my trousers to see my wounded leg.

"I don't have any more healing balm, so you might need a cane for a while," she whispers, examining me for any more life-threatening losses of blood. "Either way, you'll either have to wait here or crawl back to the castle." Her hands tightly wrap around the cloth of the bag containing the apparatus.

She must have grabbed those before she started to fight Darius. She could have just left with them while he was distracted, but she stayed.

"Don't do this," I whimper, placing my hand over hers.

She gives me a weak smile but stands, my hand falling back to my side. "I'm sure Zain will find you here. He's already looking for you." I struggle to keep my eyes open; the pain, the blood loss, the exhaustion, and now this warmth all threaten my consciousness. "This is going to change the world for the better, Renatus. I wish you could see that. I'm sorry things have to be this way."

"You made them this way. The moment we met, you set the agenda of how things would always be between us." The long-winded sentence forces me to cough.

She chuckles. "Yeah, I guess I couldn't help myself. I was just so jealous of the innocence you wore. Now I see you are just as stained as I am." I hear her start to walk away as my blurry vision can no longer see. "I wouldn't say always, Ren.

Who knows, maybe we can be friends when sides no longer matter."

Maybe, or perhaps, resentment will be the only thing that remains.

The world fades into darkness.

CHAPTER TWENTY-FIVE

MY EYES FLUTTER, soft unidentifiable shapes moving in my vision. Cold wet drops hit my face before rolling down to my lips, leaving a salty taste.

"Step back for a second. I know you want to smother him, but he needs to breathe and we don't know what is hurting him and what's not." A familiar male's voice scolds someone or something I'm not sure is even there.

The pressure on my chest elevates, and I nearly gasp from the sudden change. "Ren!" Zain's voice shouts. My guess is his hands are what now grab at my face, turning it slightly to my right.

"Zain, I said watch it!" Vasile scolds him once again.

I blink a few times, trying to push away the glazed over vision I currently have. Slowly, their faces and the environment around us come into focus. The night sky is clear above me, the lunamatrums' moon shining down onto us. A dirt path beneath me, and wild grass and flowers thriving just behind Zain.

I was trying to make my way back to Fosa, but I must have passed out.

"Don't worry, Renatus. We are going to get you back to the castle," Vasile says from somewhere on my left.

I open my mouth to respond, but my throat is sore and my mouth is too dry to allow words to come out.

Zain watches me struggle; he winces as I do. His perfectly stitched brows and teary expression are making my heart ache.

I'm going to have to tell him about me, about Xylia.

He leans down, his lips pressing gently against mine. I want to lean into it, deepen the moment, but my body will not obey my need to comfort him. Zain reaches down as we slowly separate, and he intertwines his fingers with mine. With his breath on mine, he whispers, "You have lost all privileges to adventure on your own. Shame on you for scaring me like that. Saying 'run' and 'sorry' like I am never going to see you again—" His words break into a sob and he buries his face into my neck.

I hear Vasile sigh, but it's quickly followed by a short chuckle. "Alright, alright. If we don't get moving, you might now have much time left with one another."

That's morbid, but probably true.

Zain lifts from my body and wipes his eyes. My left arm is lifted and suddenly, my body moves from its laid out position to an upright one. Vasile holds my head up by my chin, looking me over before lifting me onto his shoulder.

I choke on the pain a bit as my stab wound is lining perfectly with his shoulder. "Sorry, mate," he says, shifting me slightly until he hears the sigh of relief escape my lips.

"It's your turn to be careful, Dad." Zain's words come out uneven due to his composure, or lack thereof.

I'll make it up to him.

THE GATES OPEN before we even reach them. Vasile runs through it with me bouncing, holding back my vomit, on his shoulder.

I'm going to die if I have to endure this much longer.

The urgency I can understand, but the pain radiating through my body has had me blacking in and out every so often. I can barely remember the journey here.

"The healers and a member from the M.G.A. are waiting for you at the door. They will take him from there," a Fel Watch informs Vasile, him running along with us.

"Good. I don't think he is used to being tossed around," Vasile says, a lightness to his tone.

Very glad my pain can at least bring joy to someone else.

My body has been positioned so the only thing in sight is Vasile's feet and the ground he runs on. My breath hitches as I see him take the first step up the castle steps; my body is practically flailing around at this point. Luckily, I am thrown from his shoulder soon after and into the hands of several white gowned castle personnel.

These must be the healers.

They waste no time in stripping me of my bloody armour and ripping off the tunic underneath it as they carry me through the entrance. "How long has he been with these wounds?" the only person in a navy cloak asks Vasile.

"It has probably been close to five or six moonshifts. That's when I am assuming the fighting began, at least," Zain chimes in.

Is that really how much time has passed since I took the apparatus from him? It felt like it was hardly a moonshift.

The healers and the magicae user tasked to care for me begin to murmur to each other, discussing treatments as they turn down a corner. Zain remains in my gaze, Vasile keeping a firm grip on his shoulder and whispering something into his ear.

"Renatus!" The room silences hearing the King's raised voice. Even the healers halt in their movement forward, and I swear I can feel them consider dropping me altogether, as they can feel Kage's wrath in his tone alone.

King Felguard comes into view, marching his way straight for me. The healers quickly lower my bottom half so the King can speak to me face to face, of course allowing me to put the majority of my weight still on them.

Kage's eyes are locked onto mine, his pupils small and a scowl etched onto his face. "Uncle Kage," Zain says, pulling away from his father and in front of me.

The King does not break our eye contact, but instead shoves Zain from his path. "We will talk about you later," he hisses.

The majority of the group around me takes a few steps back, only the two holding me up remain by my side. I try to bow, but only my head lowers.

I am hoping he has already figured out that I have lost the apparatus, otherwise Vasile's point of me not making it much longer will become a reality from the punishment of death I see Kage bestowing upon me.

He grips my hair, pulling my head up so my face is matched up to his. "Where-are-they?" he asks through gritted teeth. "Who has them?" he shouts, his spit spraying across my face.

"W-we should-d talk p-privately," I strain, my voice barely audible.

"You are in no position to be making requests, traitor," Kage retorts.

I close my eyes, taking a deep breath in. "Kage, I can

explain but I am in—" Pain spreads up from my abdomen and I try to hold back a blood-filled cough.

"Take him away," the King says with disdain in his voice. He drops my head. "Throw him in the dungeon when you're done patching up his scrapes."

Mutters of compliance fill the air besides Zain, who shouts, "No!" before grabbing onto his uncle. "Please understand what was at risk, Uncle Kage."

"I understand very well what was at risk." The King points off towards something far beyond the walls in this hallway. "Xylia was at risk. Losing those apparatus means we've lost her all over again." He chokes up on his last word. He puts his hand over his mouth and looks away from Zain. "Be grateful I'm not condemning you to the same fate," he growls, causing Zain to step back.

"Kage, let's talk about all of this," Vasile says in a sympathetic voice, his hand reaching out to the King's shoulder. Kage pushes Vasile's hand off and leaves down another hall, with Vasile chasing after him.

I hope they are as good as friends as they appear to be. Not for my sake, but for the King himself.

"Renatus, I won't let him keep you down there," Zain says, stepping in front of me. He gently strokes my cheek with his thumb.

I give him as much of a smile as I can muster. "I-I'll be fine-e." My words probably sound unconvincing, but I hope he takes them seriously. He nods and rests his forehead against mine.

One of the healers holding me up clears their throat, "Sorry sir, but we need to get him taken care of."

Zain pulls away slowly and nods. "Okay," he whispers, taking a few steps back before he bolts after his father and uncle.

Please don't do something stupid.

I am escorted to the healer's wing, a long room with several beds inside of it. They set me down on the nearest one, the magicae user stepping up to me first. They close their eyes as their hand slowly makes a pass over my chest, stomach, pelvis and legs. I feel a bit of relief from the ache and wooziness caused by the mass amounts of blood loss. Once they finish their scan, they step back, allowing the rest of them to step forward and begin removing the bits of rubble still lodged inside of me. They then clean me and then sew me up.

They definitely know what they are doing. Though Sebastian from the Adamina Clan's Healers Ward could rival them all.

Occasionally, a Fel Watch will walk into the room and examine the process before stepping back out when a healer requests for them to do so. The soft candle light that flickers in the room causes shadows to be cast and dance around the room. I try to focus on the pain to stay awake.

I don't want to sleep through my last moments of freedom.

"We're almost done," one of the healer's mutters, patting my shoulder lightly.

Nodding seems the most I can do with my current energy level.

Another Fel Watch guard comes in. A healer quickly turns to them, likely relaying the same message they just told me.

I blink, well, the first half of blinking, because I am now struggling to reopen them. My head begins to spin and the eternity of my body now feels like it is buried under thousands of pounds of stone and dirt.

Maybe I am buried underneath that building. Me being found, being treated is all just a nice way of putting me to sleep, forever.

CHAPTER TWENTY-SIX

THE SUN BEATS against my eyes, forcing the darkness to retreat. My mouth feels dry and my body stiff. I can hear footsteps somewhere nearby and soft whispers a little further away. Slowly opening my eyes, I see a familiar room and faces all looking towards me. Zain standing by my bedside. King Felguard and Vasile in the doorway looking in, Madi sitting at the table in the corner, and two balls of fur cuddled at my side on the bed. I swallow hard, feeling the pressure of all the attention residing on me.

Zain smirks and hands me a glass of water. "Drink up, cause you have a lot of talking to do." Despite the mocking words, the tone is sombre and soft. I take the glass, wincing as I try to sit up.

I hear Madi sigh and stand from her seat. She walks over to the other side of the bed, grabbing under one of my arms and assisting me into an upright position. Not very gentle, but she is trying to help.

"You are lucky, kid. You came this close to breaking my kid's heart," she grumbles.

I smile at her and drink the contents of my cup rather quickly. The King steps forward and stands at the foot of the bed, looking at me with a stern look.

I remember when he and I first met. He looked scared, terrified not of the beast-filled forest he was in but of the woman who was standing in front of him.

"How are you feeling?" Kage asks, his expression unchanging.

He is very much still unhappy with me, understandably so.

I look around the room once more.

"Overwhelmed actually," I whisper, my throat still feeling strained.

King Felguard closes his eyes for a moment before reopening them.

"Renatus, the Domi Nostrae are in possession of the apparatus which I am sure you are already aware of." I nod, hearing the King's words. I feel my chest tighten, now understanding where this conversation is really going. "They've already started their assault on the Felguard Country, even before they had the items. It seems they were confident in their succession." The King places a hand on his forehead. "So much so it raises the thought of treason."

This is the war Zain left Yral for, and I'm guessing the thought of treason is landing on me.

"All of us were naïve to think that they weren't also looking for these items," his words fall into a whisper. "And it is obvious that their assault is only to keep us at bay from going after the apparatus themselves."

"You have notified the rest of the countries, letting them know what is about to happen, right?" I ask, knowing the answer is already no.

Would mean telling them about the apparatus.

Vasile steps into the room from the doorway. "I told you Kage."

"Enough!" Kage shouts, glancing over his shoulder at

Vasile. "Do you understand the consequences of people knowing something like Aruna's apparatus exists?"

"The sacrifice Xylia made is going to amount to nothing if we just stand by and let them open the doorways," Vasile argues, throwing his hands into the air.

"We risk losing her altogether by telling anyone about it," Kage says, now turning fully towards him.

Madi quickly moves to stand in between the two. "Both of you, calm down."

"You don't think I want her back? I would gladly give my life for her to live the one she deserves!" Vasile shouts, a break in his pitch. "But she wouldn't want to live it knowing it came at the costs of millions of lives, Kage."

"He's right," I mutter.

Kage growls and looks at me. "And what would you know of her?"

"I know more than you do." I look away from him to stare at Zain, whose brow is furrowed hearing my words. "Renatus is not my only name, and before you ask, it was only recently that I learned that."

"What does that mean?" Kage asks, his fists balled at his sides and shaking.

Xylia was going to marry this man, become his queen.

"I was also once Codrin, Ordell, Dagian, Anastasius and Navneet," I admit. I squeeze Zain's hand, but I feel him pull away a bit.

Zain, please give me a chance to explain.

"Codrin?" Both Madi and Vasile mutter in unison.

"How do we know this to be true?" Kage asks, holding his hand up to Madi and Vasile, who both are standing on edge hearing my confession.

I nod, understanding that doubt in my claim. "Vasile and I used to live in Kel before our parents migrated to the Admina

Clan when both of our houses were claimed by the country because we did not have the money to pay our taxes." Vasile's eyes widen and he nods to Kage, who is looking for confirmation, but I can tell Kage wants more. "Madi and Vasile first kissed after he failed the hunter's examination for the tenth time. She said that she had never met someone as stubborn as her before, and she liked that."

"One of the best days of my life." Vasile chuckles, wiping a tear from his eye as he looks at me, and I smile at him.

"Zain could have told you that," Kage says, shaking his head.

"I didn't though." Zain's voice is a whisper.

I hope you remember you are the one needing this confirmation, Kage.

Taking in a deep breath, "The night we met Kage, the night I died, you were the one controlling the feserpentline. I watched you order it to finish me off. Xylia was struggling to breathe at your feet; Vasile was still trying to get up, and there you were, the only one untouched by the creature itself." Kage's eyes widen and his mouth runs slack. "I don't know how you did it, but Xylia came up with the thought before we even went on that hunt that someone could be manipulating it. She was right."

"Kage?" The hurt in Vasile's voice makes my heart hurt. "You killed him?"

"That is out of context," he mutters, taking a step back.

"Context!?" Vasile shouts. "I don't think the context is needed. Were you controlling that thing, yes or no?"

Kage nods. "Yes, but that's because I needed to do what I had to. I was informed early on of their relationship and it would impose on her coming with me."

Vasile gasps and staggers back a few steps. "You, you murdered my best friend. You watched me weep at his grave year after year." He covers his mouth with a shaky hand. "Did Xylia, did she know?"

Kage looks to the ground with an expression I have not seen him wear before. "She knew that it wasn't a coincidence that Codrin died that night," he admits, looking away from all of us. "I didn't have much time to explain before she…" Kage's lip quivers a bit.

"I'm not mad at you, Kage. I was meant to die that night, so I could be here and present in this time." The King meets my gaze for a second before I break away to look at Zain, who is now leaning against the wall, looking at everyone in this room but me. "I mean that, Zain. There are memories and feelings, but I am not living in the past."

Zain glances in my direction and nods.

"Well, I'm mad. Mad that I have been supporting and being a friend to the man who took mine away from me," Vasile says, glaring at Kage as he leaves the room.

Madi sighs and walks up to Kage slowly. "Anything else you've been lying about?"

Kage just looks at her, biting his lip. She shakes her head and walks out, following her husband.

"Codrin, I," Kage starts, "or Renatus. All I want is her back," Kage mutters, tears begging to stream down his face. "Our conversation in the garden; I meant every word."

"I know," I whisper.

He clears his throat before sniffling a bit. "I have to go alert the realm's leaders of what is about to transpire." Kage exits the room, closing the door behind him after looking back and seeing Zain still left in the room.

That's not exactly how I wanted to tell Zain, but seemed like the moment I needed to.

"So you are my Uncle Codrin," Zain says, a twitch in his eye.

I chuckle a bit and pat the bed, inviting him to sit next to me. "We have no blood relation. I promise you."

Zain smirks and joins me. "You are in love with Aunt Xylia."

"A part of me is, along with every person I've loved in the lifetimes I've lived."

He bits his lip, as he tries to hold back a sob.

"I was so scared that I lost you. That you were taken from me." He hides his face from me with his hands. "When we found you alive, I thought that there is no way I am letting him out of my sight."

I grab onto the sleeve of his shirt and tug. He listens and carefully lays his head down on my chest. Avoiding the wounded area. I kiss the top of his head, leaving my lips there. "Does that have to change?"

He shakes his head and nuzzles into me a bit.

A sigh of relief escapes me. "Zain, I'm so sorry I didn't tell you this sooner." I squeeze him a bit tighter. "I am in love with you."

He takes in a shaky breath, his hand wiping his eyes. "Seems like I have some stiff competition."

I shake my head. "I think this is the lifetime I am meant to spend with you."

Zain sits up and looks into my eyes, allowing me to admire his. He leans in, our lips coming together. I bring up a hand and caress his face, some of his tears hitting my thumb while others fall onto my face.

"When did you become such a talker?" he mumbles against my lips.

We both let out a chuckle.

I want us to enjoy this moment before it all starts.

"I think you've taught me a thing or two."

Epilog

Kage's POV

THE BOOK SLIDES back into its place on the large bookshelf resting inside the library. I turn, seeing her for a moment. Hair shining like the sun glistening, the sharp look of her gaze and the slight curl to her lips.

Holy Awemother, do I miss her, but—

"I wish that would stop." I rub my eyes and chuckle to myself as I imagine myself becoming an old and crazed king, just like my father.

I'd deserve it. Vasile and Madi have already deemed me mad themselves after I explained to them the full extent of what I really did to sit on the throne.

Scanning through the titles, nothing seems to capture my attention. Nothing urging me to pick it up and begin reading. With Limoria at the brink of destruction, there is surprisingly little for me to do. My advisors have taken over and demand that the only exposure Limoria has of me is the heavily armed appearances I rarely make to try to ease Felguardians' panic. Since the Domi Nostrae has deemed me a priority threat, I have been forced to remain inside the castle. Only accompanied have I been allowed to even wonder about my own garden.

To infernum with those delusional extremists.

After the tenth attempt on my life, it became crystal clear that they would like nothing more than to see my head on a spike or rolling across a floor.

Would Xylia want that after everything I've done?

The doors burst open, and I jump to attention, pushing her from my mind for the moment.

"Sorry to startle you, Your Majesty. You have a visitor," Sampson says with the same expressionless face he always seems to wear.

I wish I had that talent. The heart I have is often too visible for others to see.

It lives outside of me, after all.

A young figure steps around Sampson. My jaw drops, but I close it just as quickly.

"Renatus... I was not expecting you." I raise my eyebrows and smile, surprisingly happy to see him.

Not many people stop by to visit me, understandably so. They are all busy fighting a war or have far too much disdain to even muse a meeting.

"King Felguard," he bows towards me slightly, "I apologise if I am disturbing you."

He's all grown up and looks exactly like Codrin when he died.

I wave off the apology. "Please, your visit will be the high-light of my day."

Renatus smiles and nods, taking a few steps further into the library. "I'm actually here to complete the quest you had written about. I apologise."

"No more apologies, my friend." I shake my head with a small grin. "I am happy you received my letter. I hope you find the property I've gifted to you to your liking."

Renatus' eyes widen. "I should have thanked you first."

"Thank me? You talking Vasile and Madi down from trying to dethrone me is a thank you enough, and that property I mentioned in the letter is my repayment for your kindness." I chuckle, it comes out sounding forced. Which it was.

It was clear that there was hesitation from him when that fight did break out, but he ended up stepping in and saying that regardless of what I have done in the past, I have been making up for it in my current reign.

I can tell now, looking at his broad stance, his widened and directed gaze, this is not the boy who left this castle when the war was just starting.

"Since you are here for me, I am hoping you came prepared with wondrous tales of your adventures to tell an imprisoned soul such as myself."

A chuckle leaves his lips. "Quiet the lavish cell, Your Majesty."

"Believe it or not, it does have its downsides." I wink.

I wonder closer to him, stopping at my desk, which is stationed in the centre of the room.

"Everything of interest I relayed into my reports; though, I can make one up for you. I hate to disappoint," he jokes, meeting me at the desk.

"I was quite impressed with how well you did, Ren. I am surprised you had time to go hunting for me, though I suppose it has been four years since you started your mission." He taps his fingers on the desk, listening to my comment.

"I appreciate your trust in my ability to complete it. It did take quite some time, but I was able to locate all of the doorways without being spotted by the Domi Nostrae, who were on high alert already," Renatus says, reminding me of what I already know.

He definitely is courageous, much like Xylia.

"The information was deeply appreciated by my advisors

and the other leaders of the Paxtas Order. I heard about your sabotage of their first attempt at opening the Ignisium Doorway. Quite impressive; your skills as a Forged Magicae user have grown a lot," I admit, turning towards the garden before looking back. I gesture my hand to the garden. "Would you join me for a walk?"

Ren looks out the windows and nods.

We remain silent as we move around and into the newly budding landscape. I watch as he quickly turns his attention to the frozen Queen of Felguard.

Why did I let her slip through my fingers?

He clears his throat, "As I mentioned, I did complete my search in finding the texts you requested." Ren reaches into the green-leathered satchel he is wearing, pulling out a few books.

Their titles are in languages only few yet on Vitaterrium speak. Elvish, Caeles and Infernish.

Each speaks in detail of these planes, what creatures and beings of existence live there. Could be the only defence we have if the Domi Nostrae are successful in opening the doorways.

"Do you need help translating? I created a spell that can help us understand the basics of what the text is saying," Renatus states, delicately handing them over to me.

"I appreciate the offer, but while you have been distracting the Domi Nostrae, I have been studying. Translation should be no problem." My words must impress him as his brow raises and eyes widen.

Amusing. A powerful Forged Magicae user such as himself being impressed with someone like me.

Silence falls over us as we stare at the unmoving form of the women we both have loved. He walks up and touches the smooth stone that is Xylia.

"I learned a lot while I was gone, Your Majesty," he mutters.

"Anything you think I would find interesting?" I ask.

Ren smiles and nods his head. "Yes, in fact. I spent some time hiding in Lona University after my sabotage."

I raise an eyebrow, waiting for him to continue.

Renatus smiles at Xylia before looking at me. "I could bring her back, Your Majesty."

If I was standing, my knees would be hitting the floor, but my breath has definitely escaped me.

"You... what?"

Did he steal back the apparatus?

"Xylia is not dead. Simply frozen in time," he explains.

I look at him with my eyes squinted, trying to understand how that is possible and what that means.

Frozen, trapped in the time she was that night.

Shaking my head in disbelief, I rise from my seated position. "So the apparatus," I mutter.

"Were never necessary for us to bring her back."

My heart stops hearing that there was another way to save her. The years wasted looking for the wrong solution.

If Rose was telling the truth, our child could still be alive, frozen in time with her.

"Then what are we waiting for?" I ask, taking a few steps closer, reaching up and placing my hand on the one formed from my grasp when she froze.

"For the rest of us to show up," he says, glancing at my hand holding hers before turning away from me altogether.

"The rest of who?"

"The Legends of Limoria."

INDEX

Accursed Punarjanmam - A person who, when they die, is reborn. Their memories of their past lives are locked away by a spell that was used on them in their first life.

Aruna's Apparatus - Items forged by Aruna's Natural Magicae and desire to create them. The following five scientific tools, when used together, cure death.

> **Asiferrum (Fools Blade)** - Appears as a bladeless dagger that simulates the same pain with no damage. Although, if there is prolonged application or if it is aimed at the heart, it can cause serious injury, and even result in death. The handle is curved slightly and has green scales decorating it. There is a "T" shaped guard with aesthetic supports that connect to the handle. The blade itself does exist but is phantom, which is why pain still exists without inflicting bodily damage.

> **Contritos Spirit (The Chalice of Broken Wills)** - It is silver covered with symbols from the old world. There is a single garnet on the front in a pyramid shape. The tip comes to a sharp point. When a magicae user pricks their finger and drops it into the chalice, they are forced to submit to the chalice's owner,

unable to utilise their magicae against them or their bloodline. If the magicae does not submit, they will face excruciating pain. Very few magicae users have been able to break the magicae and survive.

Copious Riviere - A luxurious riviere that is strung together with silver-based string. It is primarily made of pearls with a single sapphire in the centre of the lowest string. Its main purpose is to enhance whatever natural magicae the wearer has.

Forgee Exousia (Forged Power) - A silver-plated gauntlet that instead of fingers has chains that connect to rings. Each ring has a round shaped gem. Pinky being a ruby, the ring finger being an amber, the middle finger being an emerald, the index finger being a sapphire and the thumb, an amethyst. In the centre of the back hand is the sigil for the Forged Magicae itself. The mind, body and soul.

Lovers Cor (Lovers Heart) - A cloak that has an intricate design of the constellation of Amantas embroidered on the inside of the cloak. Amantas appears in the night sky as two lovers locked into an embrace. The legend behind it is that it is a reminder of the day the Lunamatrem and the Solismatrem met. A dark light was cast all throughout the Vitaterrium and caused many to perish as looking directly at it blinded folks and caused chaos that led to death.

The Awemother apparently separated them by night and day eternally, so they could not cause the same tragedy again. Two lovers separated, but the constellation is supposedly their remaining desire for one another. The cloak's purpose is to shield the wearer from Magicae.

Beardadils - Extremely deadly beasts that are territorial and protective of their packs. Their tufts of yellow are actually concealing pores filled with a poisonous pollen-like substance that they can shoot out at will. Normally located near the southern end of the Vermilion Forest, but there are some smaller packs located in the Allen Territory.

Cavrats - Mid-sized rodent creatures that are nearly blind. Typically live in mountains or rocky terrain. They are stark white with orange eyes with slit-shaped pupils. They have padded paws and thumbs on their front two. Generally very aggressive when food is involved or their territory encroached on.

Cognisance of Sigils - A book written to break down the language of a sigil and how, over time, they have become more complex due to the loss of ties to the places beyond the doorways. The authors are a variety of researchers.

Haldoris (Seasire) - Goddess of the Seas. Depicted as a beautiful figure with a serpent-like tail wrapped around her legs.

Idyllia - Where now stands the Ashen Land Territory was once Idyllia. A large lake with an island in the centre. The one true King built his kingdom atop of it and named it Idyllia after his first daughter and his belief that all things should prioritise peace and harmony above power and profit.

Ignisium Doorway - The door that once burst open, causing the Ashen Land to come into existence as well as what started the Ancestry War.

Incrementum - Growth spell incantation

Locquins - Large birds that have a mixture of black and blue feathers. They are extremely intelligent and are believed to have some relation to the Passerinnit race. Many countries have trained these birds to be used as carriers of important messages and help keep the different countries informed about major events and happenings.

Lureas - Sleek, and generally all black, pack animals with piercing grey eyes and large green fangs. They are incredibly fast and ferocious hunters. Native to the Northern mountains of Limoria, they tend to keep their distance from intelligent species as long as no one crosses into their territories or meddles with their pack.

Mors et nativitas unum sumus - "Death and birth are one for I"

Storing a Spell - A book about the proper practices of storing and preparing spells to use on the spot versus having to prepare the spell in the moment.

Symbols and Sigils - It reads about where sigils originate and talks about the mothers of Forged Magicae, Aruna and Ayla. It explains the making of a sigil and the history behind them. The authors are a variety of researchers.

Teleportation, Movement and Evaporation Magicae - A book that goes into detail about the complexity of a spell's evolution and the specifics of the Movement spell, Teleportation spell and the Evaporation Spell.

Terramotus - Earth movement spell

The Kindled Whip - The butt end is silver, its handle green with brown and green leather woven together and a thin silver band wrapping around in a spiral. The thong of the whip is what is truly strange. The whip is made out of wood, almost twig like, but it bends and twists like a normal whip would. The end is dipped in silver and it appears extremely sharp. The sigil is to allow a form of growth magicae to attach itself to the whip. The whip extends and lashes out further and longer than what its actual size is. The sigil also allows intent to be its aim versus any martial skill.

Understanding the Four Elements and Precious Materials - The starter guide to Forged Magicae. Breaks down how it works, basic materials to be used, tools necessary to harness magicae and examples of Forged Magicae spells. Talks a lot about how Natural Magicae ties in with Forged Magicae. The authors are a variety of researchers.

ACKNOWLEDGMENTS

Book two and I am just as amazed as when I was publishing my first. I'm a writer, yet it is extremely hard to find words for the feeling of putting your work out there for people to read. Whatever this feeling is, I think I'm addicted to it.

I want to thank my readers who have been asking and prodding about when book two was coming out, encouraging me to get my hinder in gear and type, type, type. It has been incredible to hear your feedback, love, and support for *Light of Evanora.*

To my family, who shares, gloats, and shoves my book down the throats of everyone they know! Makes me feel loved and shows your pride without you having to say it out loud.

A big thank you and shout out to my amazing and wonderful editor and publisher Chelsea Lauren with Represent Publishing. She is my biggest supporter with getting these books to the finish line. I couldn't do it without your help, and the grammar gods will second the statement.

Thank you to the incredible artists, Luke Daab, Xavier and Lidia Puccetti, for lending their talents to me to make amazing artwork. You both dazzle me with how well you bring my imagination to life through art!

Lastly, but not leastly, thank you to my beta readers for dealing with my questions and desire for you to tear my heart apart when reading through. It helps a lot to make sure I am putting my best writing out there and seeing the things I wouldn't be able to notice myself.

OTHER WORKS BY T R NICKEL

THE LEGENDS OF LIMORIA

Light of Evanora

Apparatus From Aruna